Praise for the Flower Shop Mysteries

Dearly Depotted

"Flowers and murder are unlikely but entertaining companions in another solid effort by Collins. . . . There is plenty to please here."   —*Romantic Times*

"Original and charming."   —*Midwest Book Review*

Slay It with Flowers

"You can't help but laugh at Abby because trouble sure can find her. The supporting characters make this plot even better. An enormously entertaining read."   —*Rendezvous*

"Collins has created a delightful amateur sleuth, and the plot is smooth. . . . The inclusion of a contemporary social problem gave the story extra juice."   —*Romantic Times*

"What a delight! Ms. Collins has a flair for engaging characters and witty dialogue. Try as you might, you won't guess the outcome, nor does the murderer tip a hand until the very end. Loved the flower shop setting and the first-person style of writing."   —*FreshFiction.com*

continued . . .

Mum's the Word

"Kate Collins plants all the right seeds to grow a fertile garden of mystery. . . . Abby Knight is an Indiana florist who cannot keep her nose out of other people's business. She's rash, brash, and audacious. Move over, Stephanie Plum. Abby Knight has come to town."
—Denise Swanson, author of the Scumble River mysteries

"An engaging debut planted with a spirited sleuth, quirky sidekicks, and page-turning action . . . delightfully addictive . . . a charming addition to the cozy subgenre. Here's hoping we see more of intrepid florist Abby Knight and sexy restaurateur Marco Salvare."
—Nancy J. Cohen, author of the Bad Hair Day mysteries

"Kate Collins's new Flower Shop Mystery is fresh as a daisy, with a bouquet of irresistible characters and deep roots in the Indiana soil."
—Elaine Viets, author of the Dead-End Job mysteries

"A bountiful bouquet of clues, colorful characters, and tantalizing twists. . . . Kate Collins carefully cultivates clues, plants surprising suspects, and harvests a killer in this fresh and frolicsome new Flower Shop mystery series."
—Ellen Byerrum, author of the Crime of Fashion mysteries

Other Flower Shop Mysteries

Mum's the Word
Slay It with Flowers
Dearly Depotted

Snipped in the Bud

A Flower Shop Mystery

Kate Collins

A SIGNET BOOK

SIGNET
Published by New American Library, a division of
Penguin Group (USA) Inc., 375 Hudson Street,
New York, New York 10014, USA
Penguin Group (Canada), 90 Eglinton Avenue East, Suite 700, Toronto,
Ontario M4P 2Y3, Canada (a division of Pearson Penguin Canada Inc.)
Penguin Books Ltd., 80 Strand, London WC2R 0RL, England
Penguin Ireland, 25 St. Stephen's Green, Dublin 2,
Ireland (a division of Penguin Books Ltd.)
Penguin Group (Australia), 250 Camberwell Road, Camberwell, Victoria 3124,
Australia (a division of Pearson Australia Group Pty. Ltd.)
Penguin Books India Pvt. Ltd., 11 Community Centre, Panchsheel Park,
New Delhi - 110 017, India
Penguin Group (NZ), 67 Apollo Drive, Rosedale, North Shore 0745,
Auckland, New Zealand (a division of Pearson New Zealand Ltd.)
Penguin Books (South Africa) (Pty.) Ltd., 24 Sturdee Avenue,
Rosebank, Johannesburg 2196, South Africa

Penguin Books Ltd., Registered Offices:
80 Strand, London WC2R 0RL, England

First published by Signet, an imprint of New American Library,
a division of Penguin Group (USA) Inc.

First Printing, May 2006
10 9 8 7 6 5 4

Ⓟ REGISTERED TRADEMARK—MARCA REGISTRADA

Printed in the United States of America

To my mother, Rosemary,
who always believed in me,
who was, and who always will be,
my role model for what a mother should be.

CHAPTER ONE

I jammed both feet on the brake and brought my old yellow convertible to a screeching halt mere inches from the groin of a dragon. Okay, not a dragon in the fairy tale sense of the word. This dragon was the flesh-and-blood human variety—one Z. Archibald Puffer, a former JAG officer turned law professor who was often referred to as Puffer the Dragon. He was called that not because of his last name but also because of his ability to destroy even the bravest law student in one fiery blast of fury.

My personal name for him was Snapdragon, because he had a habit of snapping pencils in two and hurling the eraser half at the head of the student whose answer had displeased him. He went through so many pencils that he bought them in bulk, made to his specifications—glossy black barrels with his initials monogrammed in silver to look like bolts of lightning: *ZAP.* I had been struck by them many times and even bore a tiny scar on my forehead from his last attack, which came with his pronouncement that I was never to set foot in his lecture hall again. That was followed in short order by my expulsion from law school, which, in turn, prompted my then fiancé, Pryce Osborne II, to break off our engagement and leave town until his humiliation over my failure had faded. *His* humiliation.

It had occurred to me back then that the old maxim of bad luck coming in threes was true. Now, as Puffer glared up the shiny hood of my reconditioned 1960 Corvette with his spiteful, ice blue eyes, and my heart pounded and my clammy hands clasped the steering wheel so hard my knuckles hurt, my gut feeling was that the Rule of Three had begun again. Which meant I still had two to go.

The irony was that the only reason I had come to the law school—a place I tried my best to avoid—was to deliver a flower that Professor Puffer had ordered. However, I didn't think now would be the best time to hand it over. He might snap it off and chuck the vase at me.

"You redheaded fumigant," he jeered, as college students gathered on both sides of the street. "You nearly killed me."

I wasn't sure what a fumigant was, but I knew it couldn't be good. "Sorry," I squeaked, slumping down as far as I could. Considering that I was short, it was pretty far.

Was it my fault he hadn't used the crosswalk? Was it my fault he was talking on his mobile phone instead of paying attention to traffic? I didn't think so. Had it been anyone else, I would have told him as much. But that steely glare brought back so many bad memories that all I could do was duck.

"Hey, there *is* someone inside," one curious student said, coming up for a look.

I raised my head just enough to peer over the dash. Mercifully, Snapdragon had moved on, but not before stopping at the curb to deliver a parting shot. "Be expecting a call from the police," he said, working his cell phone buttons. "I'm turning you in for reckless driving."

Great. Just what I needed to make my morning complete. *ZAP.*

I knew what his fury was really about. Puffer was still indignant about the night he'd spent in the slammer over three years ago on a driving-under-the-influence charge. I'd had nothing to do with it, of course—I was still downstate at Indiana University at the time—but that hadn't mattered to Puffer. What had mattered was that the Dragon had been publicly disgraced by a Knight—my father, Sgt. Jeffrey Knight, then of the New Chapel Police Department—and once I set foot in his classroom and Puffer made the connection, he never let me forget it.

So it really shouldn't have surprised me that this new trio of unpleasant events would begin with Snapdragon. In fact, my first clue should have been the strange order that had been waiting for me when I walked into my flower shop, Bloomers, this overcast Tuesday morning: one black rose suitable for funeral display, noon delivery, to Professor Z. Puffer, New Chapel University School of Law. I mean, who would order a single black flower for a funeral? Bugs Bunny?

Knowing my history with Puffer, my assistant Lottie had tried to talk me out of making the delivery. But no, I'd decided I needed to face the Dragon to conquer those irrational fears I'd held on to way too long. After all, Puffer had no power over me now. I wasn't that frightened first-year law student anymore. I owned a business, or at least I owned the mortgage for a business. It took courage to run a flower shop at the age of twenty-six. It also took money, which was something I hadn't yet managed to produce in quantity. Which reminded me. I still had to deliver the flower and collect my money.

I glanced over at the dark red rose (the closest I could get to black since there was no such thing) in its slender chrome vase, the entire package wrapped in black-tinted cellophane,

tied with a solemn black ribbon and wedged securely in a
foam container in front of the passenger seat—and tried to
imagine Puffer's reaction when he saw who the delivery person was. Maybe I should take Lottie up on her offer after all.

Horns honked behind me. I glanced in my rearview mirror and saw a line of cars waiting to turn into the law school's
parking lot, so I pulled into a visitor's space, shut off the engine, and took deep breaths to calm my nerves. What was the
big deal anyway? All I had to do was put the vase on Puffer's
desk and leave a bill. If I was lucky, he might even be in the
cafeteria, in which case I could just give everything to his
secretary, Bea, who always ate lunch at her desk.

A car pulled into the space to my right. I glanced over at
the metallic green Mini Cooper and saw Professor Carson
Reed at the wheel. Great. Of the hundreds of people I could
have seen at the college that day, I had to find the only two
on campus who held grudges against me.

From the corner of my eye I watched Reed polish off the
last of a burger, crumple the wrapper, check his teeth in his
rearview mirror, and get out. He eyed my Vette but ignored
me as he strode off, briefcase in hand.

Professor Reed was a tall, vain, handsome, single man in
his late thirties with a fondness for poetry and black clothing (including a black eyepatch and cape, if he was feeling
particularly dashing). He thought of himself as a modern-
day Lord Byron and frequently could be seen strolling the
campus grounds reciting odes to the starry-eyed female students who seemed to follow him everywhere. Sad to say,
Reed enjoyed the benefits of having his own fan club and
had left many a broken heart in his wake.

However much I found his behavior offensive, Professor
Reed had been one of the few teachers whose lectures I'd actually understood, even if I hadn't always passed his exams.
Plus, he'd written papers and often spoke on the importance
of taking a stand against injustice—a subject dear to my

heart. I'd even memorized his favorite Byron quote on that subject:

As the Liberty lads o'er the sea,
Bought their freedom, and cheaply, with blood,
So we, boys, we
Will *die* fighting, or *live* free . . .

But a few months ago, Reed became the legal adviser for Dermacol, a new cosmetics laboratory in town, and suddenly his poetic ideals were replaced by dollar signs, causing my respect for him to take a nosedive. Dermacol tested products on animals kept in wire cages, something I couldn't—make that *wouldn't*—tolerate. In fact, just a week ago, during a demonstration to protest Dermacol's policies, I was arrested for obstruction. Apparently, Reed hadn't welcomed the picket line I'd organized to block Dermacol's entrance gate and had called the police.

As I was being led away in handcuffs, I told him in a voice loud enough to carry to the reporters on hand that I'd do it again if it meant saving the lives of innocent creatures, and I'd take on anyone who advocated torturing helpless animals—including him. Then I called him a hypocritical snake in the grass for selling out to corporate greed. The local newspaper even quoted me on that.

Needless to say, Reed was no fan of mine, especially since photos of the protest made the front page of the *New Chapel News,* and the accompanying article painted him in a particularly unflattering light. For a man of Reed's arrogance, I didn't imagine it had been an easy pill to swallow, and I was certain the less we saw of each other the better. But since his office was next to Puffer's, the odds of meeting were high.

I toyed again with the idea of letting Lottie come back with the flower, but that just wasn't my style. I never shy away from a challenge—my parents would attest to that. To hear them describe it, they'd stumbled around in a zombie-like stupor for the better part of a decade due to their sleepless nights of worrying about me.

My cell phone rang, so I looked at the screen, flipped it open, and said, "Nikki, I'm so glad you called. You'll never *believe* what happened."

I knew I'd get lots of sympathy from Nikki. She was my best friend, confidante, and roommate. We had a bond so strong that when one of us was in distress, the other felt the pain.

"I don't have time for that right now, Abby. I'm standing here on the curb waiting for a guy from the gas station to put a spare tire on my car so I can make it to work this afternoon. And do you want to know why he's putting on a spare tire? Because your cousin Jillian punctured my Toyota's *good* tire. That's why."

Obviously there were times when Nikki's distress and my distress canceled that whole share-the-pain thing. "To be fair, Nikki, Jillian didn't puncture your tire. Something sharp punctured it."

"Why did it get punctured in the first place, Abby? Why?"

Two professors strolled past my car, so I whispered, "Can we discuss this later?"

"Here's why. Because Jillian parked *her* car in my designated space, forcing me to leave *my* car on the street in front of the house that's being remodeled."

For someone who didn't have time to talk, she was doing a good job of it.

"Jillian has also taken over one of my shelves in the bathroom medicine cabinet, and that's just unacceptable."

"At least you're not the one sleeping on the lumpy sofa."

"Whose fault is that?" she snapped.

There was a protracted silence on both ends. Nikki and I

had been friends since third grade—nothing had ever come between us—yet in the short time my cousin had squeezed herself into our lives, we were reduced to taking potshots at each other. Truthfully, if Jillian hadn't been a blood relation— first cousin on my father's side—I wouldn't have defended her. But having shared many sisterlike experiences with her, such as first bras, bad vacations, and painful sunburns, I felt duty bound.

"She has to move out, Abby. That apartment is not big enough for the three of us."

"I absolutely agree with you, and she will—soon. I promise."

"That's what you said weeks ago."

"So now it's even sooner. Don't hiss at me, Nik. You know Jillian is coming out of a severe depression. How many girls get jilted on their honeymoon?"

Nikki couldn't argue with that. However, she could have pointed out that not many girls had jilted four men at the altar, either, which had been a hobby of my cousin's until her recent marriage. "Fine. But promise me you'll talk to her tonight about getting her own place, okay?"

"Okay. Now do you want to hear what happened?"

"Make it fast. The guy is almost done."

As I rattled off the story, I glanced in my rearview mirror and saw a squad car pull up behind me. "Oh, great. The cops are here. Puffer called them after all."

"Get a hold of your dad, for Pete's sake, and let him handle the cops."

I'd already thought of calling my father, but somehow, being almost twenty-seven years old, I felt foolish asking him to haul me out of a scrape, especially one as silly as this. Besides, I'd already tapped him to get me released from jail after the protest march. I didn't think he'd be pleased to receive another call.

"Well, well. Would you look who we have here?" a droll male voice to my left said.

Resigning myself to embarrassment, I stowed my phone, got out of the Vette, and turned to face my bud, Sgt. Sean Reilly, a good-looking, forty-year-old, Irish American police officer with intelligent brown eyes and a perturbed scowl. Okay, we weren't exactly buddies, but over the past several months we had come to a point of mutual respect . . . I hoped.

"Top o' the lunch hour to you," I said, trying to prompt a smile. It didn't work.

"It's not the top of *my* lunch hour," he grumbled.

"I'd say not, if they have you making routine traffic stops."

My second attempt at humor didn't work, either. Reilly planted his hands on his thick black leather belt. "I don't make routine traffic stops. I heard dispatch read your license plate number and volunteered to take the call as a favor to *you*."

Ouch. And Nikki had laughed when I'd paid extra for a vanity license plate that read: PHLORIST R ME. "Gee, that was really sweet of you, Reilly. Does that mean I can go?"

"No. It means you can tell me why you tried to run down Professor Puffer."

"Let's clear up that misconception right now. I didn't try to run him down. He stepped out in front of me."

"He said you came within an inch of taking his life."

"*Pfft*. It was at least two."

Reilly's scowl deepened.

"He's a drama queen, Reilly. Okay, so maybe I was fiddling with my radio for a second. That's beside the point. The point is, he has it in for me because my father hauled him in on a DUI once."

"Did you, or did you not, almost hit him?"

I scratched the end of my nose, trying to think of a way

around the question. Clearly, I should have paid more attention in those law classes. "Yes, I almost hit him, but—"

"Uh-uh," he said, wagging a finger at me. "No buts."

"Mitigating circumstances!" I cried. Wow. I *had* remembered something. "Puffer walked out from between two cars blabbing away on his phone and never checked to see if anyone was coming."

Reilly studied me for a long moment, then finally growled, "All right. Get out of here."

"I'm free to go?"

"On one condition. That I don't get any more calls about your driving. Got it?"

"You bet." I blew him a kiss, then checked the time, saw I had five minutes to get the flower up to Puffer's office, and scrambled for the package.

A knot of fear the size of Rhode Island took over my stomach as I tucked the wrapped rose in the crook of my arm and headed toward the stately, two-story brown-brick building that housed New Chapel University's law school. The university covered an area approximately fifteen square blocks, encompassing ten buildings, three dormitories, and a handful of Greek houses. It was a small, private college, but it had an excellent reputation, and its law school held its own with any in the country—not that they could prove it by me.

I paused at the curb to let a white Saab pass. I recognized the car as belonging to Jocelyn Puffer, Snapdragon's wife, a subdued woman who seemed the exact opposite of her belligerent husband. Rumor had it that Jocelyn had come from a well-to-do Connecticut family that had disowned her when she married Puffer, not that I ever trusted rumors. Jocelyn wasn't beautiful, but she knew how to dress and was always courteous whenever I met her in town, most often at the used-book store where she worked. It was unusual to see her at the university. Then again, if I were her, I'd do my best to avoid Puffer, too.

I took a breath and continued on toward the double glass doors, but as soon as I stepped into the entrance hall and saw the sights and smelled the smells that had greeted me every day for nine miserable months, I broke out in a cold sweat. *Focus on the flower, Abby. That'a girl.*

Straight ahead was the student commons—a small area with a grouping of worn sofas, a few sets of round tables and chairs, a long table against a wall that held a big coffee urn, a stack of paper cups, and other coffee supplies, and a bottled water and soft drink machine. To my right was a hallway that led to the lecture halls, and to my immediate left was a wide, stone stairway that led up to the professors' offices—the only access other than a private elevator farther down on the right that was strictly for the use of the three professors on that side of the building. (Apparently, before six more offices had been squeezed in, everyone had been able to access it, but not anymore.) Beyond the stairway was a law library that didn't get much use now that everything could be found on the Internet.

I trudged slowly up the steps, berating myself for letting my fear of a bully like Puffer get such a grip on me. I was making a delivery, for heaven's sake, not taking an oral exam. At the top I entered the large, central secretarial pool that served the nine offices around it, three on a side, plus a computer lab, washrooms, and a conference room. To my right were the offices with the most prestige, having access to the private elevator through a shared vestibule in the back—Myra Baumgarten's, Reed's, and Puffer's. To my relief, no light showed through the glass in Puffer's door. In fact, the entire floor seemed to have emptied out, except for Professor Reed and the one person I'd been hoping to find there—Beatrice Boyd.

Known as Aunt Bea by those of us she'd consoled after

we'd limped out of Puffer's inner sanctum, emotionally bruised and verbally beaten, the fiftysomething secretary worked for two of the full-time professors, Puffer and Reed. Originally from Seattle, Bea was a product of the hippie generation and still dressed in long, colorful, cotton skirts and full, gauzy blouses belted at the waist by a fringed leather sash. She wore silver hoop earrings and turquoise rings, and never used makeup. Fortunately, her smooth complexion and big blue eyes were attractive enough without it. Her hairstyle was another throwback to the sixties—a waist-long, heavy braid of gray-brown hair, usually with a yellow pencil stuck through near the scalp like a hair pick.

I'd always thought of Bea as the ultimate earth mother, yet she'd never had children of her own. I wasn't even sure she'd ever married, although photographs of her with a man named Zed taken on various backpacking adventures were arranged on her desk. Seeing her now, I remembered the last time she'd come to my aid—when I'd learned that I'd been booted out of law school. She'd held me when I cried, wiped my tears, bundled me into her car, and shuffled me to a coffee shop, where I'd drowned my sorrows in her favorite remedy—hot, spiced soy chai tea.

It was Bea who'd urged me to forget the law and search my soul for what I truly wanted out of life. She'd encouraged me to explore the idea of buying the foundering Bloomers, where I'd worked during the summers of my college years. It had been the best advice of my life and I'd thanked her many times over for her guidance.

Unaware of my approach, she took a woven leather drawstring purse out of a file cabinet drawer and rose, a distracted look on her normally serene face. When she saw me she gave a little gasp, then covered it with a forced laugh. "Abby! You gave me a start."

"Sorry. Guess what I have? A delivery for Professor

Puffer." I held up the wrapped rose and scrunched my nose to show my displeasure.

"He's not in," she said, backing toward the stairs. "Just set it on his desk and leave the bill beside it. I wish I had time to chat, but I have an appointment."

"Sure, thanks. I'll catch you later." I watched her hurry off, hoping everything was all right—it wasn't like her to be so agitated. Then I remembered my reason for coming and turned to gaze anxiously at Puffer's closed office door. Why was I so nervous when he wasn't even there?

Holding the package in front of me like a shield, I walked toward the Dragon's lair, trying to ignore the knot in my gut. As I passed Professor Reed's office I could hear him talking in a sharp, but hushed voice. No one answered him, so I figured he was on the phone, and from the sound of it, he wasn't a happy camper.

I stopped at Puffer's door, knocked, waited a few moments, then took a deep breath and stepped inside, extremely relieved to find that Bea was right. The Dragon was gone.

His office was just as I remembered it, even down to the smell of pine disinfectant. There was a wall of shelves with the books arranged not only by color, but also by size; another wall of awards, photos, and mementos from his JAG days; a small table that held a battlefield map covered with tiny soldiers and cannons; a desk with metal legs; a high-backed swivel chair; a door at the back that led to the elevator vestibule; and, finally, the small, wooden chair upon which I had sat many times, fighting back tears while he ridiculed my papers.

The memory brought an angry flush to my face, which, on a redhead's fair skin, was bright enough to look feverish. I plunked the flower on the desk, next to his computer monitor, propped the bill beside it, and was ready to leave—when I spotted the can of glossy black pencils on the far side of his desk and couldn't resist the temptation. I glanced over my shoulder to make sure no one was there, then snatched one of the sleek tools and held it as if I were going to snap it in two, imagining the satisfaction of hurling the eraser end at Puffer's head.

Suddenly, the rear door opened and in charged the Dragon in all his intimidating glory—head up, shoulders back, spine stiff, and nostrils flaring, as if he were a general in the military embarking on a war campaign.

And there I stood like an enemy soldier within firing range, holding his pencil.

CHAPTER TWO

Professor Puffer was a medium-sized, stocky man in his midforties, with brown hair clipped close on the sides, and small, even teeth. He had on a military-style, tan poplin shirt, brown slacks, and well-shined leather shoes, and at first glance he appeared distinguished, but he banished that notion as soon as he opened his mouth. He either barked commands or snarled them, treating everyone as a recruit, his eyes mere slits whenever he had to deal with people he considered beneath him. Like me.

He quickly assessed my terror-stricken features, then sneered, "Look who came back for a visit. Betty Boob."

I'd always been sensitive about my, shall we say, generous natural endowments, so his little barb really stung. But I refused to let him know it and, frankly, felt a measure of relief that his attack hadn't been worse. I forced myself to lay the pencil on the desk—I was shaking too hard to attempt to zero in on the cup—and answer calmly, "It's not a visit, Professor. It's a delivery."

His steely gaze followed my pointing finger to the rose, and his eyebrows drew together in bafflement, as though he'd never laid eyes on a flower before. "What is *that*?"

Another insult? "Your funeral flower. It's a rose called Ink Spots and it's the nearest I could get to black."

"*Funeral* flower?" he bellowed, causing the glass panes in both doors to rattle. "I didn't order a funeral flower. What the hell are you talking about?"

I swallowed. Okay, apparently he hadn't ordered it, which made me suspect that one of his disgruntled students had. "Someone must have called using your name. I had no way of knowing it wasn't you."

"Not only *didn't* I order that rose, but I *wouldn't* order a rose—or any other flower—from you, you ill-bred, clay-brained, candy ass. Now get that abomination out of here."

Abomination? Say what he wanted about me, he didn't have to denigrate my flowers. "Excuse me?" I managed to say without too much quivering in my vocal cords. "That's one of the finest roses in my shop."

Puffer's mouth flattened so much that his lips disappeared. That usually happened right before the pencil snapping, so I took a step back, prepared to dodge the missile. "Here's what I think of your fine rose—and your witless prank." He dropped the flower into his trash can with a loud bang. "Get out of my office before I call security and have you arrested."

I fled without a backward glance—and ran smack into Carson Reed, who must have heard the ruckus and come to see what it was about. As I bounced back a step, he made a *tsk* sound with his tongue. "Causing more trouble, Miss Knight? Cooling your heels in jail didn't teach you anything?"

Being in a highly emotional state already, I knew I should ignore him and keep going, but that smug look on Reed's face was too much. "It taught me one thing, Professor.

Beware of snakes with forked tongues, who preach one thing and practice another."

His eyes twinkled, as though he were enjoying the verbal sparring. "Spot quiz. Is name-calling libelous or slanderous? Oh, I'm sorry. You probably didn't pass that test, did you?"

I knew Reed was baiting me, so, as difficult as it was, I bit back any further reply, moved around him, and continued toward the staircase.

"The answer is slanderous," he said, and when I still didn't answer, he called, "I was considering holding a rally for snakes' rights. Want to come? You can carry the snakes."

Five more seconds and I would have been in the clear, but I couldn't let that remark pass without a reply, so I stopped at the top of the stairs and turned to give him an icy look. "That's okay, Professor. Some snakes deserve to be skinned."

Ignoring his hoots of laughter, I held my head high and marched down the steps until I was out of his line of sight, then I nearly tripped over my own feet in my hurry to get out of the building, just in case Puffer made good on his threat to call security. At the bottom, I pushed open the glass doors, checked to see whether I was in the clear, then ran all the way to my car, where I sank into the bucket seat and dropped my head against the back. Could the day get any worse?

After a few moments to catch my breath, I started the motor, then switched it off again. The sun on my head wasn't nearly as hot as the anger boiling inside. The nerve of Reed to make fun of me for taking a stand against injustice! And how dare Puffer accuse me of sending the rose as a prank. Even if I were so inclined, why would I use one of my own products as a means of revenge? I let out a sigh, thinking about that beautiful flower and vase lying in the trash can, knowing they would end up in the county dump. And there was nothing I could do about it.

Or was there?

I dug my phone out of my purse and punched speed-dial number two. The phone rang five times, then Marco answered in that sexy, deep purr that always sent little vibes of pleasure straight through to my toes, even when I was in a bad mood.

"Hey, Sunshine. What's up?"

"Just a little problem. Do you have a second?"

I heard him speak to someone in the background, probably to Chris, Marco's head bartender at the Down the Hatch Bar and Grill. Then he said to me, "I'm going to take this in my office. From the sound of your voice, this isn't a little problem or one we can cover in a second. Am I right?"

Was he ever wrong?

Marco Salvare was the tall, dark, and hunk-a-luscious owner of the local watering hole two doors south of my flower shop on the town square. A former Army Ranger with a private investigator's license, he had also served a stint on the police force, but left due to his reluctance to follow senseless policies. He'd bought the bar shortly after leaving the force and since then had helped me out of a few scrapes, earning himself the honorary title of knight in shining armor— except that he didn't clank when he walked.

"Okay, shoot," he said.

I gave him my story, starting from my near mow-down of Puffer and ending with Reed's last words and my headlong dash to the car. Then I waited as Marco digested the information. Being a male, this took a while. Sometimes days.

I had rearranged my glove compartment, applied more lip gloss, and filed a nail with a snag in it when he finally offered his opinion. "First of all," he said, "I'm not going to tell you that Lottie should have made the delivery for you, because you'd only argue the point."

"True."

"Second, I'm not going to tell you that you shouldn't

have engaged in a war of words with Reed because you already know that."

"True again."

"Third, I *am* going to tell you to start the engine, put the
car in gear, and leave while you're still ahead—but you're
not going to listen."

Like I said, he was never wrong. I could ignore Reed's
jabs for the time being, but there was no way I could let
Puffer defeat me once again. I had come to the law school
determined to take back my self-respect, and by George, I
was going to do it. "Marco, you know that there are two
things in the world I absolutely hate. Injustice and bullies."

"Here it comes," he said with a sigh.

"I'm going back in there to get my flower."

"What can I say but do what you have to do?"

"Thanks, Marco. I needed that."

I got out of the car, slammed the door—that always
made me feel more in control—and headed across the
street, prepared to battle the Dragon. Boy, was I going to tell
Puffer where to get off. He could sneer, insult, and bellow
all he wanted, but there was nothing short of death that
would make me leave without my rose.

CHAPTER THREE

I pushed open the glass door and marched inside, buoyed by righteous indignation. As I started up the stairs I heard the elevator ding, signaling someone coming down from the offices above, but I didn't stop to see who got off. I was focused. I had a goal.

At the top of the stairs I turned right, skirted the deserted secretarial pool, walked past Baumgarten's and Reed's offices, and knocked on Puffer's door. "Professor?"

No answer. I took a deep breath, opened the door, and peered inside. To my amazement he was still there, his chair turned to face the back door.

"Professor, I came for my rose," I said firmly.

He didn't reply. The telephone base was empty, so I figured he was on the line with someone and was ignoring me. I tiptoed to the trash can set beside his desk, reached inside, and picked up the package, trying to make as little noise as possible, which wasn't easy, given the crackling of the cellophane. Then I darted a quick look at the Dragon to see whether he'd noticed.

He hadn't. In fact, it wasn't even Puffer seated in the chair. It was Carson Reed. And he wouldn't have noticed anyway. He was dead.

With a gasp I jumped back. Reed's head was against the back of the chair. His eyes stared straight ahead, his mouth was open, and a shiny black pencil was protruding from the side of his neck. The pencil had opened an artery from which blood had coursed down to soak his shirt collar. The phone's handset was in his lap, and his right hand was hanging off the chair, as though he'd been in the middle of a conversation when he was attacked.

Horrified by the ghastly sight, I backed up until I hit the doorframe, then I began to yell for help at the top of my lungs, even though there wasn't anything that would help Reed now. His coupon had expired. Still, I had to do something, and a solid, blood-curdling shriek was about the only thing that sprang to my shocked brain. Luckily, the yell kicked-started all those little cerebral cells. I reached into my purse, found my phone, and dialed 911.

At that moment a young male ran in, a student, no doubt, out of breath. "What happened?"

I gestured wildly toward the desk just as my call was answered. I had to clench my jaw to keep my teeth from chattering. "This is Abby Knight. I'm at the New Chapel Law School and I just found one of the professors dead."

"Puffer?" the student stammered, turning pale.

"You're at the law school?" the dispatch operator asked, repeating my information.

"Yes. In Professor Puffer's office on the second floor." I saw the student start toward the desk, so I put my hand over the mouthpiece to tell him not to get close, but it was too late. He took a look at the man in the chair, then reeled back. "Omigod. It's Professor Reed."

"Are you calling from a mobile phone, Abby?" the dispatcher asked.

"Yes." I quickly rattled off my number for her, amazed I could even recall it.

"Is anyone there with you?" she asked.

"Yes. One of the students, I think. He ran in when he heard me calling for help."

"Okay, Abby, I have officers on the way. Don't touch anything. Stay right there and talk to me. Tell me how you know the professor is dead."

"H-His eyes are staring straight ahead, and he's not moving, and there's a pencil sticking out of his neck."

The student turned to look at me, his face so ashen I thought he was going to faint. "Did you—?" He made a stabbing motion with his hand.

"Me?" I covered the phone with my hand. "I'm a florist!" Like that would make a difference. It wasn't a time for rational thinking.

"I'm going to be sick." White-faced, he sank to the floor and put his head between his knees. I was feeling queasy myself, so I stepped outside the room and filled my lungs with air.

"Abby?" the dispatcher said, "are you still with me?"

"I'm here—kind of sick to my stomach, but still here."

The police station was only a few blocks from the campus, so it was a matter of minutes until the cops arrived. As the operator kept up a stream of conversation, I heard sirens stop out front, then pounding footsteps on the stairs. I watched five blue-shirted officers swarm onto the floor, with Reilly in the lead, followed by two men in orange jumpsuits who'd probably come by ambulance. I assured the dispatcher that the police had arrived, and we disconnected.

"Over here," I called to the cops, raising my hand to give a weak wave.

Reilly did a double take when he saw me. "You look

familiar," he said, heading toward me with two men on his heels. "Five feet, two inches, freckles, red hair . . . In fact, you remind me of Abby Knight—but you can't be Abby because I told her not an hour ago to leave the school."

"Flower delivery," I managed. "It couldn't be helped." I hitched a thumb toward the open doorway. "One of the professors was stabbed in the neck. He's inside."

At that moment, the student staggered out clutching his stomach. Reilly was on him in a second. "Are you hurt, son?"

To which the student gasped, "Sick."

Reilly helped him to a chair, then he and his men and the paramedics went into Puffer's office, where I could hear him giving out brisk orders. I sank down onto the tile floor and did some shallow breathing until I felt better. When I looked up again, Reilly was back.

He crouched in front of me. "Are you okay?"

"Not so good, actually."

"Take a deep breath and let it out slowly. There you go. Now tell me what happened."

"I walked into Professor Puffer's office and he was sitting in his chair, except that when I went closer, I saw that it was Professor Reed instead, which surprised me because Reed's office is next door. That's when I noticed the pencil sticking out of his neck. . . . Reilly, I saw him alive not twenty minutes ago."

"Back up. You found Professor Reed in Professor Puffer's office? Isn't Puffer the guy you nearly clocked in front of the school earlier?"

I rubbed my temples, which were starting to ache. "And your point is?"

Reilly shook his head. "Never mind. So you came up here to make your flower delivery and found the body?"

"Not exactly. I delivered the flower, then left, then came back to get it. You'll find the package on the floor in

Professor Puffer's office. I dropped it when I saw the, um, corpse."

"You delivered the flower, then came *back* for it?"

Reliving that embarrassing scene wasn't something I felt up to doing, especially when Reilly seemed amused by it, so I said crossly, "Is that really important right now?"

"Okay. We'll save that for later. Did you disturb anything?"

"Other than dropping the flower, no. It's wrapped in cellophane, so there's no mess for your guys to clean up."

"Our lucky day." Reilly rose to his full height and stood looking down at me, shaking his head. "I don't know what it is about you, but it seems like every time we find a dead body, you're somewhere nearby."

"Tell me about it. When our mail carrier is late I break out in a sweat. I won't open the walk-in cooler until I know he's safe."

Reilly rolled his eyes as he held out his arm to help me up and lead me to Bea's desk. "Sit here and rest. You can fill me in on all the fascinating details when I come back."

"At least you can't say it's my driving this time," I said as he turned to give further instructions to the cop standing nearby.

I sagged into Bea's desk chair, but I was too rattled to sit for long. It was still sinking in that Carson Reed was dead, and that he'd been terminated in Puffer's office with one of those infamous black pencils, pointing an obvious finger of guilt directly at the Dragon.

I tried to imagine the circumstances that led up to Reed's murder—Reed stepping into Puffer's office, the two men arguing, then Puffer attacking him in a fit of rage. But what would explain Reed being in Puffer's chair? If Puffer *had* killed him, he certainly wouldn't have propped him in his own chair after he'd done the deed.

Another scenario had Reed taking a seat at Puffer's desk,

then Puffer returning to find Reed using his phone, and going berserk. But that seemed a pretty extreme reaction even for a nasty-tempered dragon.

My third scenario involved an unknown person or persons attacking Reed from behind, believing the victim was Puffer. A case of mistaken identity.

The fourth scenario was still in the works when my stomach growled noisily, reminding me that I hadn't eaten lunch. I glanced at my watch and saw that it was twelve forty. I was sure Lottie and Grace, my assistants, were wondering where I was, so I decided to call.

"I'm at the law school," I said when Lottie answered.

"You're still there? Did you have trouble delivering the rose?"

"In a way."

"Don't tell me you tangled with that pain in the ass Puffer."

"Well, yes, but that's not the problem. Professor Reed is dead—and I found the body."

"Oh, Lordy. Stay calm. I'll be right there." Lottie's answer was preprogrammed. As the mother of seventeen-year-old quadruplet sons, she was used to handling emergencies. The problem was that she tended to treat me as if I were seventeen, too.

"That's not necessary," I assured her, "but thanks anyway. The police have everything under control. I might be here a while, though. Reilly hasn't finished interviewing me yet."

"Okay, sweetie. You take care of yourself and I'll take care of Bloomers." Since she was the previous owner of the shop, and had taught me everything I knew about the business, that was no problem for her. "What about Grace?" Lottie whispered into the phone. "Do I have to tell her or can it wait until you get here?"

"No sense trying to keep it from her. She'll find out soon enough."

Lottie sighed heavily. "All right, but you know darn well she'll be spouting Shakespeare all afternoon, gearing up for your return."

She had a point. Sixty-year-old Grace Bingham was a walking archive, remembering every quote she'd ever heard. Since she operated under the theory that I roamed the earth looking for trouble, she seemed to feel that if she tossed enough of those pithy sayings my way I would miraculously reform. She didn't understand that it was out of my hands. My hair was a cosmic magnet.

"Sing a Willie Nelson song," I said. "That'll drown her out."

Lottie and Grace were about as opposite as two people could be. Lottie Dombowski was a hefty, forty-five-year-old Kentuckian with a gift for floral design, and a love of country-and-western music and anything deep fried. Lottie took life as it came and rarely grew flustered.

Grace, on the other hand, was a slender, even-tempered Brit who enjoyed classical music and expertly brewed tea. Her job was to run the coffee-and-tea-parlor side of Bloomers. She was efficiency personified, and she hated disorder.

What both women shared was loads of common sense and a high tolerance for my shortcomings. In fact, that was part of their job descriptions.

I hung up with Lottie just as the elevator dinged, followed shortly by Professor Puffer's loud voice. He was ranting at someone, so I dashed over to his office doorway for a look. Inside, Reilly was making a detailed diagram of the room, another cop was taking measurements, and the medics were setting up the gurney. At the back I could see Snapdragon trying to get past a cop barring the door. He had obviously just stepped off the elevator, which meant he'd been on the first floor, not outside. I knew from experience that the police would have blocked access to the building as soon as they arrived.

"Stand aside, sir," Puffer commanded.

"I'm not going to tell you again," the cop said. "You can't go in. It's a crime scene."

"I'm as shocked by this man's death as the next person," Puffer retorted, "but this is my *office* and I need my notes. I have a lecture to give in fifteen minutes."

At that, Reilly swung around. "You're all heart, aren't you, Professor? Tell you what. You want to see an office? How about we show you one with bars on the windows?"

Puffer's face turned an angry red. "Don't you dare threaten me."

Reilly sauntered up to him and, being taller, glared down his nose at him. "You make one more sound and I'll clap cuffs on you and haul you away. How's that for a threat?"

The two men glared at each other for a long, tense moment, but ultimately the Dragon knew he was only so much hot air. More than that, he knew *Reilly* knew, along with everyone else in the room. For once in his life, Puffer wasn't in charge.

Muttering something unintelligible, he dropped his gaze. Reilly shook his head in distaste, then went back to his investigation, while I stood there with my hand over my mouth, trying not to chortle. Suddenly, Puffer caught sight of me peering at him through the doorway and his eyes narrowed in fury. Yikes. I'd witnessed his disgrace.

Puffer disappeared from the doorway and I immediately started to sweat. He was in the back hallway and could easily cut through one of the other professors' offices and come out the front. Since I didn't feel like coping with another one of his verbal assaults, I decided a visit to the restroom would be a good idea. Quickly.

CHAPTER FOUR

I turned and nearly collided with the student, who'd evidently been watching the scene over my shoulder. "Sorry," he said.

At the same time I heard Reilly call to one of his men, "Take the professor to a room so I can interview him."

My body shuddered in relief, allowing me to focus on the twentysomething guy in front of me. Some of his color had come back, but he still seemed pretty shaken. He was dressed in typical college student style—untucked short-sleeved shirt, cargo pants, and sneakers. He had dark brown wavy hair, thick eyebrows over a pair of hazel eyes, a long, wide nose with a bump in it, a full mouth, and a chin with a deep cleft in the center. He held out his hand and gave mine a brief shake. "Kenny Lipinski. Sorry I wasn't more help earlier."

"Abby Knight. Don't apologize. It's not easy to see a dead body, especially when it's someone you know."

"I can't believe he's dead," Kenny said, pressing his

palms against his head. "Professor Reed was my adviser. He'd just secured a clerkship for me with a federal appellate judge. I hadn't even had a chance to thank him."

I gazed at Kenny in awe. A clerkship at the federal appellate level—an extraordinarily prestigious position—would open doors that would guarantee him a brilliant career wherever he chose to go—Chicago, New York, L.A. Obviously, he was a bright guy. His name was familiar, too. "Is your father Kent Lipinski of the Lipinski and Lipinski law firm?"

He gave me a guarded look. "Yeah. Why?"

I was about to ask him why he'd pass up going into his father's lucrative law practice to get into the federal court system, but then I thought better of it. The infamous and wealthy Kent Lipinski was the kind of lawyer people joked about—a slick-dressing ambulance chaser who paid people to haunt the hospital corridors and drunk tanks, trolling for clients. He had been known to lie to judges and steal files from other attorneys. He was a shameless publicity hound who was ridiculed behind his back. No wonder Kenny was looking for other opportunities.

"I was curious about something," I said. "Who's the other Lipinski? Your grandfather?"

"No. My dad. He's too important for one name." Seeing the repulsion on Kenny's face, I dropped the subject.

The elevator dinged again, so I peered through the office and saw Jocelyn Puffer walk up to the doorway on the opposite side, where she was instantly met by the cop guarding the door. She wore a long, shapeless black knit skirt, plain black pumps, a pale pink short-sleeved sweater with a matching cardigan draped over her shoulders, and a surprisingly chic black straw hat on her shoulder-length brown hair. I couldn't imagine how she'd gotten into the building—unless she'd rappelled down from a helicopter. But the fact that she was standing there meant she'd been on the first floor somewhere. I couldn't imagine why.

"I'm here to see my husband—Archibald Puffer," I heard her explain to the cop at the door as she tried to peer around him. "Did something happen?"

"How did you get inside the building, ma'am?"

"Why?"

"You'll need to come with me."

"Why do I have to go with you?" she asked, sounding both puzzled and alarmed. "Where's Archie? What happened?"

Archie? I couldn't help but snicker. Puffer was about as far away from being an Archie as I was from being an Abigail.

"Hey, you two. Step back," a cop ordered from behind. Kenny and I both moved out of the way as the crime scene investigation team passed by us and went into the office.

"Is it all right if I go back to the computer lab?" Kenny asked the cop. "I have to finish my research project."

"I want you where I can see you," the cop replied.

With a shrug, Kenny went to a desk on the far side of the secretarial pool. I sat in Bea's chair, drumming my fingers on the desktop until the cop standing outside Puffer's office shot me an annoyed look. I was tempted to call Marco and tell him what had happened, but since he had warned me not to return for my rose I knew he'd only say, "I told you so." Actually, I'd be lucky if that's all he had to say.

I called Nikki instead and got her voice mail, so I left a *you won't believe this* message and hung up. Then I used Bea's computer to do a Google search on the latest varieties of orchids. Reilly came out of Puffer's office and motioned for Kenny to follow him, so I had to wait another fifteen minutes before he came back for me. "Conference room up the hallway," he said.

The conference room was decorated in soothing neutrals

and had a clubby air to it, with dark oak wainscoting and art prints of fox hunts and other so-called sporting events. Reilly seated me in a leather bucket chair near one end of a long, walnut table, then took the head chair, looking out of place in that setting in his blue uniform. "Okay," he said, flipping open his notepad. "Start from when I last saw you in the parking lot."

I gave him the full account, ending with my 911 call.

Reilly wrote quickly, then looked up. "Did you know Carson Reed?"

"Of course. He was my professor when I went to school here." I decided not to bring up Reed's little stunt of having me arrested at the protest rally. I was sure Reilly had heard about it through the police grapevine, but, as my former boss, Dave Hammond, an excellent lawyer and part-time public defender, always said, never give the cops more than they ask for.

"Did you have an argument with Professor Reed today?"

I gave Reilly a puzzled look. "We exchanged a few words. Who told you I had an argument?"

"What did you say to him?"

"I don't remember exactly."

"Did you threaten him?"

"*Threaten* him?" There was only one person who would make such a ridiculous accusation—Snapdragon. "Reilly, look at me. Even in heels I'd barely reach Professor Reed's armpit. Check out these muscles. Do they look threatening to you?" I pushed up a sleeve and flexed my right bicep, which actually didn't look half bad, but then I noticed that Reilly's eyebrows had lowered, a sure sign that he was losing patience.

"I get the picture, Abby. You don't need to give me a graphic demonstration."

"I'm just trying to make a point. In case you didn't get it—"

"I got it." Scowling, Reilly flipped back through his notes, found what he wanted, then asked, "Why did you give Professor Puffer a death rose?"

"A death rose?" I said with an incredulous laugh. "Puffer ordered a black flower suitable for a funeral, but the closest thing I had was a rose called Ink Spots, which is *the* darkest—"

Reilly cut me off. He didn't care for wordy explanations. "The professor said he didn't order it. He claims it was your idea of a sick joke."

"Well, guess what? There's a slip of paper at Bloomers that says otherwise. If some unhappy student pranked him, that's not my fault. Do you really think I have nothing better to do than to drive around town delivering bogus flowers to ill-tempered tyrants?"

His eyebrows went even lower. "A simple no will do."

"Well, then, no. I did *not* give him a *death* rose." I emphasized the word "death" by lowering my voice to a ghostly whisper.

Reilly ignored the dramatic effects. "I'll need to see the order."

"Anytime." I folded my arms and sat back just as a cop stuck his head in the door.

"Sergeant, I'm ready to print her."

"You already have my prints," I reminded them.

Reilly gave a nod and the cop left. I expected a remark about *why* they had the prints, but Reilly only said, "Did you notice anyone in the vicinity of Professor Puffer's office when you arrived the first time?"

"His secretary, Bea. She was just leaving for lunch. The other secretaries were already gone."

"Do you know Bea's full name?"

"Beatrice Boyd," I said and spelled both names for him. "She's not married, so make that Ms."

"Did you see Ms. Boyd leave?"

"No, I saw her start down the steps. But listen, Reilly, if you're sizing up Bea as a potential suspect, forget it. She's not the killer type. In fact, she's a surrogate mother to all the students here. Do you know what her nickname is? Aunt Bea. Do you want to know why?"

"Do you mind if I draw my own conclusions?"

Someone was getting testy. At that moment, one of his men tapped on the doorjamb, then came in to whisper something to him. I strained to hear but couldn't catch it.

Reilly gave the cop a nod, then looked over what he'd just written. "Did Ms. Boyd get along with Professor Reed?"

"Bea gets along with everyone. She even gets along with Professor Puffer."

"Why do you say '*even*' with Puffer?"

"Because Puffer is a class-A jerk. It's no secret he's impossible to get along with. Bea is the only person I know who can tolerate his abuse without getting ruffled."

"Are you saying he is abusive to her?"

"Professor Puffer is abusive to everyone. That's his personality. I can't imagine how his wife stands him."

"How would you describe his relationship with Professor Reed?"

"When I went to school here they were civil to each other, but that was it. I don't know about now."

"Okay, let's go back to after you delivered the rose to Professor Puffer and were leaving the building. Did you see anyone else on the second floor as you left?"

"Only Professor Reed."

"None of the secretaries were there?"

"Nope. The room was empty. None of the other professors were there, either, but that's not unusual. They have flexible schedules and usually teach in the mornings or late afternoons. A few teach only evening classes and they rarely show up before five o'clock. But here's an idea. A group of the professors meet at the Down the Hatch every day for lunch. You can check with them to see if anyone was missing today." I pointed to his tablet. "You might want to write that down."

He glared at me instead. "When you delivered your flower, did you hear anything at all—a door closing, voices, music, the elevator—think carefully."

I gave it some thought, then shook my head. "No. Not then."

"Okay, then did you see or hear anything when you came back?"

"I heard the elevator ding as I was going upstairs, but the second floor was empty."

"So someone was on the way down?"

"That would be my guess. I didn't stick around to see who it was."

"Did you see anyone on the first floor?"

"No, but I could see only up the hallway to the commons area. Someone could have been in a lecture hall or the law library, I suppose. The building usually empties out at noon."

"This is going to be hell to investigate," he muttered. "Okay, tell me again why you returned to Professor Puffer's office."

"To get my flower. Puffer didn't want it and didn't pay for it. In fact, he dropped it in his trash can right before my eyes, so I figured I'd take it back. No sense letting it rot there."

"Why didn't you remove it from the trash when he first dropped it in?"

I leaned toward him and said quietly, "You don't know this man, Reilly. He's mean. Besides, how would you feel if you'd delivered a beautiful rose to someone who immediately tossed it, and then insulted you?"

"Upset?"

"You're darn right. He shouted at me to get out, so I got

out. But after further consideration I decided to go back for
my flower. I even called Marco to discuss it. You can check
that with him." I gave him a confident smile, knowing that
would make points for me. Reilly and Marco had been
friends since they'd worked together on the police force.

"You're telling me that Marco *agreed* you should go back
for the flower?"

Reilly just had to split hairs, didn't he? "I said we discussed it. I didn't say he agreed."

"So tell me something. When you went back to get your
flower, were you still upset?"

There was something about the way he asked that question that made me suddenly cautious. "Not exactly."

He tapped his pencil on the table. "Is that a yes or a no?"

"I don't think I can be that definitive."

Reilly rubbed his eyes, muttering, "My mother told me to
be a priest, but did I listen?"

"A priest? I don't see it."

He took in a huge chestful of air and let it out again.
"What do you say we just get this over with. Can we do that,
please?"

"Hey, you're the one asking the questions." I shrugged
and sat back.

In a tightly controlled voice Reilly said, "When you
entered Professor Puffer's office, did you notice anything
unusual—other than the body?"

Anything unusual? I summoned up the memory, but I had
been so totally focused on getting the flower that I hadn't
really paid much attention to anything around me. And then,
after seeing Reed, I wasn't exactly thinking straight. I could
have told Reilly all that, but I was tired of explaining my actions. "No."

"Did you touch anything in the office?"

"Just my flower."

"So we won't find your fingerprints on anything?"

"Nope."

"Were you in Professor Puffer's office when you made the 911 call?"

"Yes, but I used my cell phone."

"Then you left his office?"

"I felt queasy, so I stepped outside for some fresh air. Kenny was just about to toss his cookies and I didn't want to do the same."

"You're speaking of Kenny Lipinski? Do you know Kenny?"

"I met him today for the first time. He heard me calling for help and came running in."

"From where?"

"Probably from the computer lab. He said he needed to go back to finish his research."

"Did you hear or see him in there earlier?"

"No. The lab is on the far end of the secretarial pool and the door is usually closed. There's no window in it, either, so it's not easy to tell if anyone is inside."

Reilly jotted that down, then flipped back a page, read over his notes, and glanced up at me. "Okay, let's talk about this exchange of words between you and Carson Reed."

I didn't like the way he kept focusing on my conversation with Reed. "It was nothing, Reilly, not even worth mentioning."

He pinned me with a cool look. "Then you shouldn't mind telling me."

Yeah, right, except that I did mind. But I didn't want him to know his questions were making me nervous so I tried to downplay it. "Professor Reed made a remark about my not learning a lesson. You know how educators are—always trying to teach people something."

"That's not an exchange of words. I want the exchange, Abby."

"I gave you the gist of it."

Reilly let out an exasperated sigh. "You're making this interview last a lot longer than it has to, but if you want to sit here the rest of the afternoon trying to dodge my questions, then fine. I'm game."

I frowned at him, but all he did was wait. Reilly could be extremely patient when he had to be. Unfortunately, I couldn't afford to lose any more of my day. As Grace was fond of saying, time was money. I had orders to fill, flowers to arrange, customers to appease.

Still, I wasn't about to concede the battle without letting Reilly know I was unhappy with his question, so I huffed loudly. "Fine. But you have to understand what led up to our little *exchange*. So here's the story. Write fast. Professor Reed is the local counsel for the Dermacol Cosmetics Company, which, by the way, tests its products on live animals. Live animals, Reilly! Fluffy kittens. Playful puppies. You have a dog, don't you? What if someone smeared mascara into his eyes until they bled? Or poured wrinkle cream down his throat until he puked?"

Reilly looked as though he was mentally counting to ten. "I'm not here to discuss Dermacol, Abby. I'm here about a murder. Okay?"

I'd have to work on him about Dermacol some other day. "Okay. So anyway, my roommate heard that there was going to be a protest rally at Dermacol, so we decided to go. While we were marching, Professor Reed showed up with Dermacol's CEO and they held an impromptu news conference for the reporters that were there. I spotted a delivery truck coming in, probably there to deliver more animals, so I organized a human chain to block the back gate. Professor Reed called the police and I was arrested. That brings us to today. Reed heard Puffer yelling at me, so he came out of his office to taunt me about the arrest."

"Are you stating that he started the exchange?"

"Of course he started it. He was trying to provoke me,

probably so he'd have a reason to have me arrested again. I tried not to let him get to me, but he did."

"There's a surprise," Reilly muttered as he wrote. "What did you do then?"

"I made a comment about him being a snake."

"A snake you wanted to skin alive?"

"Is that what Puffer told you? Didn't I say he was a jerk? All I said was that some snakes should be skinned."

"Did you mean it as a threat?"

This conversation was going in circles and I was getting angry. It was clear that Snapdragon had done his best to make me look like a suspect, no doubt to take the heat off himself. "Reilly, what's wrong with you? I made a smart remark. Let it go."

He tapped his pencil on his notepad. "Let's look at what we have here. We have a dead professor. We have a witness who claims you threatened the professor. We have you at the scene of the murder with access to the murder weapon just before the professor died. We have your statement that you returned to the school angry. And then we have you at the scene immediately after the murder. I'm supposed to just let that go?"

"I could say almost all of those things about Professor Puffer, too. He had access to the pencils and he was there before and after the murder." I was really getting testy and I'm sure my voice showed it.

Then I remembered something that immediately sobered me. Not only had I had access to the pencils; I had held one in my hands. But I kept my mouth shut. If that particular pencil wasn't the instrument used to kill Reed, there was no need to throw more suspicion on myself.

"We're not discussing Professor Puffer," Reilly snapped. "We're discussing you."

"Did you tell Puffer that when he started pointing his finger at me?" I retorted hotly. "Okay, sure, Professor Reed and I didn't agree on the animal rights issue, and we did have a slight dispute today, but this is me, Reilly. Abby Knight, daughter of a cop, upstanding businesswoman, defender of justice. What are you thinking?"

He gave me a look that made me wish I hadn't asked. "I'm thinking," he said, crossing his arms over his chest, "that you shouldn't leave town."

CHAPTER FIVE

My mouth fell open. Don't leave town? Was Reilly implying that I might have killed Reed? "You're not serious, are you?"

The look he gave me said he was quite serious. I stared at him, stunned, for about fifteen seconds, then I scraped back the chair and rose. "If you want to know anything else, you'll have to call my attorney, Dave Hammond."

Reilly flipped his notepad closed and got to his feet. "Okay, then, I guess we're done."

We were done all right, but not because he said so. I plowed out of the conference room and headed for the staircase, only to find myself escorted downstairs to the entrance by one of Reilly's men, who then opened the door and stood there waiting for me to depart. Through the glass doors I could see a crowd gathered on the lawn. Some students had even spread blankets and brought food. Minivans from television stations as far away as Chicago were parked along the street, and reporters and photographers were standing around waiting for some action.

Then I noticed Bea standing off by herself, looking grim, so I stepped outside and headed over to talk to her, only to find myself immediately surrounded by reporters. Microphones were shoved under my chin and cameras were focused on my face as they fired questions at me.

"Give us your name."

"Do you go to school here?"

"Is this a hostage situation?"

"Will you give us a statement?"

"Are you the flower delivery girl who was seen entering the building around noon?"

I wasn't going to answer them—but I couldn't let that last question go. "I am *not* a delivery girl," I said to the cluster of mics. "I'm a florist. I own Bloomers, on the town square."

"Is anyone hurt inside?" someone called.

This was followed by more shouted questions. I finally pushed past them and marched toward the street, fully expecting to be followed all the way to my car. But then I heard one of them shout, "There's another one," and I glanced around just as Kenny came out and was quickly swallowed by the press. I hurried to the parking lot, jumped into the Vette, backed the car out of the space, and took off, feeling new sympathy for celebrities.

Attorney David Hammond sat behind his old oak desk and took notes on a yellow legal pad as I recited my story. A slightly paunchy man in his late fifties, Dave had never quite got the hang of matching a shirt and tie to his suit. Today he had on a white shirt and navy striped tie with cocoa brown trousers. The suit coat hung on a hook on the back of his door.

His lack of style didn't matter to his clients, who adored

him. Dave had a keen mind and a big heart, and he refused to charge by the nanosecond. He hated big corporations and loved to skewer insurance companies, sloppy detectives, and lazy attorneys who wouldn't return phone calls. He was also a damned good defense lawyer, as I'd learned when I clerked for him.

"I should have guessed where Reilly's questions were leading and kept my mouth shut," I said. "How foolish am I for thinking any friendship we had would make a difference in how he treated me?"

"He's being a cop, Abby. You know your father would have done the same thing."

"Yeah, but still . . . Don't leave town?"

"Did you have plans to leave town?"

"Well, no. But what if I wanted to?"

"Forget about that for now. Here's what you have to do. Number one, keep your mouth shut. Number two, keep your mouth shut. And number three?" He made a rolling motion with his hand, signaling me to supply the answer.

"Keep my mouth shut."

"That's right. Don't talk to the police, don't talk to reporters, don't even discuss the details of the murder with your mother. And for heaven's sake, keep a low profile so you don't draw the police's attention."

"Dave, I will keep my profile so low that ants will crawl over me."

"That's what I like to hear. I don't think anything will come of the interview you gave Reilly. It's too circumstantial. Having said that, I also have to caution you that stranger things have happened, as you know. However, I wouldn't stay up nights worrying about it."

"I'll leave that for my parents to do." I smiled for the first time in hours. "Thanks, Dave. I feel better. Do you want a retainer?"

"First, I'm going to pretend you didn't ask that," he said.

He loved to number things. "Second, a retainer for what? There's no case against you."

I went around the desk and gave him a hug. Then I left, feeling as though a twenty-pound weight had been lifted off my back. As I cut diagonally across the courthouse lawn, I waved happily to Jingles, the window washer, as he carried his bucket and squeegee to the next store on his list. I almost stopped to chat with him, but then I remembered Dave's warning, so I zipped my lips, lowered my profile, and kept on going.

Though Chicago was only a little over an hour's drive away, New Chapel's town square had managed to retain most of its old-fashioned flavor. It had brick-edged side-walks, quaint streetlights, family-owned shops and restaurants, and a big, limestone courthouse that sat in the middle of a huge lawn shaded by many oaks and maples. It also had the biggest gossip mill in Indiana. At least it seemed that way to me.

As proof, by the time I had crossed the square and stepped through Bloomers' bright yellow door, everyone I had ever known in my life had called to find out exactly what part I had played in the drama unfolding at the law school. The stack of messages waiting for me behind the front counter was an inch thick, and as I flipped through them, I saw that a good half inch were from my mother.

"You'd best call her immediately, dear," Grace said in her crisp British accent, coming out of the coffee parlor with a cup of her special brew for me. "Or else risk a surprise visit, and I doubt you're quite up to that after the tribulation you've been through."

Grace was dressed in a pair of beige slacks and print blouse with a blue cotton blazer over it. As usual, not one hair in her short, layered gray cut was out of place. She handed me the coffee, but before I could take a sip, she peered into my eyes, moved my head from side to side, and turned me in a circle to satisfy herself that I had survived my ordeal.

"Is that Abby?" Lottie swept through the curtain at the back of the shop. She was wearing her usual summer getup—bright pink blouse and white slacks molded snugly to her size-fourteen frame, and pink loafers. Matching pink barrettes held brassy curls off her broad face in a style that continued to be a source of embarrassment to her teenaged sons. Her husband, Herman, however, thought she looked like a queen.

"Sweetie, I'm so glad you're all right," Lottie cried, giving me a big bear hug. She leaned back to look me over. "When you said you found the professor's body, I didn't realize he'd just been killed. You could have walked in on the murderer. Lordy, I don't even want to think about what could have happened to you."

"How did you hear about that?"

"There've been news bulletins every five minutes on the radio, and Herman said the TV stations interrupted their programs to broadcast live reports."

No wonder my mother had been calling. If the news reports had upset Lottie even after I'd talked to her, I couldn't imagine what they'd done to Mom. I could feel myself tensing, so I held the cup of coffee to my nose, closed my eyes, and inhaled the bittersweet aroma. Grace made the best java I'd ever tasted, fixed just the way I liked it with a good shot of half-and-half. Just the smell was enough to calm me. I filled the women in on my visit to Dave, cautioned them not to give out any information on the murder, then started to the back to do my daughterly duty.

"After you've rung your mum," Grace called, "I'd like to share a few thoughts with you."

Uh-oh. The quote lady was ready.

The phone rang and Lottie went to answer it. "Bloomers,"

she said in her big voice. She listened a moment, then covered the handset with her palm and whispered, "Guess who."

"Hmm. Let's see . . . Mommy dearest?"

Grace and Lottie knew I loved my mother. They also knew there were times when she drove me crazy, and I had a feeling this would be one of those times, best suffered from a distance, the most desirable location being Nome, Alaska. The only thing that I had going for me now was that until three thirty that afternoon, she was confined to her classroom.

My mother was a lively, bright, well-loved kindergarten teacher who had raised my two brothers and me with a firm but gentle hand and had seen my father through the adversities of surgery and a crippling stroke. A year ago she'd decided to take a sculpting class, so, as a Christmas gift, my father bought her a potter's wheel. That was the beginning of a series of clay pieces that could only be described as bizarre. Even worse, she had decided that Bloomers was the perfect place to display her creations, so every Monday for the last two months she had lugged in her latest sculpture for me to sell.

Two weeks ago she had turned her talents, such as they were, to making mosaics, which had sounded like a great idea—at first. After all, how many bizarre creations could be made from little clay tiles? Except that she wasn't using *clay* tiles. She was using *mirrored* tiles. She hadn't brought any of her creations in yet, but I knew it was only a matter of time.

When I'd joined my parents for dinner on Sunday, Mom had already tiled the brass umbrella stand by the front door, the living-room lamps, the old wooden trunk they used as a coffee table, all the vases and candlesticks in the house, a giant wooden salad bowl, a soup tureen, the place mats on the dining-room table, and both sides of the swinging kitchen door. She'd even mirrored the hall mirror. There had been so much reflection in the house that I'd had to wear sunglasses during the meal. I wouldn't even enter the bathroom for fear of seeing body parts distorted in a way that would cause nightmares for years. I couldn't begin to explain how much I was dreading next Monday.

I carried my cup through the curtain to my desk in the workroom and sat down, but before I picked up the phone I swiveled the chair for a quick look around the room. My gaze swept the long countertops, the shelves on the wall that overflowed with containers of silk flowers, the big, stainless steel, walk-in cooler stuffed with fresh blossoms, the long, slate worktable in the middle of the room, then back to my desk, with its familiar cat pencil cup, framed photos, small computer monitor, and a pile of paperwork waiting to be filed.

I called that glance around the room my sanity second because it always brought me a feeling of well-being that allowed me to face just about anything. It wasn't merely a workroom to me. It was a tropical paradise—fragrant, peaceful, inspiring, colorful . . . I couldn't even begin to describe all the feelings it evoked. All I knew was that at Bloomers I had finally found a place where I fit, a place where my light could shine, where neither my height nor my measurements nor my ability to cite case law mattered.

I had only one major fear—failure. It had happened to me once too often not to leave scars. Since I had taken over the shop, business had picked up, but it still wasn't great, especially because my main competition was a floral and hobby megastore out on the highway. I made enough to pay my assistants and buy my supplies, but beyond that I took out only what I needed for bills, and I was always looking for more ways to boost sales. However, selling mirrored mosaics wasn't one of them.

"Hi, Mom. I'm fine. No need to worry."

"Abigail, tell me it's not true. You didn't really find another dead body, did you?"

"Do you want me to answer truthfully or do you want to sleep tonight?"

"Hold on. We're going to do a conference call with your father."

"Mom, that's not necessary. I'll talk to you both later, when you get home from school."

"Do you really think my nerves will hold out until then?"

"Okay, fine," I said, and settled back to wait for my father to get on. It took him a little longer to do things. More than three years ago he'd lost the use of his legs after a felon's bullet struck him in the thigh and an operation to remove it had caused a stroke. With therapy he had regained most of his speech, but he was still in a wheelchair. He'd retired from the police force shortly after the shooting and was currently teaching himself genealogy. He hoped to write a biography of the Knight family one day, starting with his great-grandfather, who'd come over from Ireland. Having heard many of the stories, I had a feeling the bookstores would probably shelve the book next to *Ripley's Believe It or Not*. We had some quirky skeletons in our closet. Thank goodness the oddball gene had skipped my generation.

I heard a click and then my mother said, "Okay, Abigail, your father's on. Go ahead."

As I launched into a sanitized version of my afternoon, Lottie came in to finish a topiary made with deep-coral alstroemerias, ming fern, and jessamine foliage. I watched her work her magic as I talked, and finally ended my story with Dave Hammond's comforting assurance that the matter would probably come to nothing. My mother apparently tuned out that last part.

"Oh, dear God!" she cried. "Jeffrey, you have to call someone to make sure Abby's not a suspect. You still know people on the force."

"Maureen, calm down. No one said she was a suspect. It's not like they told her not to leave town."

Gulp.

"But she was questioned, Jeff. Our baby! That's just not right."

"It's standard police procedure."

Their debate raged on, so I finally said, "I'd love to stay and chat but I have orders to fill. Love you both," and hung up. I'd dodged the bullet temporarily.

"Is she freaking out?" Lottie asked.

"She can't yet. She's at school." I turned to get up and there was Grace, holding the lapels of her blazer—her lecture pose.

"That's a new jacket, isn't it?" I asked her. "I really like it over that blouse."

I heard Lottie cough and knew she was trying to cover her laugh at my attempt to divert Grace's attention.

"Thank you, dear. Yes, it is new. And I'd like to share something that William Shakespeare wrote in the *Second Part of King Henry the Fourth*."

The phone rang. "Excuse me a minute," I said and turned to pick it up before Lottie could get it. No offense to Grace, but I wasn't in the mood to hear from any of King Henry's parts, even the more interesting ones.

It was Marco. "Are you all right? I left a message for you to call."

"I'm fine. I just got back to the shop. Reilly put me through quite a grilling."

"Whoa. Why would he put *you* through a grilling?"

I took a quick glance over my shoulder and saw Grace waiting patiently. "This might take a while," I whispered to her. The bell over the door chimed, so she left.

"I found the body, Marco. Can you believe Reilly actually told me not to leave town?"

"Wait. *You* found the body?"

Marco must have been the only one in town who hadn't heard the news, and by the tone of his voice I knew I needed to put a good spin on it. "Remember when I told you I was going back for my flower and you said to do what I had to do?"

"I'm coming down." There was a click on the other end.

I hung up and glanced over at Lottie, who was tying a sage-colored satin ribbon at the base of the topiary. "Marco's on his way. I guess he'd rather hear the story in person."

"Herman is like that, too. He can't concentrate unless he can see me; otherwise his mind wanders. Is that your stomach growling?"

"I didn't eat lunch."

She put down her pruning shears and headed for the tiny kitchen in back. "I'll microwave a bag of popcorn. It'll tide you over until supper."

While Lottie was gone I pulled an order for an arrangement of silk flowers for the insurance agency next door and gathered supplies for it, starting with a wicker basket. The bell chimed four times while I worked, and each time I held my breath, expecting to see Marco stride through the curtain. Instead, I kept hearing what sounded like turkeys gobbling. I finally went to the curtain to take a peek.

"Here you go," Lottie said from behind me, the buttery smell of popcorn preceding her. "What are you looking at?"

"Customers."

"Is someone trying to steal something?"

"I can't tell."

"What do you mean you can't tell?"

"It's too crowded."

"Crowded?" Lottie came up behind me for a look. "Lordy," she whispered in an amazed voice. "It's like a plague of locusts."

We peered out together, watching as at least a dozen

women prowled the shop, examining flower arrangements, picking up knickknacks, and checking price tags on the wreaths that hung on the brick walls.

"I haven't seen it this busy since Valentine's Day," Lottie said in a whisper. "I'd better work the register so Grace can take care of the coffee parlor. I see people heading in there."

The bell chimed, and over the top of the ladies' heads I saw Marco step inside. He glanced around, clearly surprised by the crowd. Then he spotted me and headed my way. He didn't look happy.

CHAPTER SIX

I backed into the workroom, pinched my cheeks for color, and hurried to the table to resume my work. No need to let him think I was watching for him. How pathetic would that look? When he came in, I was perched on a stool, arranging silk flowers. I glanced up at him and couldn't stop a smile from spreading across my face. No matter what kind of trouble I was in, seeing Marco always strummed my heart strings.

He had thick, dark hair that was kind of curly but not too short or too shaggy. He had deep-set dark eyes that could strip away your outer layers and see into those secret places in your soul, strong Mediterranean good looks, and a body sculpted from the rigorous training of the Army Rangers and maintained through workouts at the local YMCA. But what really made him sexy was the confidence he exuded from every pore. It was like an aphrodisiac, only without the slimy oyster. Add that famous Salvare smile to the mix—

a slight upturn of his mouth—and grab hold of something solid, baby. As the French would say, *ooh-la-la*.

Marco and I had been seeing each other ever since he'd come to my rescue after a hit-and-run driver smashed my Vette a few months back. It was the beginning of a beautiful and, hopefully, permanent relationship—when we're both ready for the permanent part. I seemed to be moving toward it faster than he was, although he was starting to show glimmers of promise.

Marco wasn't glimmering now. He had pulled up a stool and was studying me with an intense gaze, waiting for me to talk. I offered him popcorn, trying to raise his smile, but he shook his head. He wanted facts. He was in his PI persona. "Tell me what happened."

I took a bite of popcorn to appease the hunger monster, then launched into my story, which was starting to suffer from too many tellings. "All in all it was a horrible experience, Marco, a terribly gruesome sight, and I hope I never have to witness anything like it again. Professor Reed had his faults, but I certainly didn't want to see him dead. And then to have Reilly treat me like a suspect, well, that was just over the top. Dave Hammond doesn't think it will come to anything, but I can't help worrying a little."

Marco didn't bat an eye or make a sound. The only indication of his feelings was a tiny tic in his jaw muscle, and I knew exactly what it meant. "I know," I said. "I should have taken your advice and left the college. But I had to go back for that flower or I couldn't have lived with myself. My dignity was at stake."

"Did Reilly actually tell you you're a suspect?"

"Not in so many words."

"So you're not a suspect."

"Officially—no. But he told me not to leave town. How would *you* read that?" I offered him popcorn again.

That time he took a handful and chewed it, looking

pensive. After a few moments he said, "I agree with Dave Hammond. Reilly's interest in you probably isn't anything more than a formality."

I perked up at that. "You think so?"

"I think so. But to satisfy my own curiosity I'd like to nail down a few more details about what you saw. Go back to when you found Carson Reed's body. The eraser half of a pencil was sticking out of his neck. Did it look like there'd been a struggle?"

"No. More like he'd been taken by surprise."

Marco pursed his lips. "If someone had stabbed me, my first reaction would be to yank out the weapon. So something must have kept him from doing so. You didn't notice a gash, or any blood running from his head, or anything binding his hands?"

I forced myself to revisit the gruesome scene. "No on all counts."

"Okay. You said Professor Puffer came up to the second floor on the elevator, followed shortly by his wife Jocelyn. So both of them were in the building before the police arrived?"

"Right. I didn't see Puffer in the student commons area when I went in, but that doesn't mean he wasn't in the law library. As for Jocelyn, I heard a cop ask her how she got inside, but I didn't hear her answer. Why she was there at all is a puzzle. When I attended the school, she rarely set foot in the place, which wasn't surprising given the way Puffer verbally abused her—and that was in public. I can't imagine how he treats her in private."

"You mentioned that you saw her before noon, then not again until twelve fifty, leaving a gap of almost an hour." Marco drummed his fingers on the table as he pondered the matter. "When she came off the elevator, how did she look and sound?"

"Flustered, but I saw her for only a minute, then a cop took her away."

"Did she see Reed's body?"

"I don't think so. There were too many people in the way."

"Did she seem upset to find cops in her husband's office?"

"She seemed more baffled than anything else."

Marco took a handful of popcorn. "What was Puffer's reaction to Reed's death?"

"He didn't seem upset, just angry because a cop was blocking his way. He kept insisting that he should be allowed inside because it was his office and he needed his lecture notes. Reilly had to threaten to take him to the police station to get him to back off."

Marco absorbed the information. "What about this student—Kenny Lipinski? What was his reaction?"

"Like mine. Shock first, then sick to his stomach. Professor Reed was his adviser and had just secured a clerkship for him with a federal appellate judge. That probably doesn't mean anything to you, but law students would kill for a shot at that position."

Marco lifted an eyebrow. "Interesting way of putting it. I suppose other students were vying for it?"

"I see where you're headed. Maybe one of them was upset over not getting that clerkship and took it out on Professor Reed."

"It's one possibility. You said there were other offices on the second floor. Were any of the professors in them?"

"The offices were dark and the doors were closed, so my guess would be no."

"The secretary—Beatrice Boyd—how did she get along with Reed?"

"As I told Reilly, Bea gets along with everyone. She's a sweetheart. All the students love her." I reached for one of the napkins Lottie had left on the table and wiped my buttery fingers.

"Do you know of any reason Professor Puffer might have wanted Reed out of the way?"

"As much as I would love to turn the heat on Puffer, no, I don't. But I wouldn't rule him out, either. He had the means and the opportunity, which would seem to make him the obvious suspect, wouldn't it? So why would Reilly order me not to leave town? All I did was discover the body. If I were the murderer, would I hang around to alert the police?"

Marco reached for more popcorn and tossed the kernels in his mouth. "So your question is, why would he throw you in the suspect pool? Well, let's see. Did you give him straight answers?"

I brushed a daisy petal off the table. If I said yes, I'd be lying, which I didn't like to do. If I said no, there would be the inevitable question as to why I didn't give Reilly straight answers, and frankly, I did it because that was my nature, and yes, I knew better. So I said, "Do you mean straight, as in linear?"

Marco didn't have to utter a word. His expressive eyes did the talking for him, and they said he knew I was dodging yet again. "Sunshine, you know Reilly likes everything quick and to the point. Why yank his chain, especially during a murder investigation?"

"I wasn't trying to yank his chain. I simply didn't want to be pinned down to a specific answer for fear he might misconstrue what I said."

"In other words, you didn't want to give him any information that might make him think you could have killed Reed."

"Bingo."

"But it happened anyway. Otherwise he wouldn't have told you not to leave town."

Bingo. I plopped my chin in my hand and sighed unhappily. "What should I do?"

"Nothing. You haven't been charged, and the cops have a whole bunch of people to interview before they start narrowing down their list of suspects." He wiped his hands on the napkin, crumpled it into a ball, and twisted around to make a perfect shot into the trash can in the corner. "I'd still recommend keeping a low profile. You don't want to draw attention to yourself while the police are investigating. *Capisce?*"

"Yes, I understand." Did *he* understand that he was the sexiest man who'd ever walked the planet, especially when he spoke Italian to me? Did he know how much I wanted to hop on his lap and nuzzle that hard jaw?

"I'll let you get back to work," he said, ready to slide off the seat.

"Wouldn't you like some more popcorn before you go?" I dug in the bag and produced two buttery kernels.

"No, thanks." Clearly he was unaware of the passion he had inspired. "I'm going to talk to Reilly before he goes off his shift and see if he'll tell me where he's going with this case, what his thoughts are."

At that moment I didn't much care what Reilly's thoughts were because *my* thoughts had wrapped themselves around the hunk sitting almost knee to knee with me, in his leg-hugging Levis and tan T-shirt, stretched tight over those totally masculine pecs. I hopped off the stool, sidled up to Marco, and said in a seductive voice, "Are you sure you don't want some?"

He gazed at me for all of one second, then the left side of his mouth curved up slightly—and I knew I had him in the palm of my hand, right beside those kernels. "I might be persuaded," he said in that low, rumbling purr.

I fed him one kernel followed with the second, watching those taut throat muscles do their job. Then Marco curled his fingers around my wrist and brought my hand to his mouth. His smoldering gaze on mine, he used his tongue to flick away the last trace of butter, teasing every nerve in my body into a fever pitch of excitement, so that I had to lean against the table to steady myself. Then he put his other hand around my waist and brought me up against his hard chest, tilting his head so our lips could meet.

At the very moment of impact Lottie burst through the curtain and went straight to the radio she kept on the counter. "Sorry, kids, but I think you should hear the latest report." She turned up the volume to bring in the newscaster's voice.

"To repeat our breaking news story, Carson Reed, a professor at New Chapel University School of Law, was found dead shortly after noon today, the victim of a brutal attack. According to an anonymous source, Reed's body was discovered by local businesswoman Abigail Knight, who was there to deliver a floral arrangement. Police haven't released any details and won't comment about potential suspects."

"Well," I said, trying to make light of it, "that shouldn't raise my profile too much."

"When asked for a comment," the news anchor continued, "Ms. Knight, a former student of Carson Reed's, would only say, 'I am *not* a delivery girl. I'm a florist. I own Bloomers, on the town square.'"

A huge silence descended on the workroom. I glanced at Lottie, who was shaking her head in dismay. Marco was more verbal. "I'm surprised you didn't offer up your Social Security number while you were at it."

I dropped my head into my hands. Things were spinning out of control and I felt helpless to stop them. "That would explain the sudden rush of customers," I muttered through my fingers. "I'm the new curiosity in town."

Lottie started to turn off the radio, but Marco said, "Wait."

With the news bulletin over, the two talk-show hosts,

Rob and Rick, of the corny afternoon radio program *Rob and Rick's Radio Schtick* resumed their banter: "Sounds like Abigail Knight is a florist with an attitude, Rob."

"Is she ever! I remember Abby from New Chapel High School, when she took on Coach DePugh for using a live eagle as mascot at the homecoming game."

At that I dropped my hands. "The bird was a hawk, not an eagle. And Rob was a big geek."

"Hey, Rob," his cohost said, "is that the same Abby Knight who was arrested last week for leading a protest march at Dermacol Labs?"

"I didn't lead it!" I exclaimed hotly.

"She sure is, Rick, and if I remember correctly, Carson Reed was Dermacol's spokesman. How's that for a coincidence? Listeners? What do you make of this? Give us a call at four-six-one-two-four-six-one. Hello, who is this?"

"Uh, yeah, this is Doug. My wife works at Dermacol. Sounds mighty suspicious to us that this rabble-rouser florist has a showdown with Mr. Reed, then all of a sudden she finds him dead. She sounds like a troublemaker to me."

"A troublemaker?" I cried. "A rabble-rouser? Do I have to listen to this?"

"It's better to know what people are saying," Marco told me.

"Thanks for your opinion, caller," Rick said. "And who's up next?"

"This is Bill, and I have to say, thank God for Dermacol Labs. They're paying me a decent income and giving me good benefits."

"Not to mention torturing animals," I snapped.

"Danged activists would just as soon shut down the lab," the caller continued, "so that people like me have to stand in soup lines because of some harmless testing."

I was ready to tear out my hair. "Harmless? He's insane.

Why can't he get a job somewhere else? Why does *not* working there mean standing in a soup line?"

"Calm down, Sunshine. People don't think logically when emotions run high. Remember, they're all scared right now. There's a killer on the loose."

"I say we shut down that woman's flower shop and see how she likes it!" the caller finished.

"Okay, Bill," Rick said. "Thanks for the input. Hello, caller three."

"I just want to say that Professor Reed was a wonderful man," a young woman said tearfully. "All his students adored him. That woman had no right to take him away from us just because he flunked her."

"I didn't take him away!" I shouted at the radio.

"Hey, Rick," Rob said. "We're not being fair to Abby."

Thank God someone finally realized that.

"So why don't we give Abby a call and see what she has to say for herself?"

"It's about time," I said to Marco, who was rubbing his eyes, looking as if he'd rather be anywhere else.

Marco pointed his index finger at me. "You are not to say a word."

"I have to let them slander me like that?"

"Yes."

I couldn't do it. It went against my nature. I had to defend myself.

CHAPTER SEVEN

The phone rang and I started to go for it, but Marco and Lottie both yelled, "No!"

"It might be a customer."

"Grace will get it," Lottie said, and sure enough, a second later we heard her answer up front. Then she stuck her head through the curtain. "Abby, dear, someone named Rob is on the line. He said he's from a radio station and you know him."

"She's not here," Lottie said.

"Then I shall tell him you're out making a floral delivery."

"No!" all three of us yelled, startling Grace.

"We don't want him to call back," Marco said. "Just say she has no comment."

On the radio, Rob said, "Ms. Knight is afraid to talk to us, Rick."

"You're a scary guy, Rob," Rick joked. "Okay, folks, this notice was just handed to me. Looks like there's another protest rally in the works, this one organized by a group of Carson Reed's students. You'll never guess where they're going to march, Rob."

"I know this one. In front of Abby Knight's flower shop."

"You got it. Okay, folks, you heard it here. There will be a gathering of Professor Carson Reed's students at Bloomers, on the town square."

Marco shut off the radio. In the front, we could hear Grace on the phone, deflecting calls. Another line lit up, so Lottie answered it at my desk, forcing herself to say in her usual cheerful manner, "Bloomers." She listened briefly, then said, "She doesn't have any comment," and hung up. "That was a reporter from the *New Chapel News*."

The ringing started again and two more lines lit up. "I'll get those up front," Lottie said and hurried through the curtain.

When I let out a heavy sigh, Marco started rubbing my back. "You'll survive this, Sunshine."

"How?" I muttered. "I can't defend myself. I have to keep a low profile."

"You don't need to defend yourself. You didn't do anything wrong. As soon as the police arrest their suspect, you'll be vindicated."

"I hope so."

"Hey, with Dave and Lottie and Grace on your side, not to mention yours truly, how can you go wrong?"

I lifted my head to gaze into those gorgeous brown eyes and smiled in spite of myself. "Thanks."

"No problem. Now, let's rehearse your line: 'No comment.' "

"No comment," I repeated dutifully, walking my fingers up his arm. It was impossible to think seriously for very long with him that close.

"Good. Remember it."

"Want to permanently etch it in my brain?"

He gave me that little grin. "Try me."

I put my hands on his face and guided him in for a two-point landing on my lips. This time we made it with no interruptions, only bliss. Marco's lips were firm and smooth as they moved against mine, and his mouth had the salty, creamy taste of butter that made me hungry for more—kisses, not butter.

"Did that do the trick?" he asked, giving me that sleepy-eyed gaze that drove me wild.

I traced a fingertip across his iron jaw. "For now. I might need a refresher later, though."

"Why don't you come down to the bar after you lock up tonight. We'll have supper and I'll fill you in on what I learned from Reilly. And then"—he wiggled his eyebrows suggestively—"more etching."

"Sounds like a plan to me."

As I parted the curtain so Marco could walk out, several customers spotted me and clamored, "There she is! Hey, Abigail, over here!"

One woman waved money, while another shouted, "I want to place an order."

"I was next," another woman said and tried to elbow past her.

"I'm right behind her."

"Hey, Abby, remember me? I'm a friend of your mother's."

"Escape while you still can," I whispered to Marco, then, as he warily circled the frenzied mob to get to the door, I fought my way to the counter and began to take payments and evade questions. After a solid hour of it, the shop finally quieted down, letting me get back to the workroom. Nothing busted stress like surrounding myself with fragrant blossoms.

I finished the arrangement I'd started earlier, then pulled an order that called for an arrangement for a formal dinner party. I opened the big cooler and stepped inside, letting my

thoughts drift as I absorbed the many varieties of flora, waiting for an idea to hit me. The weather would stay warm
through most of September, so I decided to stick with a summer theme. And what came with summer? Lots of sun and
big, fluffy white clouds. That brought to mind lazy afternoons at the Dunes, warm sand, seashells, and stones washed
smooth—all shades of white. What could be more formal
than that?

The off-white lily called Sahara was cool and classy, as
were the delicate lilies of the valley. I pulled some, then
added stems of artemisia, salvia, echinacea, and dusty
miller, and laid them all out on the worktable. I scanned the
shelves above the counter for the appropriate container and
spotted several possibilities—a warm beige ceramic vase,
another vase that looked like it was made of pale coral, and
a clean-lined, square, glass vase. I chose the glass and filled
a third of it with a mixture of white sand and tiny seashells.
In twenty minutes I had my creation done, and as I stood
back to admire it, Lottie came through the curtain.

"What do you think?" I asked her.

"It's gorgeous. And you need to leave now, through the
back door."

"It isn't five o'clock yet and we've got a bunch of orders
to fill."

"Do you want to talk to the reporter waiting outside? I
think his name is Mackay."

"No. Did you tell him I have no comment?"

"It didn't work. He parked himself on the lawn across the
street and is waiting for you to leave. But he won't be expecting you to leave early, or through the back door, and he
probably doesn't know your car or he'd be watching it."

"Let me just finish wrapping this first."

Lottie took the wrapping paper out of my hands. "I'll do
it. You just go."

I slung my purse over my shoulder and headed for the

kitchen. "I'm having dinner with Marco at the bar, so I'll slip in sometime afterward to finish the orders."

"Wait!" Lottie pulled a blue and pink cotton print scarf out of her tote bag, wrapped it around my head, tied the ends under my chin, then examined her handiwork. "Put your sunglasses on. Perfect."

Feeling like a spy, I peered cautiously out the back door. The alley was clear so I hurried to the end, turned the corner, and dashed to my car, parked by the American Legion Hall. I pulled up the ragtop but left the windows down for air. The old farmer who'd originally owned the Corvette hadn't opted for frivolities such as air-conditioning.

Congratulating myself on outwitting the reporter, I started the engine, fastened my seat belt, and adjusted my mirror, catching sudden sight of my reflection. Dear God. I looked like Nikki's grandmother. I was about to remove the scarf when I heard someone call my name. I checked the rearview mirror again and saw one of the reporters who'd been at the law school striding across the parking lot, waving his arms and calling, "Wait!" as he headed right for me.

Apparently, I hadn't outwitted him.

CHAPTER EIGHT

Instantly, I shifted into reverse, hoping to get out of the lot before he reached me, but he was moving too fast. He stopped directly behind the Vette, and since I couldn't very well run him over—well, I *could*, but I was in enough hot water with Reilly as it was—I swivelled around to glare at him through the back window and motion with my hand for him to move away.

"I'd like to talk to you," he called. "Just give me five minutes."

"Vy you vant to talk to me?" I called back in a pretty fine imitation of Nikki's grandmother's husky Slavic accent. "Go avay from car."

The next thing I knew, he was peering in the open window. "You're Abby, right?"

He wasn't bad looking if your taste ran to guys with silky, dark brown hair long enough to pull back in a ponytail. On the plus side, he did have striking sea-foam green eyes framed by a handsome set of brown eyebrows. But the real clincher was his wide, captivating smile. I couldn't help wondering whether his teeth were naturally that white or he bleached them.

Since I was hardly in the right frame of mind to be captivated by a guy who chased me down in a parking lot, I said, "Olga does not know thees Abby." I eased the gas pedal down and the Vette started to roll backward.

"I'd really like to talk to you, Abby—or Olga," he said, keeping pace with me. "I'd like to hear your side of the story."

My side of the story? "Go avay. Olga ees busy voman." I shifted into drive and took off, but not before he tossed his business card into the car. "My cell phone number is on it," he yelled. "Don't lose it. You're going to want to talk to me."

Don't hold your breath, buddy. I paused at the street to make sure it was clear, then sped away with a squeal of tires. I whipped off the scarf, ran my fingers through my hair, and turned on the radio. But instead of playing the usual variety of songs, all the local stations were reporting on the murder—and my connection to it. Annoyed, I shut it off and drove in silence, hoping the killer would be found quickly and my life would get back to normal—such as it was.

As I pulled into my parking space at the apartment building, my phone rang. I shut off the motor, checked the screen for an ID, and saw it was Nikki.

"Omigod, Abby. I went on my break and got your message about the murder. How horrible! Are you all right?"

"Let's just say I feel very close to your grandmother right now."

"I have no idea what you're talking about."

I got out of the car, plucked the reporter's card out of the back—convertibles should always be litter free—and glanced at the printing. It read: CONNOR MACKAY, REPORTER. *THE NEW CHAPEL NEWS*. Beneath that was a phone number and an e-mail address. *Mackay. Hmm.* Not a local name. Probably from out of town.

Without giving Connor Mackay another thought, I tucked the card in my purse and said to Nikki, "If you have five minutes I'll tell you what happened."

"I have six, so go ahead."

As I headed for our apartment, stopping to check the mailbox and dump the junk mail into the trash container, I caught her up to speed on my meetings with Reilly and Dave Hammond, Rob and Rick's radio show, and my sudden notoriety. "Tell me, Nikki, how am I supposed to keep a low profile now?"

"You can start by instructing Jillian not to blab anything to anyone. Otherwise, if a reporter shows up at the door, she'll probably invite him in for a drink. Then you can remind her about my shelf in the medicine cabinet. And don't forget you promised to talk to her about moving out. Oops. I'm being paged. Gotta go."

At that moment my neighbor, Mrs. Sample, came around the corner with her Chihuahua, Peewee, on his leash. The Samples were a friendly, middle-aged, childless couple who adored their pet, a tiny, fragile animal who wore little sweaters and booties Mrs. Sample herself had knitted—as she had told me many times, along with other, equally fascinating tidbits.

"Peewee, look who's here," Mrs. Sample cooed, scooping up the yapping minibeast before he could nip off a hunk of my flesh. For a reason known only to the dog, he resented me—or at least my ankles. "We saw your picture in the paper today, Abby, and we just can't imagine why anyone would think you had anything to do with the murder. Can we, Peewee?" She waved the dog's paw at me to show his concern, as if I couldn't see his flattened ears and exposed fangs.

I thanked her for the support, then proceeded upstairs to

the second floor, last apartment on the left, and stood outside fumbling in my purse for the key. Before Jillian had moved in, Nikki's white cat Simon had always waited for me on the other side of the door, meowing eagerly for his food. Now, because he had a disdain for strangers—and no one was stranger than Jillian—he mostly kept to Nikki's room, where he spent his day lounging in the window, plotting his revenge on the fat brown squirrel that perched on a branch outside to snicker at him.

I missed the sight of that cute little kitty face, with its big golden eyes gazing up at me so trustingly. I missed the feel of that soft, furry body weaving between my ankles as I stumbled to the refrigerator for cat food. Now the only body that got in my way was my cousin's, and it wasn't soft or furry. A gym membership and weekly waxing appointments saw to that.

Jillian had studied fashion design in college and now ran her own wardrobe-consulting business. She called it Chez Jillian, meaning "at Jillian's home," which was pretty laughable considering she didn't have one. Yet she was good at what she did and had a loyal clientele who happily let her empty their closets and fill them up again. I thought of her as the New Chapel version of Stacy London, the cohost of *What Not to Wear,* only not as diplomatic. But at least the shopping trips got her out of the apartment, the length of time depending on traffic conditions between here and Chicago. Jillian would shop only in Chicago.

I unlocked the door but couldn't get it open more than a foot. "Hello?" I called, sticking my head through the opening. "Jill?"

"Just a minute, Abby."

I was facing a rack of clothing. I parted a group of blouses to peer up the short hallway to the living room beyond. Off the living room was another hallway that led to our two bedrooms and a bathroom. To my immediate right was our galley kitchen, containing a small refrigerator, stove, microwave, double sink, cabinets, a work counter, and an eating counter with two stools.

I wedged the upper half of my body inside the door, then inserted one leg as my tall, gorgeous, twenty-five-year-old cousin clicked up the tiled hallway on her high-heeled sandals. "Hold on," she said, shifting the portable rack so the door would open.

I practically fell inside, but caught myself on a metal pole. "What's this?" I asked, pointing to the blouses.

She sighed dramatically as she began pushing the rack toward the living room. "Tell me you actually need an answer to that question."

"I know they're clothes," I said, following her up the hallway. "Why are they here?"

She parked the rack and went into the living room. "I'm trying out a new venture."

"What kind of venture?"

"Home shopping."

I edged past the blouses and gazed around in surprise. A rack of jackets and coats now hid most of the bookcase that stood against a side wall, and another rack of dresses and slacks filled the space in front of the picture window, where a long console table was supposed to be, along with our phone and answering machine. "Did you just say *home shopping*? As in people shopping in *my* home?"

"*Our* home." She moved a few hangers, then checked off something on a list fastened to a clipboard.

"No, Jill. This is Nikki's home and my home. *You* are a houseguest."

"So were you at one time."

"But I had a good reason for staying."

She sighed tiredly. "I have the same reason, Abby."

I couldn't argue that. We'd both been dumped by Osbornes. She had married Pryce's younger brother Claymore. I glanced around the room. "Where did you put the phone?"

She pointed toward the bookshelf. I knew it was the bookshelf only because I could see the very top of a row of books. "And the answering machine?"

"Same place."

I fought my way through the coats to check the machine. Two calls. I hit Play but couldn't hear the message because of the muffling effect of the clothes. "Jillian," I began.

"One call from Grace, one call from Nikki."

"You listened to them?"

She stopped making check marks. "Do you want me to run out of the room with my fingers in my ears every time someone leaves a message?"

What I wanted was for her to run out the door—and stay out—but I had to find a way to tell her that wouldn't cause an emotional breakdown, like the one she'd had when she first showed up at our door, weeping hysterically. She'd had her luggage with her but not her husband, which was a bad sign considering she was supposed to be in Hawaii on her honeymoon. Apparently, Claymore had realized too late that he'd made a mistake.

The outcome was that my cousin, the serial jilter, had become the jiltee, and she hadn't taken it well. To make matters worse, my aunt Corrine, instead of being sympathetic to her daughter's plight, had put the blame squarely on Jillian's shoulders, causing a big rift between them. I wasn't about to interfere, especially since my aunt had finally paid—handsomely, I might add—for Jillian's wedding flowers. I was a firm believer in Grace's saying: Don't bite the hand that feeds you.

Nevertheless, Jillian had turned to me for help, so I gave her my bed, thinking it would be for a night, not a nightmare. Even Nikki, whose heart was usually overflowing with sympathy, had stopped feeling sorry after two weeks' worth of living with Princess Jillian. "Adult women shouldn't need babysitters," she had grumbled on several occasions.

What Nikki didn't understand was that Jillian only appeared to be an adult. Inside she was still the self-conscious, withdrawn, twelve-year-old girl she had once been, with scoliosis so severe that her spine had looked like the letter S. When she was fourteen, a seven-hour surgery and three months in a body cast had corrected her physical problems and let her grow into a beautiful woman, but emotionally Jillian seemed stuck as an eternal teenager, flighty and selfish, with an endless capacity to fall in love but not to stay in love. That she'd actually made it down the aisle with fiancé number five had shocked us all.

That she'd turned up a week later, alone, hadn't.

With growing annoyance, I climbed out of the clothes rack and faced my cousin, who, as usual, was dressed in designer duds. Today it was a lime green silk top with off-white slacks. Her long, smooth, copper-colored hair was caught up in a twist and fastened with an enameled barrette shaped like a butterfly. That was one of many differences between us. Jillian was always well dressed, even on weekends, whereas when I was at home, it was a comfy old T-shirt, cutoff blue jeans, and bare feet for me. "Okay, just so I understand, you're going to have your customers come *here* to shop? In this tiny living room?"

"No, silly. The racks won't all fit in here. Two are in your bedroom and one is in Nikki's room."

I could only imagine the fireworks when Nikki came home from a long shift, tired and ready to crash onto her bed—and couldn't even find it. I took the clipboard out of Jillian's hands and guided her to the sofa, which was amazingly devoid of clothing. "Jill, sit down and listen to me. I have something important to tell you." I waited until she had carefully arranged her slacks so they wouldn't wrinkle, then

I crouched in front of her so she had to look directly at me. "Okay, here it is. You can't run your business from here."

She blinked rapidly, trying to make sense of my statement. "But I *am* running my business from here. The clothes will be delivered here, my clients will come here to try them on, and I'll never have to leave the apartment."

Dear God.

I massaged my temples, trying to think of a way to explain my feelings in simple-to-understand language that would get my point across without my having to choke her. "Okay, let me put it another way. Get these racks out of the apartment."

She leaned forward, concentrating intensely. "Go on."

"That's it, Jill. Just get the racks out of here."

"And put them . . .?" she prompted.

"I don't know. I haven't thought that far. How about your mother's basement? It's nicer than most people's living rooms."

She made a scoffing sound. "You know my mother and I aren't speaking."

"Then get a room at the New Chapel Inn until you can find your own place. I don't really care where you put them, as long as it's somewhere other than in this apartment."

Her big doe eyes tilted downward, her lower lip trembled, and she was suddenly that insecure little girl with the crooked back. "So you don't want me here? You're kicking me out?"

"I'm not kicking you out. Well, yes, I am, but I'm trying to do it in a nice way."

Jillian sat back with a knowing look. "It's Nikki, isn't it? I've been sensing bad vibes from her ever since I told her she was hogging the medicine cabinet."

It was a wonder Nikki hadn't thrown us both out. "Okay, look," I said, sitting down beside her. "It's not just Nikki. It's me, too. I'd really like to have my bedroom back. This sofa isn't the easiest thing to sleep on. Face it, Jill, there's not enough room in the apartment for the three of us—or the nine of us, if you count the racks. Not only that, but you love to shop in Chicago. Why would you even want to work from here?"

"When it snows, the expressways are treacherous."

"That's never stopped you before. Besides, it's only September. Snow never falls before the end of November."

"I like to plan ahead."

"Since when? You put your wedding together in a month and a half."

She folded her arms and sniffed. "I know. And look how that turned out."

"I'm not buying your story, Jill. Something else is going on. You're hiding out here. Want to tell me why?"

"No." Jillian pouted for a moment, then sighed in resignation. "Fine. I'll get my own apartment. Happy now?"

I was ecstatic, but all I said was, "It's best for all of us." Then we hugged. Problem solved. Now I could turn my attention to more important matters.

"So tell me about the murder," Jillian said.

"You know about it?"

"Duh. You can't turn on the television without hearing the reports."

"Why didn't you say anything?"

She looked stumped for a moment, then shrugged. "I guess I was preoccupied. So who do you think did it? I mean, you obviously didn't . . . did you?"

Ignoring her question, I gave her a brief account of my afternoon along with strict instructions to avoid talking to reporters. Then I fought my way through the jackets, got the answering machine, and took it to my bedroom to listen to the messages.

The first call was from Nikki. "Tell Jillian the new tire is going to cost one hundred forty-three dollars." She hung up without saying good-bye. Obviously she had left it before she got my news about the murder. And since Jillian had already heard the message, I didn't have to deliver it. Worked for me.

The second message was from Grace. "Abby, dear, a reporter came here looking for you. He said he spoke with you earlier today and was just following up on it. His name is Connor Mackay and his phone number is—"

I hit Delete, crawled past a rack of dresses, and sat on the side of my bed. I had to leave for Marco's bar in fifteen minutes, but until then I could lie down and let the stress of the day wash out of me and memories of Marco's delicious kiss wash back in, like the tide. I stretched out on my back and closed my eyes and, within minutes, was so into the whole beach imagery that I could even hear the sound of waves washing up onto the shore, smell the pungent fish odor, and feel the gritty, warm sand beneath me.

I was just about to drift out to sea when a heavy missile landed on my stomach. My eyes flew open as I gasped for air. There sat Simon, licking a paw.

"Simon," I wheezed, struggling to sit up, "I'm not a landing pad. Look at all the room beside me." He paused to glance at me, as if to say, *So?*

The phone rang and I yelled, "Jillian, would you get that for me, please?" I scratched Simon behind the ears, listening as my cousin said, "Yes, this is where Abigail Knight lives."

"No, she doesn't!" I cried, sending the cat scurrying under the bed. I dashed down the hallway just in time to hear Jillian say, "I'm sorry. She's not taking any calls right now. Would you like to leave a name and number where she can reach you?" She glanced up at me and gave me the okay sign. "Thank you," she said brightly, and hung up. "How did I do?"

"Next time don't admit that I live here. In fact, just say you don't even know who I am."

"Got it."

"So who was on the phone?"

"A reporter."

"What was his name?"

"Were you planning to call him back?"

"No."

She shrugged. "Then it doesn't matter."

Valid point. The phone rang again and Jillian said, "Let me get it." She cleared her throat as she picked up the handset. "Bonjour," she said in a cheery French accent. She listened a few moments, then replied, "I am sorr-eee. I do not know zees Abby Knight." She hung up with a giggle. "That ought to confuse him."

"Who was it?"

"Didn't we already have this conversation?"

"Jillian!"

"Okay, it was some guy named Connor Mackay."

"Gee, what a coincidence. He chased me out of the parking lot not fifteen minutes ago."

"I have to say, Abby, he had a pretty wixy voice."

"What's wixy?"

"Wickedly sexy. *You* need to get out of the flower shop more often. Anyway, he said you're going to want to talk to him soon."

"How arrogant of him." I headed for the kitchen to get my purse from the counter.

"He didn't say it in an arrogant way," Jillian called.

"Oh, right. *Wixy*."

"No, more like . . ."

I paused, my hand on the doorknob. "Like what?"

"Threatening."

CHAPTER NINE

I gave my cousin a scowl. "Connor is a reporter, Jill. He's not going to threaten me."

"Okay, fine. Don't call him. Just don't blame me if something bad happens. Where are you going?"

"To Down the Hatch."

"No, really."

"To find inner peace."

"Awesome. Bring some back for me."

The Down the Hatch Bar and Grill occupied the first floor of a narrow brick building that had been built around 1900 and, like Bloomers, came with high, tin ceilings, wood floors, and loads of charm. Marco's bar was where the judges and attorneys from the courthouse across the street gathered for lunch, and was an evening hangout for the college crowd, who thought the kitschy fisherman's theme—a fake carp mounted above the long walnut bar, a bright blue plastic anchor on the wall above the row of booths, a brass bell near the old-fashioned cash register, and a fishing net hanging from the beamed ceiling—was retro-cool.

When I walked in, Marco was talking to his chief bartender, Chris. He saw me come in and signaled that he'd be right there, so I slid into the last booth and scanned the plastic-coated menu, although I could have recited it by heart.

Within a few minutes Marco appeared, bringing two Miller Lites with him, his five-o'clock shadow giving him a dangerously appealing look. He sat across from me and handed me one of the tall, cold glasses just as Gert, one of the waitresses, stopped at the table, her order pad in one hand and a pencil in the other. Like the fake carp, Gert had been a fixture there for decades. In fact, there was even a strong resemblance between them, especially around the gills.

"Sorry to hear about the murder, kid," she said to me in her gravelly smoker's voice. "You doin' okay?"

"Thanks for asking, Gert. I'm okay."

"All righty, then. You kids gonna eat?"

"Italian beef sandwich au jus," I told her. "With lots of jus."

"Open-faced turkey sandwich for me," Marco said. "Hold—"

"—the slaw," she finished for him as she tore off the order and headed for the kitchen.

"Any news from Reilly?" I asked Marco.

"Two important items. Carson Reed had been stunned by a blow to the head before he was stabbed—they haven't determined the source of the blow yet—and they got two clear fingerprints and a blurry partial off the end of the pencil. Reilly said Puffer's prints could account for one of the sets, since he owned the pencils. It'll be interesting to see who the other set belongs to."

I nearly sloshed beer over the rim of my glass. I hadn't told Marco about picking up the pencil, and since that bit of information would probably sound better coming from me than from, oh, say, the police, I decided I'd better fess up now. So I waited until he was in the middle of taking a long pull of beer, then I said quickly, "I hope the prints aren't mine."

He stopped swallowing. "What?"

"I said I hope they're not mine."

He blinked twice, giving his gray matter a moment to absorb it. "Is there a chance they *are* yours?"

"Okay, first, promise you won't tell Reilly."

Marco gazed at me in disbelief. I sensed no promise would be forthcoming. "You handled the murder weapon?"

"Let's be clear on this. I *might* have handled the murder weapon. Before Puffer came in, I took a pencil out of the cup and pretended to snap it in two, just to see what it felt like."

"But then you put it back."

"Yes." I nodded eagerly, then, noting a look of relief on his face I clarified, "On the desk. Not in the cup."

Seeing his relief vanish, I hastened to explain. "I didn't put it back because Puffer walked in and caught me with it, and I was so rattled that I set it down on the closest surface, which turned out to be the near corner of his desk because the cup was all the way on the far corner, past his computer monitor. Anyway, it's possible that the murderer used a different pencil."

"The murderer is going to grab one from the pencil cup way over on the far side of the desk rather than use the one lying right there in plain sight?"

I sagged against the seatback with a desultory sigh. "Probably not."

"Did you tell Dave Hammond what you did?"

Hmm. Had I told Dave? Could I give Marco an unqualified, one hundred percent yes? Not really. Those couple hours after the murder were kind of hazy. So maybe ninety percent . . . Okay, eighty-three . . . Make that a definite fifty. Not very good odds, especially because Marco, being a male, would naturally be able to recall every detail, including what brand of shoes Professor Reed had worn—if he'd worn shoes. I hadn't noticed. How mortifying.

The paper napkin beside my plate suddenly needed my undivided attention. I shook it out and laid it across my lap, making sure to smooth out every last wrinkle.

Marco sighed. "You didn't tell Dave, did you?"

"I'll call him first thing in the morning."

"Wise move."

Gert brought our sandwiches, so we paused the conversation and dug into the food. But then I started thinking about the fingerprints, and my appetite did a nosedive. I swallowed the bite and pushed the plate to the side.

Marco looked at me curiously. "Is something wrong with the beef?"

"The beef is great. My nerves aren't. I have a terrible feeling my prints are going to be on that pencil."

"Okay, let's look at it rationally. Even if your prints *are* on the pencil, you have a good explanation for it, and you have a witness. Puffer can verify that he saw you holding it."

"You think Snapdragon will back *me* up?" I pushed the plate farther away so I could lean my head in my hands. "This is getting worse by the second."

"Take it easy, Sunshine."

"You don't understand. It's the Rule of Three, Marco. Two bad things have happened, which means I have one to go."

"Come on, Abby. You're not the superstitious type."

"This isn't a superstition. It's real. I became a believer a year ago. Trust me, the Rule of Three never fails."

"Then why haven't I experienced it?"

"You have. You just weren't counting."

"Right." He chewed a bite of food, thinking. "Okay, what

about this? Yesterday I stepped into the shower and discovered I didn't have hot water. Turns out the ancient water heater finally gave up the ghost. Then right before the dinner rush, my dishwasher quit on me. That was yesterday. Today, nothing."

I gaped at him in horror. "It doesn't have to be all in one day. It just has to be three bad events in a short period of time. You're really in for it now."

"We'll see," he said and engulfed a huge bite of his sandwich.

"Don't say I didn't warn you." Watching him wolf down the food, I decided I was hungry after all, so I pulled the plate toward me and started eating again.

"Here's a thought," Marco said. "To take your mind off things, let's go over to the Green Parrot later for a little dancing."

Dancing with Marco, gazing up at that darkly handsome face. *Ahh*. Remembering how good it had felt to float across the floor with him at Jillian's wedding reception, I couldn't help but sigh dreamily. I was definitely up for some of that. "Sounds great, but first I have to go back to the shop and finish a small stack of orders. It should take about two hours."

Gert stopped at our table and pointed to the television mounted in a corner over the bar. "Hey, doll, you're on TV again."

I turned for a look and there, doing a live report from the lawn in front of the law school, was one of the reporters who'd fired questions at me. In a small square in the upper right corner of the screen was an image of me, freckles and all, taken from my high school yearbook. I scooted out of the booth and moved closer to hear what was being said.

". . . should be noted that local florist and animal rights activist Abby Knight was apparently the last one to have seen Carson Reed alive and the first to find him dead. This follows on the heels of Knight's arrest at a protest march against Dermacol Labs, for which Reed is legal counsel. This is Don Dell reporting live from New Chapel, Indiana."

The scene switched back to the newsroom, where the male news anchor, with perfectly styled gray hair, said, "In an ironic twist, Knight, the owner of Bloomers Flower Shop and a former student of Carson Reed's, had gone to the law school to deliver a funeral arrangement."

"It was one flower," I protested as the anchor moved on to another topic. I turned around and every eye in the bar was on me. I slunk back to my seat, trying to ignore the gapes and whispers, as Marco started on the remaining half of his sandwich as though nothing had happened.

I put a hand on the side of my face to block the curious stares. "Marco, everyone is staring."

"Nah," he mumbled through a mouthful of turkey and bread.

I turned my head and saw three guys at the bar leering at me. One even wiggled his eyebrows. I grabbed the menu and used it as a barrier. "No, Marco, they really are staring."

He glanced at the bar and the men instantly looked away. "Ignore them," he advised.

"I can't eat with people watching me. Juice will drip down my chin. Lettuce will wedge itself between my front teeth. Crumbs will stick to—"

"Grab the beers and come with me." Marco scooped up his plate and mine and started up the hallway that led to his office, a modern room done in silver, gray, black, and white. We settled on two black leather sling-back chairs facing Marco's sleek black desk and made short work of our food.

"Feel better now?" Marco asked as we finished our brews.

"Yes, thanks, but I'll feel best when the murderer is found."

"You know what I think about that?" Marco said, taking the glass from my hand. He tugged me over to sit on his lap, then put his arms around me. "I think you should stop thinking about the murder. You've got more important things to do right now."

I leaned my forehead against his. "Yeah, like finishing all those orders waiting for me."

"Actually, I was referring to that kiss we'd started earlier."

"I was hoping you'd bring that up." I tilted my head up and our lips connected, an Irish-Italian fusion. Marco's mouth was hot and hard against mine, and I could smell a hint of the soap he used on his skin, a little bit spicy, a little bit sweet, and a whole lot intoxicating.

Why not stay here all evening and practice these kisses? the little imp inside me whispered. I was all set to agree with her when my practical side stepped in. *Right. Then you'll be up half the night knocking out those flower arrangements, and you know how testy you get when you haven't had your sleep.* I was nothing if not practical.

"I suppose," I said after a few long, slow, sexy kisses, "I should get my orders done so we'll have time to go dancing." I was kind of hoping he'd try to talk me out of it, but Marco was even more practical than I was.

He pulled back to look at me with those bedroom eyes, tracing the outline of my lips with his index finger. "I suppose you're right. How about if I walk you down to Bloomers?"

As options went, it wasn't as good as staying there and kissing him, but I took it anyway.

Except for the bars and restaurants, all the businesses around the square closed at five o'clock, so the sidewalks were fairly deserted as we strolled hand in hand up the block. Marco waited while I unlocked the door and disabled the alarm, then he stepped inside to scope out the premises—a habit he'd picked up from his Army Ranger training.

"It's clear." He checked his watch. "I'll be back in two hours. Lock the door behind me."

Suddenly, there was a squeal of tires in the street outside, followed by a loud crash. We rushed out the door to find out what had happened, as did patrons of the several eating establishments on the square. Around the corner, on the south side of the courthouse lawn, a badly rusted Pontiac Grand Am had smashed into a car parked in one of the angled spaces, and now sat with its front end crumpled and steam coming out from under the mangled hood. As I watched, the door creaked open and a teenaged boy emerged, appearing dazed but not injured. The other doors opened and three more boys got out, all looking bewildered.

Marco muttered something that sounded like, "That's Mike Arr!" as he started across the street at a fast jog. I followed, thinking he'd recognized one of the teens. It wasn't until I got closer that I realized he was actually saying "my car." The teens had crashed into Marco's dark green Chevy. Hadn't I warned him? There was no avoiding the Rule of Three.

The police station was across the street, so within moments cops came pouring out the door. An ambulance arrived next and two EMTs examined the boys to make sure they hadn't been injured. Meanwhile, Marco was on his cell phone, trying to reach a towing service. He put his hand over the phone and said, "Looks like we're going to have to reschedule our date."

"That's all right. I have lots to do. I just hope your car isn't too badly damaged." I couldn't resist adding, "And in case you weren't counting, that was bad luck number thr—"

He held up his palm to stop me. "Don't go there."

I went to Bloomers instead.

Making sure to lock the door, I headed for the workroom, where I popped an Enya CD into the portable player on the counter and pulled the first order from the spindle. It was for a birthday basket of fresh flowers in bright, autumn colors.

I went to the cooler to pull orange lilies, yellow button mums, red carnations, preserved fall leaves, and a thick handful of wheat. Then I spread them out on the worktable and let the creative side of me take over.

I had just finished the fourth order when the phone rang. I checked the caller ID and saw an unfamiliar number, so I ignored it. It rang again, same number on the screen. Out of curiosity, I dug through my purse, found Connor Mackay's card, and—bingo. It was a match. "You're out of luck tonight, Mackay," I said as the answering machine picked up. He was persistent. I'd give him points for that.

I cleared away nine more orders, then glanced at the clock to see that it was almost midnight. Hurriedly, I packed the arrangements into the cooler, locked up, and took off, hoping I'd beat Nikki home so I could make sure the clothing was out of her bedroom. But it didn't work out that way. When I got back to the apartment, Nikki was standing over the sink, still in her hospital duds, eating ice cream from the container.

"Hey," she mumbled. "Why are you out so late?"

"I had orders to finish. Listen, I'm sorry about the home shopping thing. I told Jillian to clear out the clothing ASAP."

"Home shopping thing? What are you talking about?"

I glanced down the hallway and saw that the racks in the living room were gone. "Wait there," I told Nikki and hurried to check both bedrooms. No racks there, either. In fact, no Jillian. Her clothes had even been cleaned out of my closet. "She did it, Nikki!" I called. "She finally moved out." I sank down onto my bed with a huge sigh of relief.

"Not all of her moved out," Nikki called from the bathroom. "She's still using my shelf."

The answering machine was beeping, so I hit the Play button and heard Jillian's excited voice. "Abby, I found an apartment. You'll never guess where."

"New Zealand, I hope," Nikki said, coming in to sit beside me on my bed.

"You know the vacant unit up the hallway?" Jillian continued. "The superintendent, that nice Mr. Bodenhammer, is letting me rent it by the month. Isn't that great?"

"Since when is Mr. Bodenhammer nice?" Nikki interjected.

"We'll be neighbors!" Jillian's message continued. "I borrowed your sleeping bag and a spare pillow until I get a bed. I'll see you at breakfast."

She had moved only three doors away. Talk about a good news/bad news message. But the important thing was that I had my bed back. Now, if I could just find the murderer and get my life back.

CHAPTER TEN

The next morning, I retrieved the *New Chapel News* from outside the door and unrolled it to see a bold banner headline that read, PROFESSOR MURDERED; KILLER SOUGHT. I kicked the door closed and went to sit at the kitchen counter to read the story below, praying my name wouldn't be mentioned. But beneath a black-and-white photo of Carson Reed was a long article in which both Professor Z. Archibald Puffer and I were named as being first at the scene. There was no mention of Puffer's wife or of Kenny Lipinski being present. Lucky them.

The reporter had obviously talked to Puffer, because he came off smelling like the proverbial rose, whereas I came off smelling. Period. Not only did Puffer lie about himself and Reed being friends, but he also made it sound as though I had an ax to grind—or a pencil to sharpen, as it were—with both professors. He went on to relate my unexpected flower delivery and retrieval and said that if he were investigating, he'd test the rose for toxicity.

If that wasn't damning enough, alongside the main story was a grainy photo of me at the protest rally, shaking my fist at Reed, and an accompanying article recounting my vow to take on anyone who advocated torturing helpless animals, including Reed. Also included was my quote calling him a hypocritical snake in the grass, and the details of my subsequent arrest. I came across as the Mad Florist of New Chapel, running around with poisoned roses and sharpened pencils. If it hadn't seemed as if I had a motive before, it certainly did now—revenge.

I shoved the newspaper aside. Dave Hammond was *so* not going to be happy when he saw that article. If my profile got any higher, I could light a match and set Lady Liberty's torch on fire. I checked the byline to see who I could thank for adding to my notoriety. The reporter in question was none other than the persistent, wixy Connor Mackay.

Wixy, indeed. Weevil was more like it, as in boll weevil, as in *what a worm*! Did he think making me look guilty in the press would prod me to spill my guts? Was that what he'd meant by "You're going to want to talk to me"? Boy, did he have me pegged wrong. The only thing I had any desire to spill was boiling oil—on his head.

I checked the time on the kitchen clock and breathed a sigh of relief. Mom never read the paper until she was having breakfast, which meant I was off the hook for at least twenty more minutes, plenty of time for a cup of strong coffee and a slice of toast.

As I scooped ground beans into the filter, added water, and hit the On button, I heard a key in the lock, and a moment later my cousin appeared, looking slightly out of sorts from her night on the floor.

"Coffee," she rasped, opening the cabinet in search of her favorite mug—which used to be my favorite mug until she commandeered it.

"I'm making it right now. What are you doing up so early? Noon is a long way off."

Jillian rubbed her lower back and flexed her shoulders. "Do you know how hard the floor is? My spine is killing me. I was too excited to sleep anyway. I have *so* much to do, starting with ordering bedroom furniture. Aren't you excited about my new place?"

"I'm so weak with excitement it's making me hungry," I said as she pulled a tub of whipped butter, a jar of strawberry jelly, and a loaf of whole wheat bread from the refrigerator. "In fact, would you put bread in the toaster for me, please?"

Jillian dropped in a slice for each of us, pushed down the lever, then sat at the counter to wait. She spotted the newspaper and pulled it toward her, her eyes bugging. "That's your picture! You made the front page!" But then, after skimming the article, her eyes bugged even further. "Omigod, Abby, this makes you look so—"

"Guilty?"

"I was going to say freckled." She gave me a sympathetic look and reached out to stroke my hair away from my face. "And guilty. I'm so sorry."

It was a rare and touching moment until I realized she was restyling my hairdo. I sniffed the air. "I think the toast is burning."

"I'm on it. You sit right there and rest."

I was about to protest that I didn't need a rest, but then I decided to let her play house mom for once. And as long as she was in a generous mood . . . "Would you do me another favor? The phone is going to ring in approximately"—I checked the clock on the microwave—"twelve minutes. It'll be my mom. Tell her I know about the article, and that it's all a misunderstanding. I'll be talking to Dave Hammond later this morning to get it straightened out. In the meantime she is not to worry. Got it?"

Jillian snickered. "Your mother not worry? Right. Like

that's a possibility. Okay, I'll tell her, but you'll have to do the same for me, because my mother will probably call here, too."

I gazed at my clueless cousin in wonder as she handed me a cup of coffee. "Jillian, I can't answer the phone for you. It might be *my* mother calling."

She shrugged. "Then I guess the machine will have to pick up the calls."

"The ringing will wake Nikki. Look, why not answer in your French voice?"

"Mais, oui! I can pretend to be the maid. *C'est magnifique!"*

I was going to say she could pretend to be my friend Michelle from Quebec, but Jillian was so pleased with her idea that I didn't bother to point out the incongruity of my employing a maid when I could barely pay my bills. But that was my cousin—tons of education, no common sense. "Okay, Jillian, if Dave calls, tell him I will phone him at his office at nine o'clock."

"Should I use my French accent?"

"It doesn't matter, as long as he can understand you."

"Parfait."

With that problem solved, we sat at the counter and ate our burned toast slathered with butter and jelly while she explained her grand designs for her apartment.

"Who's going to pay for the furniture?" I asked when she'd finished.

"I have a credit card."

"You don't think Claymore should pay? I mean, he did desert you, after all."

"No, I'll pay." She was being very cavalier about it, which made me think she had something up her sleeve. But I didn't have time to pump her further. I wanted to be at Bloomers early to get started on the orders I hadn't finished. Plus, I hoped to avoid my mother's call.

The weather was warm and sunny, so I dressed in cropped khaki pants and a bright, striped, short-sleeved shirt. I picked up my purse, saw Lottie's scarf waiting to be returned, and recalled the problem I'd had leaving the shop the previous day. With that front-page article in the paper, I had no idea what to expect today. But did I want to don that ugly scarf again? No offense to Lottie, but, well, ick. I thought of grabbing my familiar blue Cubs hat, but everyone knew me in it. I wanted to wear something *not* like me.

"Hey, Jillian," I said, as she read the style section of the paper and sipped the last of the coffee, "do you have a hat that would hide my hair so I can slip into work unnoticed?"

She lowered the paper. "Trying to keep a low profile at this point is rather futile, don't you think? Besides, it would take a whole lot more than a hat to disguise you. Maybe if you bound your breasts and wore six-inch heels . . ."

"Jillian. Humor me. A hat. Before I club you with my un-bound breasts."

She heaved a sigh of resignation, then made an elaborate and quite noisy show of folding the newspaper and setting it aside. "Fine. But you'll have to allow me a few minutes to find something that will coordinate with your outfit."

"I don't care if it coordinates as long as it hides my face and hair."

"Don't *ever* say you don't care in my presence again." She shuddered. "I feel so violated."

I rinsed out the coffeepot while I waited for her to return. She was back in a few minutes with a rolled-brim, loosely woven, ecru cotton hat, which she scrunched down over my head so far I could barely see. She tucked my hair behind my ears, adjusted the hat, and took my sunglasses out of my purse and put them on me. Then she leaned back to study the finished product through narrowed eyes, as though she were studying a painting. Smiling proudly, she said, "See there?

It coordinates with your outfit *and* it hides your face and hair."

I didn't have time to go to the bathroom mirror for a look, so I trusted that she was right. When I checked my image in my car's rearview mirror on my way to the shop, all I could see of me was a nose and mouth, and about two inches of red hair hanging from the back of the hat, which I could hide by pulling up the collar of my shirt. That was low profile enough.

Lottie and Grace hadn't arrived yet, and it was too early to call Dave Hammond's office, so I started in on the normal morning chores. When the ladies arrived at eight o'clock I had things well in hand and had even started an anniversary arrangement.

"Sweetie, how are you doing?" Lottie asked, coming through the curtain with Grace right behind her. "We saw the newspaper article this morning."

"How utterly dreadful of them to attack you in print," Grace said, checking me over as though I might be sporting bruises. "What you need is a soothing cup of chamomile tea. I'll go brew it right now."

While Grace bustled off to the parlor, Lottie and I sat down to discuss the orders that had come in overnight. Five minutes later, Grace appeared with a tea tray and a worried frown.

"The bobbies are here, Abby."

The police. Damn. For a little while I'd actually forgotten about the murder. I took a quick sip of tea, then hurried up front, where Reilly and another cop were waiting.

"What's the good news, Reilly?" I asked, hoping for something other than his scowl.

"We need the order for the flower you delivered to Professor Puffer." Reilly kept his gaze above me, as if he were embarrassed to be treating me like a suspect, as well he should have been.

"No problem," I said lightly, then went to the workroom, where Grace was waiting with the small yellow form in hand. I turned it over to the second cop, who was holding out a manila envelop so I could drop the paper inside. Both men gave me a quick nod, then walked out, leaving me feeling like I had cooties.

After a start to the day like that, I had little hope for improvement. But at ten minutes before nine o'clock, Grace came back to the workroom and said in amazement, "There's a queue of customers outside the front door waiting for us to open."

A line in front of Bloomers? That was a first. I glanced at Lottie, who said, "Let's open."

Grace unlocked the front door and people poured in. Within minutes, all the white wrought-iron tables in the coffee parlor were filled and Grace and Lottie were hustling to keep the java flowing. That left me to handle the shop, but I quickly realized the customers weren't shopping so much as gawking at me and whispering among themselves. Obviously, they'd read the morning newspaper. I went from feeling like a giant cootie to feeling like a one-woman freak show.

Lottie came across the room to whisper in my ear, "Customers in the parlor are asking for you. Do you want to switch places with me?"

I peered through the doorway and half a dozen hands fluttered in the air, waving at me to catch my attention. "Abby, over here!" several women called.

"I think I'll stay where I am," I muttered to Lottie, waving back.

The phone rang, so I hurried to the counter to answer it. "Bloomers. How can I help you?"

"Abby, I need to talk to you," I heard Marco say.

At that moment, a woman came rushing over, a cell phone pressed to her ear. "I'm standing right beside her. Hold on." Then she aimed it at me and I saw it was a camera phone. "Can you see her?"

I turned my back on her to whisper to Marco, "I'm a little busy at the moment. We're jammed with customers. Can I call you back later?"

"Not a chance. This won't wait. Have Lottie cover for you and get to another phone."

"Okay. Hold a moment, please." I forced a sunny note in my voice so customers nearby wouldn't think anything was amiss, but since Marco had sounded unusually grim, I wasn't feeling much of the sunshine myself. I hit the Hold button, wove through the throng, sidled up to Lottie, and said quietly, "I have to take a call in the back. It's urgent."

She glanced at me with a worried frown. "Okay, sweetie. Go ahead."

I started across the shop and a bright light went off in my face, bringing me to a sudden stop. I blinked to clear away the green halo and saw a woman lower a camera, then call to someone behind her, "I got her, Lou."

"Oh, good!" Lou called back. "Now take one for Betty."

Before I became a trophy for Betty's photo album, I darted through the curtain and bypassed my desk phone in favor of the kitchen wall phone. I wanted to be as far away from those nosy customers as possible. "Okay, Marco. What's up?"

"The cops have identified the prints on the pencil."

My stomach tensed. "Puffer's and mine?"

"Puffer's prints weren't on the pencil, Abby. Yours were the only ones there."

CHAPTER ELEVEN

"My fingerprints can't be the only ones on the pencil," I said to Marco, trying to keep the worry—make that hysteria—out of my voice. "Reilly told you yesterday they found two sets and a partial."

"Reilly screwed up, Abby. He spoke too soon. I think he was *hoping* to find prints other than yours."

"*He* was hoping? I had a few hopes in that direction myself. What about the partial print?"

"Wasn't enough there for a match."

"But because there *is* a partial, that means another person touched the pencil, right?"

"The blurred print could be yours, too."

So there was my third event—my fingerprints, no one else's, on the murder weapon. The Rule of Three could not be broken.

The hysteria I'd kept out of my voice was now tunneling into my brain, so I blocked it with a dose of Knight logic. "I don't care if my prints are the only ones. I know I'm innocent and the cops have to know that, too. I mean, they can't actually think I'd kill anyone. Right?"

Silence. Always a bad sign. I glanced up at the phone's base on the wall and saw a light flashing on line two. "Wait, Marco. I have another call." I scrambled to my feet, punched the second button, and answered not quite as cheerfully as before, "Bloomers. How can I help you?"

"Abby? It's Dave. Something has come up and I need to talk to you right away. When can you get down here?"

Oops. I had forgotten to forewarn him about my fingerprints. By the tone of his voice I was betting the prosecutor's office had already contacted him. "Dave, I've got a store full of shoppers right now. Can't we discuss this over the phone?"

"I need you here, Abby. Right away."

I'd never heard him sound so grim, and that made me worry even more. "Okay. Give me five minutes."

We hung up and I saw a third line blinking. I answered with a hurried, "Bloomers," and heard, "Abby, how are you today? Connor Mackay here. Did you have a chance to read my article in today's—"

Before I singed his eardrum with a few choice words—and risked seeing myself quoted in tomorrow's newspaper—I ended the call and went back to Marco's line. "Dave wants to see me right away, probably about the fingerprints. I'm going to his office now."

"Let me know what he tells you."

I returned to the workroom for my purse, feeling as if I were caught in a nonsensical dream and couldn't wake up. Lottie came through the curtain, saw me put my purse on my shoulder, and asked, "What happened?"

"I have to go see Dave."

"Why, baby?"

"Because I forgot to tell the cops I'd handled one of Professor Puffer's pencils and now my prints have turned up on the murder weapon."

"Oh, Lordy." She came at me with her meaty arms out-stretched and gave me a hug, rocking us both back and forth as if I were five and had just been told my tonsils were coming out. Then she held me at arm's length and stared me in the eye. "You're going to be fine, you hear me?"

"Of course I'll be fine. I'm innocent."

"That's the way to keep those spirits up. You know we're firmly behind you, sweetie, whatever happens."

Whatever happens? Why did I feel like I was about to ski down the side of a steep mountain? Without skis.

"Use the back door," Lottie said. "There are two reporters up front asking for you."

That was one of the problems of living in a small town. There simply wasn't much happening, so when something as big as a murder came along, the newspapers and local cable TV stations were beside themselves with excitement. Finally, something to report other than garage sales! Great.

I jammed Jillian's hat on my head, slipped out the back way, took the alley to the corner, then crossed the street and ducked down another alley to reach Dave's building. I couldn't get in the fire escape door in the rear, so I had to go around to Lincoln and use the front door. As I kept my head down and my eyes focused on the ground, two pairs of women's sandals suddenly loomed in front of me. I stopped with a gasp and looked up into the faces of my mother's bridge friends. Quickly, I pulled the hat lower and attempted to scuttle past, but it didn't work.

"Oh, look! It's Maureen's daughter," one of the ladies said. "Abby, dear. How are you?"

So much for the hat disguise. "Hello, Mrs. Nowlin, Mrs. Warner. Beautiful day, isn't it?" I tried to move around them—I had only another two yards to go—but the ladies closed ranks.

"We read about the murder," Mrs. Nowlin said in a grave voice, belying the delighted gleam in her eye. "We just wanted to let you know our sympathies are with you. It takes a brave soul to stand up for oneself against a cad such as Carson Reed."

"The worst kind of cad," Mrs. Warner added. "How shameful of him to advocate for that awful cosmetics lab."

"And have you dragged off to jail!"

"We don't blame you for striking out against the injustice of it all."

"Or for losing your temper."

"He must have pushed you to the edge."

"Could you plead insanity?"

I stared at my mother's friends in disbelief. "I didn't kill Professor Reed."

"Of course you didn't *kill* him," Mrs. Warner said, using her fingers to put quote marks around the word *kill*. "You simply put a stop to his—"

"Baser tendencies," Mrs. Nowlin finished. "If you need character witnesses—"

"Call us," Mrs. Warner said.

They gazed at me like a pair of Siamese cats waiting for the mouse to make a move.

I didn't know what to say. My mind refused to accept that these two middle-aged women who had known me for years thought I had killed a man. I stepped around them, walked the two yards to Dave's door, and went inside. The world had gone mad.

Dave's secretary ushered me straight into his office. Seeing the somber look on his face, I thought it might be wise to chat him up a bit. I took a seat on one of the chairs on the other side of his desk, pulled off the hat, and combed my fingers through my hair. "Can you believe that article in this morning's *New Chapel News*? There wasn't even a mention of Jocelyn Puffer or of Kenny Lipinski being there. And can you believe Puffer had the nerve to point the finger of guilt at me? Can he get away with that?"

Dave opened the manila file in front of him. "Professor Puffer didn't say anything libelous. He was careful to only hint at your guilt."

"So there's nothing I can do to stop him?"

"Not unless he crosses the line. But that's not why I asked you here. I just got a call from the DA. Guess whose prints they found on the pencil? And don't give me that coy look. Why didn't you level with me yesterday about handling the weapon? How can I defend you if you don't tell me the truth?"

He was really steamed, something I'd witnessed probably twice in all the months I'd clerked for him, but I knew it was only because he cared about me. "Dave, honestly, I wasn't hiding anything. I really did forget to tell you about the pencil."

"You *forgot* that you handled the murder weapon? Is there anything *else* you forgot?"

"No, Dave," I said, feeling like a little kid being scolded.

"Do you know how this looks to the police? Now they want to talk to you again. But I won't expose you to that unless I'm one hundred percent certain you're not involved."

My mouth dropped open. If Dave thought I was involved, what chance did I have?

"I know how worked up you get over your causes, Abby, and I know this guy Reed pushed your buttons. You wouldn't be the first one to get so angry you went off the deep end."

"This is *me,* Dave, the little florist who loves all living things. How can you think I would kill anyone, even if he pushed these so-called buttons of mine?"

"Forget what I think and starting considering what twelve of your fellow citizens might think. I don't care what you did, Abby, but I need you to be straight with me because I have to make sure it never comes to a matter of a dozen people deciding your fate."

"Dave. Hello. I touched a pencil when I delivered a flower.

They can't send me to prison based on such a flimsy scrap of circumstantial evidence as that."

"Maybe you forgot one of the more important lessons of the law. Prisons are full of people convicted on circumstantial evidence. And at this point, young lady, let me tick off the circumstantial evidence they have against you: access, motive, opportunity, and fingerprints." He sat back and lifted his hands. "Bingo."

Stunned didn't begin to describe what I was feeling. "This is ridiculous. The police know me. They know my father. The prosecutor isn't going to charge me with murder. "

"Fine, Abby, I'll write to you when they put you away."

His normally cheerful face was solemn. He wasn't kidding. I swallowed a lump of fear and said shakily, "I'll do whatever you say."

"Tell me how the devil your prints got on that pencil. And don't say you merely touched it, because that would indicate just the tip of your index finger, and they found prints from both hands on it."

"That's because I held it with both hands, like this." I proceeded to demonstrate.

He sat back with a frown of concentration as I related the experience of walking into Puffer's office, spotting the infamous black pencils, and what happened after that. When I finished, Dave said, "I might be the only person who believes you, but, strangely, I do. For God's sake, from now on tell me everything, okay?" He turned to reach for the phone. "I'll call the prosecutor and set up an appointment. With any luck we can take their focus off you and put them on the real culprit's trail."

While Dave was on the phone, I couldn't help but think about the total absurdity of the whole situation, all because of some student's stupid flower prank.

"We're set," he said, turning back to me. "Three o'clock

this afternoon. Be here ten minutes early and we'll walk across to the police station together."

"I just hope they feel exceeding foolish after they hear my explanation." With a huff, I stood up and headed for the door, then paused, remembering my encounter with my mother's friends. "Is it okay if we take your car this afternoon?" At his nod, I pulled Jillian's hat over my hair, then paused again. "And can I leave through the fire exit?"

As I slipped out into the alley, I phoned Marco and told him about the meeting. His advice was for me to stay composed no matter how the cops tried to get under my skin— as if I would let that happen—and above all to be open and friendly. No problem, I told him. I was always open. (Too open, if you believed my parents.) And I could absolutely do friendly.

What I couldn't do was get back to Bloomers.

CHAPTER TWELVE

"Grace," I whispered into my cell phone, peering around the corner into the alley behind my shop, "there are two shady characters hanging around the back door."

"Reporters, no doubt. We've had them buzzing about all day. You'd best stay away if you don't want to talk to them."

I ducked back when one of the men turned his head my way. "But we've got orders that need to go out this afternoon, and I can't put them all on Lottie's shoulders."

"One must exercise patience, Abby. It's a virtue. As Shakespeare said so well in *Othello,* 'How poor are they who have not patience! What wound did ever heal but by degrees?'"

I wasn't sure about healing wounds, but wounding a few heels sounded like a fantastic idea, and I knew who I'd start with—Connor Mackay, who was responsible for my new predicament. But that wasn't Grace's point. For her the issue was patience, of which I had a limited amount. So limited, in fact, that one reason I never had a manicure was that I had a difficult time waiting for the nail polish to dry. (Another reason was the cost.) But in my present situation, it was a matter of principle.

"I refuse to let a few newshounds chase me away from my shop, Grace. Bloomers is my livelihood. I'll just square my shoulders and march past them. I'll dare them to try to stop me."

"Before you charge into the fray, would you allow me two minutes to try something?"

Could I refuse a woman who spoke like Queen Elizabeth? "Sure. Go ahead."

I put my phone away and waited. Moments later the back door opened and the men moved forward, one with a camera at the ready. At once, Grace appeared, holding a big aluminum bucket. Before either man realized what she was about to do, she heaved the contents—water with lots of leaf and flower clippings in it—into their faces.

As the pair coughed and sputtered and wiped greenery out of their eyes and off the camera, I darted past them, into Bloomers, just as Grace said to them in her regal accent, "Good heavens. I didn't know anyone was lurking about out here. So sorry." And slammed the door.

Well done, Gracie. Huzzah.

I spent the rest of the morning and afternoon cloistered in the workroom. I didn't want to complain, because I was doing what I loved best. Still, knowing that there were people hanging around outside, waiting for a glimpse of the "notorious florist," I felt confined, even a little claustrophobic. For reasons only small-town minds could understand, I had become a draw for the curious, the news starved, the gossips, and a few wackos, two of whom had decided to keep a vigil in front of the shop, one carrying a sign that said JUSTICE FOR REED, the other one carrying a sign saying SAVE THE FLORIST in bloodred letters. Actually, it had read SAVE THE FOREST before he'd squeezed in an L and altered the E.

The student protest group had yet to arrive. Ironically, business had never been better.

"Sorry I can't help out front," I told Lottie when she came in to gather fresh flowers for the display case. "Everything will go back to normal after Dave and I meet with the police."

"I don't doubt that for a moment," she said in such a way that I couldn't tell whether she was relieved or disappointed. I decided not to ask. Sometimes it was better not to know those things.

"Your mother phoned during her recess break looking for you," Lottie said, "and I could tell she was working herself into a hush puppy–sized lump of worry."

Not that I'd ever seen a hush puppy, let alone knew what to do with one, but any worry coming from my mother wasn't good. At her worst she didn't eat, sleep, or even create her works of, well, art. She went to school, then came home to fret and pace. Over the years she'd worn an actual — though somewhat erratic — path through the green carpet in her bedroom, flattening the shaggy pile like a lawn mower run amok.

Mom blamed it on a gene she'd inherited from her mother, and somehow I knew that little devil was lurking in my DNA, too, just waiting for a child to spring forth from my womb to keep the chain intact. Luckily, I was a long way from that stage in my life. In fact, I was so not ready for motherhood that I refused to even sit in a rocking chair in case it gave my repressed biological urges any ideas.

"Jillian was supposed to talk to my mother this morning to prevent Mom from freaking out," I told Lottie.

"I don't mean to intrude, dear," Grace said, slipping through the curtain like a silver-haired phantom, "but do you actually believe your cousin has the ability to be a calming influence on your mother — or on anyone, for that matter?"

Obviously Grace *did* mean to intrude or else she wouldn't have. But she did have a valid point. "You're right. I don't know what came over me. Maybe it was the shock of seeing my name, not to mention my freckles, splashed across the front page of the morning paper."

"That'd do it for me," Lottie said with a firm nod, settling the matter once and for all.

To circumvent my mother going into a state of hysteria, I called the school right then, instead of waiting until after the meeting. I also had an ulterior motive. Since recess was long over and she was back in class, I didn't actually have to speak with her. I simply left a message saying that everything would be fine by suppertime. Then, seeing that it was fast approaching two thirty, I decided to plan my escape route so I wouldn't be late for the meeting.

Ten minutes later, wearing Jillian's hat and keeping my head down, I had Grace open the back door and toss out more water, just in case any reporters were still lurking. Then I darted into the alley and ran toward Marco's bar, intending to cut through from back to front, emerge onto the sidewalk, and make the short jaunt to Dave's office.

The water hadn't even finished splashing when I heard a man yell, "There she goes!" just as I ducked into Down the Hatch's back door. With my pursuers not far behind, I flew past the kitchen, up the short hallway past Marco's office, then continued to the bar area, where I called to Chris, "A little help, please?" and hitched my thumb over my shoulder.

As I dodged patrons in a headlong rush to get to the front door, Chris stepped out from behind the bar and purposely blocked the men's path. My last glimpse of them was of their frustrated faces as they watched me pass the picture window outside. I chortled with glee—then ran squarely into a tall, lean body, knocking my hat askew. I stumbled back a step, then looked straight up into a pair of sea-foam green eyes, the very same eyes that belonged to the weevil who had maligned me in the paper.

Connor Mackay bent down for a look at the face beneath

the hat, then said, "Abby Knight!" in a way that would have been quite flattering if I hadn't known what a worm he was. "I was just thinking about you, and here you are."

"Hmm. What a coincidence." I tried to sidestep him, but he moved with me.

"You know what they say. There are no coincidences. We were destined to run into each other today."

I darted a glance over my shoulder to see whether the reporters had broken free. "Look, I'm kind of in a hurry right now. Do you mind?"

He merely smiled, not Marco's corner-of-the-mouth sexy grin, but a wide, engaging smile that made it impossible to ignore him, even though I was trying my hardest. "Then I'll make this quick. Want to have dinner with me tonight?"

An ego as overinflated as this man's needed puncturing in the worst way. And was I ever up for that. "I'm sorry," I said, looking puzzled. "Have we met?"

He laughed the laughter of the truly amused instead of the seriously deflated. "Yes, we have, Abby—or Olga, or whomever you're pretending to be today. Connor Mackay from the *News*—and I know you remember me because I'm an unforgettable guy."

I hated to admit it, but he *was* pretty memorable. I pretended to ponder the matter. "Sorry. The name isn't ringing any bells."

"Well, I'm not one to hold grudges, so now that we've been reintroduced, how about that dinner? I'll treat."

Connor was not only egotistical, he was also as transparent as plastic wrap. "Right. Your treat. And tomorrow every bit of information you wring out of me will be in print, another chapter added to the garbage you wrote for today's paper. I don't know how you stand to look at yourself in the mirror."

He gave an easy shrug of his shoulders. "I work with the information I have, which is why I keep asking you to talk to me. You remember me asking you to talk to me, don't you?"

Now he was being flip. I stepped closer and put my index finger against the middle button of his blue chambray shirt, pressing it as I talked to stab home my message. "Here's the thing, Mr. Unforgettable. I'm not wowed by your coy tactics or your creative storytelling or your college-boy good looks, and I don't know what you hope to gain by following me around town *pretending* to run into me. I think you are an idiot of the highest order and I wouldn't give you an interview if you flew me to *Paris* for dinner. So why don't you crawl back into your dank little hole and spin lies about someone else?"

There was a long moment of stunned silence, then he said in a very even voice, "Actually, I was on my way to the courthouse to cover the trial of the man who robbed the jewelry store last January—but I'll keep what you said in mind. If you have a change of heart about talking to me—no, make that *when* you have a change of heart—you know how to contact me."

He nodded politely and strode toward the street, while I tugged my hat down as low as it would go and slunk into Dave Hammond's office, wishing I'd kept my mouth shut. An ego had been deflated all right, but it hadn't been Connor Mackay's.

At three o'clock that afternoon, Dave ushered me from his car straight into the police station, where we were shown into one of the conference rooms—a small, windowless, rectangular box with dingy white walls and a black-and-white tile floor that was stained and cracked from decades of use. In the room was a standard, government-issue steel desk, gray metal folding chairs around a long table with a cheap, pecan veneer, and an old coffeepot on a hot plate on a stand in the corner. All the comforts of home.

I was surprised to see Chief Prosecuting Attorney Melvin Darnell there, but then I reminded myself that this was a murder case, and the chief prosecutor was an elected official who had to keep his name in front of the public as the Protector of the Realm so he'd be reelected. And what better way to exhibit his abilities than in a highly publicized murder case?

Mel, as he called himself, was well over six feet tall, with thinning blond hair and a wholesome, country farmer appearance. He prided himself on being a man of the people, the dependable next-door neighbor you'd entrust with your house key. His campaign slogan was "All's well that ends Mel," a corny play on an old saying that, sadly, had been a highly effective strategy, although Grace still shuddered when someone uttered it.

Mel was sitting beside Detective Al Corbison, a paunchy, middle-aged, bald man with tobacco-stained teeth and no sense of humor whatsoever. Corbison was inserting a cassette into an old-fashioned black tape recorder in the middle of the table. Both stood up to shake hands with Dave. They merely nodded at me.

To show them I wasn't bothered in the least, I gave them a cool smile, pulled out a chair across from them, and sat down. As the men took their seats, I put Jillian's hat on the table in front of me and leaned back. I wanted them to see how unconcerned I was. I wanted them to feel ashamed of themselves for what they were about to put me through. I also wanted a good cup of coffee, but by the looks of the thick sludge in the bottom of the pot, that wasn't going to happen.

Corbison pushed the Record button, then stated the date, time, and people present. Feeling like I was an extra on the set of *Law and Order,* I had to cover my mouth to keep from chuckling out loud. It was way too surreal for me to take seriously. But when Corbison started reading me my rights, I stopped chuckling and started smoldering. They were carrying things too far.

"Do you understand your rights as they were read to you?" Corbison asked.

Did he think I was an idiot? "Gee, I'm not sure I got all of it. Maybe you'd better run through them again."

Mel tilted his head, as if he didn't get my sarcasm, while Corbison glared and Dave gave me a warning nudge with his elbow, so I said grudgingly, "Yes, I understand."

Both men opposite me took a moment to read over their respective notes, then the detective handed me several typed pages that I recognized as being the information I'd given Reilly at the law school. "Look over your statement and tell me if it's true and accurate."

Dave bent his head to read the pages with me. I skimmed through them, then said to Corbison, "They're true and accurate."

"Then why isn't there anything in your statement about you handling the murder weapon?"

Corbison looked way too pleased with himself, and I just had to put an end to that. I hated smugness. "Because you didn't ask if I left anything out. You asked if it was accurate. It *is* accurate. It just isn't complete." It was my turn to look smug. *Take that, Al!*

I could feel Dave's eyeballs on the right side my face and knew he was trying to bore a hole into my brain so he could leave a message. I was guessing the message would say, *Stop that right now!* I took a quick glance at All's Well Mel and he didn't look quite as farmer friendly as before.

"Let's talk about the fingerprints," Corbison said with more smugness.

"Mine or the murderer's?" I replied.

Corbison smiled cagily. "Maybe they're one in the same."

Or maybe you're an imbecile. I decided to ignore Corbison in favor of Farmer Mel. "You can't be serious about me being a suspect. I'm a hometown girl, a florist, for heaven's sake. I grow things. And I'm very pro-justice. I've even solved a few murder cases. I'm sure you know my father, Sgt. Jeffrey Knight, who was wounded in the line of duty three years ago. So, seriously, guys, why are you focusing on me instead of on the obvious suspect—Professor Puffer? The man is infamous for using his pencils as weapons. See this scar?" I pulled back one side of my hair to show them a tiny, white, crescent-moon shape near the hairline. "Puffer did that. And if he can do that, well, it's pretty obvious he has serious anger-management issues. So, come on. Level with me. What's really going on here? Why are you trying to make me look like a killer? Is this a game you're playing to catch the real murderer? Am I bait?"

Corbison shot to his feet, bracing his hands on the table and leaning toward me, an ugly look on his face. "You think we're playing games?"

"Easy, Al," Mel cautioned, laying a hand on his forearm.

"I'd like to have a minute with my client," Dave injected. Just as well. The fury in Corbison's face had really shaken me. Clearly my little speech about being the hometown florist had fallen on deaf ears. I had become a perfect stranger—or maybe a not-so-perfect stranger—who was capable of murder.

Dave waited until the tape had been stopped and the men had gone, then he said, "Look at me, Abby. Look at my face. Do you see any amusement in it? These men are not playing games and you can't, either. This is your life we're talking about. People in town are frightened. A professor has been murdered, of all places in a law school. This is unprecedented! I've been listening to the radio talk shows and everyone is up in arms. They're after blood. There's a murderer on the loose and people want justice, vigilante or otherwise."

I couldn't think of a thing to say. Then again, my mouth

was so dry I doubted anything but a rasp would have come out anyway.

"This atmosphere creates enormous pressure on the police and the prosecutors," Dave continued. "Do you remember the old saying from your law school days about a prosecutor being able to indict a ham sandwich? Well, it's true. And there's enough circumstantial evidence here to indict you—and may well be enough to convict you. People have been convicted on a lot less. So drop the smart-ass attitude and get serious. When they come back in, answer their questions with no editorializing and no sass. Got it?"

Had it, but couldn't get over it. I cleared my throat and managed, "So I really am a suspect."

Dave sighed. "That's what I've been trying to tell you. The prosecutor is here for one reason—to look for what he would need to take this to trial: your tone, your demeanor, your body language. So watch it, okay? Be straight with them. No pithy comments. No exasperated sighs. No rolling of the eyes. Nothing but straightforward."

He wouldn't have to tell me again. I knew my saucy attitude was a form of protection to fend off that scared-silly part of my brain that was whispering, *These men are out to get you! You could actually wind up in prison.* It was called denial. But I couldn't afford to deny the truth of my situation any longer. I was in serious trouble and I had to be the model of cooperation to get myself out of that trouble.

The men returned and the recording was started again. I sat meekly with my hands in my lap as Dave said, "Sorry for the delay. Let me state for the record that we're here to give you total and complete cooperation. Abby will hold back nothing. If I thought she was involved, we wouldn't be here. Hopefully, she can help you find the murderer in this case."

"Let's start over," Mel said in a friendly voice, while Corbison sat back with a frown and glared at me. Apparently they had decided to do the good cop–bad cop routine. "Tell me how your prints got on the pencil."

I took a deep breath and began my story for the umpteenth time, trying to include every detail, whether I thought it was important or not. Then I sat back and waited.

"Let me get this straight," Corbison said, stepping up to bat. "Professor Puffer dropped your flower in the trash, and you were so angry you went back to his office to get it."

"It was a beautiful flower in a handsome vase. I couldn't stand to see it go to the dump."

"On a scale of one to ten," Corbison said, "how angry would you say you were?"

I pondered his question for a moment. "Angry enough to override my fear of the man, so I'd say . . . a six. I take a lot of pride in my flowers, and this flower was a perfect rose known as Ink Spots, a very dark red, velvety—"

"At the protest rally," Corbison said, cutting me off, "you confronted Professor Reed. Why?"

"Because he was defending the type of heartless, greedy company he used to rail against. Do you have any idea what they do to those poor, helpless animals? It would make your skin crawl, literally, just like the toxic chemicals do to their fur, and—"

"How did you feel when Professor Reed had you arrested?" Corbison asked.

I was a little perturbed by the way he kept cutting me off, but I kept it to myself. "Shocked. Hurt."

"Angry?"

"Well, of course. Professor Reed was a sellout. He told us we shouldn't be afraid to take a stand against injustice, then he had me arrested for taking a stand against injustice. Wouldn't you be a little angry?"

"On a scale of one to ten?"

I shrugged. "Six."

"So you felt the same amount of anger toward him as you did toward Professor Puffer after he trashed your lily?"

"It was a rose, and no, not the same. More like a seven with Reed."

Corbison said, "And when Carson Reed came out of his office to taunt you about the arrest, how did you feel?"

Did I really want to tell him I was angry again? I looked at Dave but he didn't say anything. He probably didn't want to appear to be coaching me.

"Answer the question, please," the prosecutor said evenly.

In a very quiet, controlled voice I said, "Yes, I was angry."

"You'll have to speak up for the tape," Corbison said.

"Angry," I said louder.

"On a scale of one to—"

"Eight." I was really sick of that scale.

"What was Professor Reed doing when you returned to get the flower?" Corbison asked.

"Nothing. He was dead."

"Are you sure?"

Was I sure. "Well, let's see . . . there was a pencil sticking out of his throat, and his eyes were staring like this"—I demonstrated by opening my eyes as wide as I could get them—"and he wasn't moving, so, yes, I'm sure."

Corbison leaned forward expectantly. "Or maybe he was alive when you came back and you were so *angry* that you picked up the pencil and stabbed him in the throat."

I pressed my lips together and folded my arms over my chest, then thought better of the body language and put my hands back in my lap and said firmly, "I didn't kill him."

"But I'll bet you wanted to," Corbison said, as if he could egg me on.

"Killing someone isn't what pops into my head when I'm angry. Besides, I told you he was already dead when I came back."

Corbison scratched his neck and looked doubtful. "Eight is a very high amount of anger."

"Look, I could have felt a twelve toward him, but I still wouldn't have killed him."

"Did you think about it?"

"No!" I looked to Dave for help. Corbison was clearly badgering the witness—in this case, me. Why wasn't Dave objecting?

"Don't you think skinning a snake would kill it?" Corbison asked.

"Yes, but you're taking my comment totally out of context. And for the record," I added, leaning toward the tape recorder, "I'm opposed to skinning any creature."

Corbison sat back with his arms folded and a look of triumph on his face. "So you did think about killing Carson Reed."

"Have you not been listening?" I snapped, then felt Dave's hand clamp on my arm. I took a deep breath and slowly let it out, trying hard to keep the famous Knight temper from boiling over. "I did not kill Professor Reed, nor did I think about killing him."

Corbison and Mel put their heads together to discuss something in whispers, then Corbison said, "All right. That's all for now, but keep yourself available in case we have further questions."

I snatched my hat off the table; we stood up and walked out.

"The second half went much better," Dave said as we headed toward his car.

I jammed the hat on my head, doing a slow sizzle. Had we been at the same meeting?

"Are you okay?" he asked, glancing at me in concern.

Okay wasn't quite the word I'd use to describe my feelings. Righteous indignation came close. "Corbison was badgering me, Dave. Why didn't you stop him?"

"And make it seem like you had something to hide? Listen, if they can't shake you with their badgering, they'll start looking elsewhere for their suspect."

"Yeah, well, I have a strong feeling they've looked as far as they're going to."

"Think about this," he said, sliding into the driver's seat. "With the evidence they have, they could have arrested you, but they didn't. Take that as a good sign."

"I'm trying. I really am. But we both know if the police don't turn up any better leads, they'll come back to me."

He didn't argue, which meant he agreed, which meant I was in an oceanful of hot water. "Well, then," I said, fastening my seat belt, "I guess I need to make sure that doesn't happen."

"Abby, be very careful. You don't want to be charged with obstruction because you interfered with the police investigation. And you don't want to put yourself in a position of danger."

"I'm not in a position of danger now?"

"You know what I mean. Let the police do their work, and have a little faith in the justice system."

"Yeah. Right. The justice system. We both know how well it worked for my dad. He was paralyzed for life and the drug dealer who shot him was out of jail in nine months."

"Abby, let me tell you something. If I didn't put my faith in the system I couldn't do my job." He reached over to pat my shoulder. "It isn't like you to be so pessimistic. Come on. Think positive. I have total belief in you and in what you've told me. Remember, the truth will out."

Only if the truth had a chance to *get* out. The problem was, the killer was doing his best to bury it—and me with it.

CHAPTER THIRTEEN

Dave parked his car in a small lot around the corner from his office, then we headed up to Lincoln and turned in opposite directions, Dave for his office and me for Bloomers. I crossed the street to the courthouse lawn and plowed forward, keeping my head down and looking at no one. I thought I was doing well, too, until I spotted a band of sign-carrying protesters marching in front of my shop. I came to an immediate halt, glanced around for cover, and dived behind a sturdy maple tree. Tugging my hat as low as it would go, I peered around the trunk to take a better look.

Besides the wacko with the SAVE THE FLORIST sign, there were three more with SAVE THE ANIMALS / DOWN WITH DERM-ACOL signs. But the JUSTICE FOR REED group had grown to ten, and they were shouting their slogans at everyone who walked or drove by. Deciding it would be in my best interest to avoid any more protest marches, I called Lottie to tell her about my current situation—actually, all of my current situations—not to mention my new mission in life, which was basically to save mine and have one. Lottie agreed that I should have a life and assured me that Grace did, too, although we both knew there would be a quote forthcoming before the whole fiasco was finished.

"I'm sorry I can't get to the shop. I feel terrible leaving you two with all the work."

"Don't sweat it, sweetie. We're making money as fast as we can take it in. I've been to the bank twice today and had to call suppliers to get more flowers."

"That's good news, but I'll bet you're swamped with orders, so I'll sneak in tonight—"

"No need to bother with that. I've already asked my cousin Pearl to come help out in the shop tomorrow so Grace and I can keep up."

"Oh. Okay. That's fine." Why did that make me feel worse? Business was booming at Bloomers, something I'd been praying for since I first took on the mortgage a mere five months ago. I should have been overjoyed. Instead I felt—unnecessary.

"You just concentrate on finding the killer, sweetie, and leave Bloomers to us. And don't be going on a big ol' guilt trip, either. You didn't do this on purpose. Hold on, Abby. Grace wants to say something."

The phone was passed and then Grace said, "Sorry to bother you, dear, but, speaking of guilt, your mum rang twice, the last time five minutes ago. Your father rang ten minutes ago. Same message from both. Call them back."

"Okay, I will." But not yet. First I had to share the bad news with Marco so he could bolster my spirits. "Thanks, Grace. Stay in touch."

I checked to make sure no one had noticed me, then I hit the speed-dial code for Marco.

"Hey, Sunshine," he said, answering on the second ring. "How'd the meeting go?"

"The question isn't how it went, but where it went. The answer is, down the toilet."

"I'm at the bar. Come over."

"Make sure the back door is open." I slipped the phone in my purse and took a roundabout route to Down the Hatch, stopping to peer down the alley before stepping into it. The coast was clear, but I didn't dare tarry. Ahead, Marco had opened his back door, so I slithered along the side of the building, hurried past him, and headed straight for his office.

He locked the door and took a seat at his desk as I sat in one of the sling-back chairs and stuffed the hat in my purse. "Give me the details," he said.

I recounted the minutes of the meeting, and when I finished I said, "I know you won't be in favor of this, Marco, but after the grilling they gave me, I've decided I need to take matters into my own hands. I've got to find the killer."

"I agree."

"So please don't try to talk me out of it. . . . Wait. Did you just agree with me?"

"Do you think I'd leave your fate up to a prosecutor's political whim? Not a chance, baby. We're going to find the killer together."

I smiled a genuine smile for the first time that day. Marco was absolutely the greatest. To show how much I appreciated him, I jumped up and went around the desk to give him a hug. Also, to feel those rock-hard pectorals. They were the greatest, too.

"Are you going to grope me all afternoon, or are we going to get busy saving your shapely behind?" he asked teasingly.

I craned my neck for a glimpse of my backside. "My behind is shapely? Really? In these pants?"

Marco gave me a look that males have perfected that said, *I'm sorry I brought it up.*

"Never mind. You're right, Marco. This is serious business. Everything in good time." I put my shapely behind in the chair. "Okay, here's what I was thinking. Professor Puffer should be first on our list of people to investigate. He had the means and the opportunity to kill Carson Reed. Plus, he's trying awfully hard to make me look guilty."

Marco opened a desk drawer and removed a yellow legal pad. I leaned closer and saw that it was the notes he'd taken when I talked to him on the phone just after the murder. Adding to them, he wrote the heading *Suspects,* then put Puffer's name beneath. "What about a motive?"

"Not clear. Maybe a professional rivalry. Reed was younger than Puffer by ten years, yet he has—*had*—tenure and Puffer didn't—*doesn't*." Death and verb tenses—not easy to master.

"How did that happen?" Marco asked.

"I'm not sure. Maybe because Puffer got a late start—he was a JAG officer before coming to New Chapel. I do know that he applied for tenure several times and was turned down, and I also know that he and Reed were not friends, despite what he told Connor."

"Who's Connor?"

"The reporter who wrote the front-page story in today's *News.* He keeps bugging me to give him my side of the events."

"But you haven't, and won't."

"Of course not. My motto is—" I pretended to zip my lips.

"Good." Marco added Jocelyn Puffer, Beatrice Boyd, and Kenny Lipinski to his suspect list, then showed it to me. "Should anyone else be on here?"

"If it was a case of mistaken identity, how about all of Puffer's students?"

"A case of mistaken identity?" Marco looked doubtful.

"You're right. I'm reaching. But the rose bothers me. What if someone sent it to Puffer as a warning? What if the killer went to Puffer's office to make sure he got it, spotted the flower sitting in the wastebasket and freaked out, not realizing the wrong man was in the chair? After all, the back of the chair was tall, and Reed was facing the other way."

Marco shoved the pad of paper toward me. "Make a diagram of the office."

I flipped to a clean page and sketched the room, then pointed out the features. "Here's the desk. Here's the chair facing the back door. Here's the front door. Here's the wastebasket."

Marco studied it. "If the killer was close enough to see into the wastebasket, he would have been close enough to see Reed."

"Not necessarily. The rose showed well above the rim of the wastebasket. The killer could have spotted that from as far away as the front door. He might have rushed in, socked Reed from the rear, then stabbed the pencil into his neck, saw who it was, and fled out the rear door, taking the elevator down to the main floor."

"That's really a stretch, and besides, if it's a case of mistaken identity, you can rule out Puffer as the murderer because he would have known who was in his chair."

"Oops. Then forget that theory because I can't rule out Puffer. He's my number one suspect. Let's go back to square one."

Marco toyed with his pen. "Here's what I don't like about Puffer being the killer. First of all, he'd be stupid to kill someone in *his* chair with *his* pencil. Second, you said he didn't act nervous or worried, which makes him either innocent or a clever sociopath."

"I'll vote for the second option. What better way to get away with murder than to make yourself look too obvious— like you were set up? He's shrewd, Marco, and his temper is volatile enough that he could easily have flown into a rage and killed Reed."

"We'll need to question him to see if we can establish a motive."

I shivered at the idea of confronting him. "You might want to work on that one alone."

"I'll see what I can do. Let's move on. Number two is Puffer's wife, Jocelyn. You told me you saw her at the school before noon, yet she didn't show up until after the cops arrived. So we need to find out how she got into the building and where she was between the time you first saw her and the time she showed up at her husband's office."

"I'll talk to Jocelyn. She's always been pleasant to me. I just don't see her as a suspect."

"Remember this. The one you least expect is the one you'll overlook. If anything at all sounds the slightest bit fishy, start digging. Talk to her friends, coworkers, neighbors. Establish a pattern of behavior for her and see if she's been deviating from it. Who knows? Maybe she and Reed were having an affair and he threatened to tell Puffer."

"Jocelyn is not even close to Reed's type. He preferred lively, pretty, *young* women, which Jocelyn isn't. She's a fifty-something drudge who's been browbeaten by Puffer into a grim, colorless shell. It's common knowledge that he inspects their house every morning to make sure it's perfectly tidy. He bounces quarters off the sheets, Marco, to see if they're taut enough. That would make anyone grim."

"She still needs investigating, Sunshine, to find out where she was during that gap of time. That reminds me; I need to check with Reilly to see if they sealed off all of the building's exits and if anyone tried to get through." He made a note to himself, then moved back to his list. "Next up is Beatrice Boyd. I know you said she was able to get along with everyone, but that doesn't mean she couldn't have had a bone to pick with Reed."

"If she had a bone to pick, she'd bury it in the backyard and move on. She's very even tempered, not the type to cower or complain or get flustered. I've seen Puffer in a rage over some silly little thing and she never even blinked." I paused, thinking back. "Except she did look a little ruffled when I arrived with Puffer's floral delivery."

"Did you ask her why?"

"I didn't want to be nosy. Stop rolling your eyes. I know when not to pry. She was in a hurry—late for an appointment, I think she said. That must be why she seemed rattled. She's a punctual person."

"Is she married?"

"No. I don't think she ever was. But she's sort of adopted her niece Hannah, who came here from Minnesota a year ago to attend college."

"Any possibility of Beatrice having an affair with Reed or being jilted by him?"

"Zilch on that idea. Bea may look like a free spirit, but she's as old maid–ish as anyone can be. And she's a lot older than Reed."

"Still, I'd like to know more about that appointment." Marco checked his notes."What about Kenny Lipinski? He was on the scene right after the murder. Coincidence?"

"That thought crossed my mind, too. He said he was researching something in the computer lab, so he'd have to log in and out, which will be easy enough to verify. But why would he want to murder his adviser, especially one who'd secured a federal clerkship for him?"

"Something to investigate. What about another student wanting that clerkship?"

"I'm sure there were several who were hoping to get it, but being passed over for it isn't exactly a motive to kill the professor. Kill Kenny, maybe, to take his spot."

"All the same, it would be helpful to find out who else was in line for it. It takes only one nutcase who feels cheated to lash out at the person he believes is responsible."

"If you're looking for a nutcase, Puffer's your man. Wait till you meet him."

Marco jotted one last note, then looked up at me. "Will you have time to see Jocelyn before the memorial service tomorrow?"

"What service?"

"One o'clock in the afternoon at the university chapel. It was in the paper."

"I didn't read any farther than the front page. I was blinded by all the freckles. Do you think I should go?"

"I think *we* should go. It'll give us a chance to observe the other suspects. Wear something inconspicuous and we'll sit in the back. I'll pick you up at noon."

"It's a date. In the morning I'll pay a visit to the bookstore where Jocelyn works. That should be a quick one to check off our list."

"The other interviews will have to wait till next week." Marco put away his notes and shut the drawer. "Classes at the law school have been canceled until Monday in Reed's honor. That was in the paper, too, by the way." He came around and took my hands, raising me to my feet. "We're going to find this killer, Sunshine."

"I hope we do it soon," I said with a sigh. "I won't be of much help to you behind bars."

His mouth curved up in that intriguing Marco grin that made my breath catch and my toes curl. He drew me into his embrace and gazed down into my eyes. "If they put you behind bars, I'll just have to break you out."

Standing there with Marco's arms around me, his powerful virility radiating warmth into every fiber of my body, I was ready to break out—of a few garments. I gave him a flirtatious smile and said in a sexy voice, "Promise?"

One dark eyebrow lifted slyly. "I think we can do better than a promise." Then he tilted his head down to meet my lips. Oh, yeah. That was better, all right. Warm, strong hands sliding down my back; firm, manly lips nuzzling, nipping, teasing with little darts of his tongue, melodious chimes ringing in my ears . . . Wow. That old saying was true! His kiss really *was* setting off bells.

Wait. That was my phone.

Almost at once Marco's desk phone rang, too. It had to be a conspiracy.

"Hold that thought," he whispered against my lips, then reached across the desk for the handset. While he was on his call, I dug my phone out of the recesses of my purse and looked at the caller ID. Mom. Who else? She had a sixth sense that seemed to vibrate at critical moments, *Abby alert! Dangerous kissing ahead. Call at once!*

Marco held his hand over the phone. "It's my kid sister. The local cable news station has been running footage of you taken at the protest march. She thought I should know."

"Swell. That's bound to help things." I tucked my phone away. My voice mail could handle Mom for now. One problem at a time.

Marco thanked his sister and hung up. "Looks like you're a local celebrity."

"I don't want to be a local celebrity. I want to arrange flowers. I want to come and go without having to dodge reporters. Most of all, I want to know why your sister thought you should know about my TV coverage. Does she think we're an item?" I gazed at him hopefully.

Marco had a fleeting expression of panic on his face as he stammered out something about my name coming up once or twice in conversation. So he *had* been talking about me—to family yet. Another glimmer of hope. But had she called out of concern for me, or to warn him to stay away from me because I was bad news?

Suddenly, there was a knock on the door, followed by Gert's gravelly voice. "I don't want to panic anyone, but I thought Abby should know what's happening outside the bar."

Whenever anyone said not to panic, that meant there was a good reason *to* panic. So naturally I was on the verge of panicking when Marco intervened by giving my shoulders a reassuring squeeze and saying quietly next to my ear, "Gert likes to exaggerate. Don't worry. It'll be fine." Then he swung the door wide. "Come in, Gert."

The scrawny waitress stuck her head in and gave me a sympathetic look. "I hate to be the one to tell you, Abby, but there's a mob of angry people on the sidewalk outside and they're calling for your arrest."

CHAPTER FOURTEEN

"They're calling for my arrest?" That was definitely a time to panic.

"It's probably a stunt to get in front of the cameras," Marco assured me. "Don't worry about it."

Easy for him to say. He wouldn't be the one wearing an orange jumpsuit. I sank into one of Marco's chairs with a groan, picturing hundreds of outraged citizens carrying pitchforks and flaming torches, while a posse in ten-gallon hats strung a noose over a limb on one of the maples edging the courthouse lawn. (I wasn't sure where the posse had found their ten-gallon hats—Indiana wasn't exactly known for its cowboys—but imaginations don't always use logic.)

"Exactly how large is this so-called mob?" Marco asked Gert.

"Twenty people, give or take. Some are carrying signs, and there's a crew from the cable news station and a couple guys toting professional-looking cameras."

Marco eyed her skeptically. "How did they find out Abby was here?"

She paused to cough up thirty years' worth of nicotine-induced phlegm. "They're not here. They're in front of Bloomers. We're just getting the spillover. The bar is full, by the way."

I was so glad to be of help. Damn that Connor Mackay and his article. I dropped my head in my hands. "How am I going to get around town? I can't spend the rest of my life—whatever is left of it—running down alleys, dodging angry mobs and crazed reporters."

"You need a good disguise," Marco said. "Gert, keep her company. I'll be right back."

"Say, doll," Gert said, crouching in front of me, "I was thinking of planting daisies along the front of my house. What do you know about them? Any particular kind I should look for?"

Without even thinking about it, that part of my brain dedicated to flowers rattled off, "Dendranthema rubellum 'Clara Curtis.' Salmon pink, very winter hardy, about fifteen inches high." Then the rest of my brain sighed morosely. Lottie and Grace must be going crazy at the shop. And I couldn't get down there to help.

"I'm back," Marco said. "Try this on." He handed me a man-sized black rain poncho, which I slipped over my head. He adjusted the drape, pulled up the hood—which completely swallowed my head—then leaned back to study me. "That should work. Let's give it a try."

The poncho was so big that it puddled on the floor around me. I couldn't even find my hands. Before I went out again, I'd have to come up with a better costume than this, not that I didn't appreciate Marco's efforts. I gathered the voluminous cape as best I could and stumbled behind him to the back door, waiting while he checked outside.

"All clear." Marco peered into the hood. "Hang in there,

Sunshine," he said softly. "You'll be okay." Then he pressed his lips against mine.

For some silly reason, tears filmed my eyes. I wanted to be more than okay. I wanted to be declared innocent. I wanted the people in town to believe in me again. I wanted to get back to my flowers and have only my normal worries—money and, well, money. But I appreciated Marco's show of support and would have put my arms around his neck if I could have freed them. "Thanks," I whispered tearfully.

"Call me tomorrow after you talk to Jocelyn."

I lifted the hem so I wouldn't stumble and darted out into my new reality—the alley. As I scurried away, hugging the shadows, dodging garbage cans and waste bins, I had a new-found empathy for rats. Meanwhile, somewhere in town, the real rat was happily cleaning his whiskers, safe in the belief that he or she had gotten away with murder.

I made it to my car with no interference, but couldn't get *into* my car with so much material draped over me. So I removed the poncho, put it in my trunk, then drove home cautiously, top up, not wanting to exceed the speed limit or blow any stop signs. All I needed was to be pulled over for a traffic violation and have someone from the media find out. I could see the headline now: LOCAL FLORIST CAUGHT FLEEING TOWN.

As soon as I had pulled into my parking spot, my cell phone rang, so I checked the screen, saw Mom on it, and decided I'd better answer before she filed a missing-persons report. I forced a cheerful note in my voice. "Mom! I was just thinking about calling you as soon as I finished what I was doing." That was vague enough to be plausible.

"I've been worried sick all day, Abigail. Do you have any idea how upsetting it is for us to see our daughter painted by the media as a murderess?"

Did she have any idea how upsetting it was to *be* that painted daughter?

"People are saying the most horrible things about you and it makes us sick. I'm frightened for you, Abigail. I've never seen people so up in arms. Please tell me you got everything straightened out at your meeting."

"Well . . . not exactly."

"You didn't get it straightened out? I knew I should have had your father use his influence. Hold on while I call him."

"Mom, wait! This isn't as simple as taking care of a traffic ticket or bonding me out after a protest march. This is serious. The prosecutor is involved now. If Dad tries to pull strings and someone finds out, people will be even angrier than they are now, and they might take out their anger on me. Besides, I don't want to stress Dad and possibly bring on another stroke."

There was a long silence, then she said ruefully, "You're right. We certainly don't want that to happen. However, if there's anything I can do—"

"Thanks, Mom, I appreciate it, but Dave said not to worry. He totally believes justice will be served."

"But *you're* worried. I can hear it in your voice."

"That's why I've enlisted Marco to help me investigate." I got out of the car, locked it, and headed toward the apartment. "But you can't tell anyone, especially not Dad. Just tell him Dave Hammond is handling everything."

"Abigail," she said, her voice starting to get scratchy, "I love you. Please be careful."

"Don't worry. You know me. Caution is my middle name."

I heard her groan. "Now I'm really worried."

At that moment a white van with the letters WWIN-TV on the side pulled into the parking lot. I ducked behind a pickup truck and said quietly, "Mom, I need to hang up now. I've got some reporters to dodge." I shut the phone, clamped my purse beneath my elbow, and took off for the front door like a quarterback making a run for the goalposts.

When I burst into the apartment and slammed the door behind me, breathless from my dash up the steps, Jillian was using her laptop at the table. She gave me a glance, then went back to the screen. "I can't decide which headboard to buy. Come take a look."

"Jillian," I said, trying not to wheeze, "I just ran up two flights of stairs to outrun a camera crew from WWIN, and that was just one of many bad things that happened today. The last thing I want to do is pick out a headboard. Now if you really want to help—"

She swivelled to stare at me. "Are you serious? A camera crew from WWIN? I'll bet it's for their program *Whoosier Who's in the News*." Shoving back her chair, she ran to the window that looked out over the parking lot. "Are they still out there? Maybe I can snag an interview to plug my home-shopping business."

I tackled her as she flew toward the door, hanging on to her arms to drag her to a stop. "If you leave this apartment to talk to those reporters, I'll tell them you were jilted on your honeymoon."

Jillian swung to face me, her eyes slits of outrage. "You wouldn't!"

"Watch me."

She glared for a long moment, bosom heaving, then snapped, "Fine. I won't go out there, but I hope your conscience bothers you for depriving me of free advertising."

"If it will make you feel better, I swear to you, my conscience will never be the same."

"The only thing that will make me feel better," she said, straightening her blouse, "is if you tell me which headboard you like." She took a seat at the table and waited for me to join her.

I thought about locking myself in the bathroom and having a nice, hot soak in the tub, but she'd only pick the lock with a straightened paper clip, take a seat on the edge of the tub with the computer on her knees, and drive me crazy in there. I didn't know how mothers with little children managed.

There was only one thing to do and that was to select the stupid headboard and be done with it. So, after studying the photos on the screen, I pointed to a really cool rattan one in caramel with dark brown trim.

"I knew you'd choose that one." She put the cursor on a little box that said BUY NOW and clicked on it.

"Jillian, you checked the white wrought-iron headboard, not the rattan one."

"I know."

"Why did you do that?"

"Because we have opposite tastes."

In Jillian's world, that made perfect sense. She bookmarked the page and sighed contentedly. "That's one item off my list. What do you say we have dinner and you can tell me all about your bad day and I'll tell you all about my good day?"

"Fair enough. Are you cooking?"

Jillian thought a moment, then nodded. My cousin's idea of cooking dinner was to warm up a container of veal ragout that she had ordered from a restaurant. Apparently she was serious about not leaving the building, which was odd when I stopped to think about it. Jillian had always loved to be out and about. But since there was enough in my life that needed investigating at the moment, I put that thought aside and instead told Jillian about my interview with the police and my instant celebrity status of the worst kind.

"That really sucks, Abby," she said as we cleared the kitchen table. "Maybe you should call that wixy Connor and give him your side of the story so people will leave you alone."

"Are you talking about the guy who, according to you, threatened me?"

"I said he *sounded* threatening, not that he actually did threaten you."

"I'm supposed to keep a low profile, remember? Dave wouldn't be happy if I started blabbing to the press. Besides, Connor might twist my words and make me look even guiltier."

"He didn't strike me as that kind of guy."

"You didn't even see him, Jill. You only heard his voice—which you just said sounded threatening."

She flipped back her long hair. "He was merely trying to get you to call him. Actually, he's a very decent guy."

"And you know that how?"

"His voice. I can tell a lot by a person's voice."

"Right. That's why you agreed to go out on a date with a man who turned out to be a convicted felon doing time for auto theft. Lucky for you, the warden intervened."

"How was I to know the guy taking my telephone order was a prison inmate? Never mind about that. Do you want me to pull together a few disguises for you?"

"They have to be better than your knit cap."

"That hat was your idea. Just put yourself in my hands for an hour and I'll design personas that will change you so completely your own mother won't recognize you."

A tall order for a short person like me, no irony intended, but there was no harm in letting her try. "That would be great, Jill. Thanks."

"And in return," she said happily, starting for the door, "you can help me choose the rest of my furniture. I'll be right back."

It was a small price to pay for freedom.

While she was gone, I washed and dried the dishes and

fed Simon, who had scampered into the kitchen as soon as his little cat radar had informed him that the maniac was out of the house. He gobbled the food, shooting anxious looks at the door, and finished just as Jillian returned with an armful of clothing. The last I saw of him was the tip of his white tail as he shot around the corner heading for the safety of Nikki's bedroom window.

For the next hour I played store mannikin while Jillian concocted my disguises, pulling outfits from her racks of haute couture, which included some pretty bizarre getups. We followed that up with another hour of Web shopping, after which I decided to try out one of my new personas so I could go to the shop. I really wanted to go to my shop. I needed to dig my fingers into rich, dark loam, inhale the fragrance of sweet roses, and abandon myself in a fit of creativity that would soothe my stifled soul. I'd inherited that from my mother, too.

With Jillian looking on, I checked my appearance in the bathroom mirror and pronounced it very cool. Wearing a black Fedora hat, belted trench coat, slacks, and boots with three-inch stack heels, my red hair tucked safely out of sight, I looked like a private eye straight out of a Humphrey Bogart movie.

I tilted the brim down over one eye and said in my best Bogie accent, "Stand back, *schweetheart*. The feisty florist is coming through."

Jillian merely shook her head as if she thought I was pathetic.

The cable news crew had decamped sometime during the evening, leaving the coast clear all the way into town. I played it safe by taking Jillian's gold Volvo instead of the bright yellow Corvette, and parking a block away from the shop. But I still had to use the front entrance to get inside Bloomers because of the security alarm. Luckily, there were only a few people on the sidewalk and they appeared to be heading into Marco's bar. Still, I kept my head down as I slipped into the first recessed doorway, then darted into the next one, which, happily, was mine. I worked the lock, shut the door behind me, and punched in the code to shut off the alarm.

For two hours my hands flew and my soul sang as I created one masterpiece after another—a fall cornucopia display for a bank lobby, a fiftieth-wedding-anniversary bouquet, several new-baby planters, birthday baskets, and one dining-room-table arrangement of which I was particularly proud.

Using an eighteen-inch-long copper container, I gathered large, off-white spider mums, deep red roses, yellow sunflowers, orange carnations, and yellow, two-toned roses, with green button mums and variegated ivy as filler, cut the stems short, and created a low, plush mound of autumn color that looked good enough to eat. I attached a note addressed to Lottie that said, *An Abby Knight original. How do you like it?* Then I placed it on a wire shelf in the walk-in cooler. I put the stack of orders on the worktable with another note that said, "All finished. Call me tomorrow and let me know how it's going."

Then I shut off the lights, put on the black hat and coat, reset the alarm, and quietly eased open the door and slipped outside, pulling it shut behind me. I felt whole again. I felt confident and useful and—

"Police!" a deep voice commanded from behind. "Hold it right there."

—scared.

CHAPTER FIFTEEN

"**P**ut your hands in the air, turn around slowly, and step out where we can see you," a policeman commanded.

My heart gave a shudder. They must have thought I was a burglar. Either that or they'd decided to arrest me for murder after all.

Wait a minute. Didn't I know that voice? With my hands raised I said shakily, "Reilly, is that you? It's me, Abby. See?" Since my hands were already in the vicinity of my head, I used them to lift the hat, freeing my hair.

There was a sharp exhale of breath, then he said, "Damn it, Abby. What the hell are you doing sneaking around in the dark in that getup?"

"Is it all right if I put my hands down?"

"Yes," he snarled.

I lowered my arms and turned. Reilly was alone, dressed in denim jeans and a collared knit shirt. The only thing that identified him as a cop was the gun in his hand, which he immediately tucked into the back of his pants.

With a sigh of relief, I put the hat back on my head and tucked my hair beneath it. "I had to wear a disguise because I've been hounded by reporters all day. Looks like I fooled you, too."

"You almost got knocked flat on your ass is what you did." He stepped up closer to study me. "Reporters are hassling you?"

"A TV crew even followed me home tonight. Gather round, folks. Come see the homicidal florist. Watch her wield her knife on the poor, defenseless bleeding hearts." I sighed dejectedly.

He gazed at me as if he actually felt sorry for me. Then a shutter seemed to fall behind his eyes and he became the cop again. "Look, the next time you decide to slink around here in the dark, let me know so I can make sure no one arrests you for breaking and entering. Okay?"

"Sure thing. Thanks, Reilly. Are you working undercover tonight?"

"No, I just stopped at the bar for a sandwich. I'm on the graveyard shift this week. Do you need me to walk you to your car?"

He meant it kindly, but my independent nature was too strong to accept his offer. "I can handle it, but thanks." As he turned to go, I said impulsively, "Reilly, do you honestly believe I could have murdered someone?"

"It doesn't matter what I think. I just do my job."

"No, it does matter what you think. That's the problem with you guys. You need to think more often."

Reilly turned and walked away as I called, "It's why Marco left the force, you know. He decided it mattered what he thought, too."

People were coming out of Marco's bar, so I turned up the collar of Jillian's trench coat, went home, and crawled into bed, still thinking about people like Reilly and my dad, who just did their jobs, no questions asked. What made them different from the Marcos of the world, who needed to make their own decisions? Or people like me, who seemed to be constantly battling dragons—big ones, little ones, pencil-hurling ones—

"Abby, help me!" Jillian cried, barging into my bedroom just as I was drifting into a nice, deep sleep. "I lost a dog."

And annoying ones. I had to get my apartment key back.

"Shush, Jill," I whispered. "You'll wake Nikki."

"Nikki isn't home yet. You have to help me, Abby. I don't know where else to turn."

I knew I'd be sorry I asked, but there was no way out. I sat up, leaned my pillow against the headboard, and waved a hand at her. "Go ahead. I'm listening. How did you lose a dog?"

Jillian plopped down on the side of the bed, bouncing me an inch off the mattress. "You know how Mrs. Sample dotes on her Chihuahua?"

"You lost Peewee?" I shrieked, causing her to put her hands over her ears. "Jillian, if anything happens to that dog, the Samples will never forgive us!"

"I didn't lose him on purpose. Here's what happened. Not long after you left, Mrs. Sample came over to ask if you would check in on Peewee tonight and tomorrow morning because she and Mr. Sample had to go somewhere—I can't remember where—to the hospital maybe. He might be ill. Anyway, that's not important. What's important is that I said you would, but then you didn't come home, so I took Peewee out for a walk, and somehow he got away."

"You told her *I* would check up on her dog? What were you thinking? You know that mutt hates me. All right. Okay. Never mind about that. How did he get off his leash?"

Jillian started twirling a lock of her hair, always a sign that something bad was coming. "It's a harness, not a leash—and before you hit me with the pillow, let me explain. Mrs. Sample said Peewee won't go outside without his sweater, but he snapped at me when I tried to shove his legs in the sleeves, so no way was I going to tackle the harness. I herded him into the elevator and out the front door onto the grass, figuring it would only take him a few seconds to do his business, then I'd herd him back inside. But he kept sniffing under a bush and didn't seem to be in a hurry, so I made a phone call. Then I turned around and he was gone. But he can't have gone far, can he?"

"How long was it between the time you made the call and the time you turned around?"

She shrugged. "Ten minutes."

I got up and tugged my khakis over my pj bottoms. "Did you look behind the building?"

"I looked everywhere. I even asked these two cute guys if they'd help."

I pulled a T-shirt over my head. "What cute guys?"

"I didn't know them. They must live in the building. They were getting into a gray minivan, so I ran over and explained the problem, but they didn't have time to do more than make a quick inspection of the parking lot."

I slipped on my flip-flops, grabbed a flashlight from the kitchen junk drawer, and headed for the hallway. It was the perfect end to a perfect day.

We searched all around the building, under the cars, and behind shrubs, and when Nikki got home, we enlisted her help, too, but there was no sign of Peewee. Jillian was so distraught that I didn't dare tell her I had a strong hunch we'd never see the little dog again, for fear of losing the rest of the night's sleep.

An hour and a half later we clumped back upstairs and gave Jillian a list of whom to call in the morning—the animal shelter, local veterinarians, the police, and the Samples. Then Nikki and I retreated to our apartment to eat Nikki's newest dessert craze—raspberry fruit bars—while I updated her on my day. We discussed my disguise for the next day and the questions I needed to ask Jocelyn Puffer. Then, bleary-eyed and sugar sated, we stumbled off to our respective rooms for some sorely needed slumber.

But as I lay there drifting off to sleep I kept thinking about the vehicle Jillian had seen. I couldn't remember ever seeing a gray minivan in our parking lot. Was it a coincidence that the two guys were there when the dog disappeared? More important, why was I staying up to worry about a dog when my own neck was on the line?

At nine o'clock the next morning, I peered at the strange-looking woman in my bathroom mirror—the one in a Bill Blass silk charmeuse kimono in a subdued black floral print, wrapped across the front, tied at the waist, and falling just to her knees, her hair covered by a black and silver braided silk scarf turban, her earlobes sporting three-inch silver hoops, her eyes exotic smudges of dark brown shadow, her lips coppery-pink petals, her face glowing with bronzer, looking like she'd spent a month in the sun—and wondered who the hell would be dumb enough to fall for this disguise. I mean, my face was still my face, tanned, turbaned, or not.

I glanced down at my legs, encased in long, black, high-heeled boots. I did feel very exotic . . . and tall . . . and there weren't any freckles or red hair to give me away—a good thing, too, since another Connor Mackay story had made the front page of the *News* that morning. I tucked in one last strand of hair and made a face at myself. Hmm. Maybe I wouldn't be recognized after all.

In his article, Connor had interviewed a few of Carson Reed's associates, including law professor Myra Baumgarten and good old Z. Archibald Puffer. None could understand why anyone—with the possible exception of me—would want to murder Reed. After all, he was an all-around great guy, a stupendous professor, and a supportive colleague. And Puffer was more than happy to mention my dispute with Reed, which Puffer claimed dated from my dismal attempt to become a lawyer, long before the protest at the cosmetics lab.

Naturally, Puffer hadn't mentioned *his* role in my short stay at the law school, nor did he state that the only reason I'd gone to the school the morning of the murder was because of him, not because of any beef I had with Carson Reed. Why would he?

The second page of the newspaper had been filled with letters to the editor raging against the injustice of a law professor, especially one as noble as Carson Reed, being struck down in his prime by one disgruntled animal rights activist who fronted as a florist. Where were all the people who had marched alongside me at Dermacol? Why weren't they writing letters on my behalf? Had the entire town turned against me? I was so furious that I dug out Connor's number and almost called him to set the record straight. Then I imagined what Dave would say and reluctantly put away the card to get on with the business at hand—proving myself innocent.

Nikki was still sound asleep—something a person who worked afternoon shifts could do—so I tiptoed down the hallway, retrieved my purse from the kitchen counter, and let myself out of the apartment. I had already checked the parking lot from the window and hadn't seen any reporters or TV vans, so I felt pretty confident that I was in the clear. But just to play it safe, I used Nikki's little white Toyota to drive into town, parked on a side street, and casually strolled up the block toward Lincoln, where Books of Olde, the rare and used books store, was located.

From that vantage point I could look diagonally across the square and see that the marchers had returned to Bloomers, and it looked like their numbers had grown. I wondered briefly whether my side had picked up any supporters at all.

Suddenly I heard, "Hello, young lady. Visitor in town, are you?"

I spun around and there stood Uncle Sam, dressed in his navy blue tailcoat, red-and-white striped trousers, white shirt with red bow tie, and white stovepipe hat decorated with a blue band of stars, just like the Uncle Sam of history. He even had a long white beard, his very own chin whiskers.

His real name was Joe Starke, a lifelong resident of New Chapel and zealous patriot who had decided to spend his retirement years patrolling the town square passing out miniature U.S. flags, or driving up and down the streets in his monstrous white 1986 Pontiac Parisian, a full-sized flag flying from his window and John Philip Sousa marches blaring from his radio. On national holidays he wore his Korean War medals pinned to his lapels, gave spontaneous speeches on street corners, and marched in the parades, invited or not. He loved New Chapel and was the happiest man I'd ever met. Because Joe was such an amiable guy, everyone in town humored him, but no one ever took him seriously.

This morning he was standing in front of Books of Olde, a small plastic bag filled with tiny flags in his hand and a confused look on his face, as though he should know me but wasn't able to place my face. I raised my hand to say hello, then remembered I was incognito and simply let it go at that. Unfortunately, Joe took it to mean that I didn't speak the language.

"Stranger in town, are you?" he asked, and when I nodded, he began enunciating his words slowly and loudly. "Where. Are. You. From?" He looked around the square with his hand shading his eyes, as though he was searching for land.

Deciding that it might be quicker to pretend I didn't understand, I thumped my chest, walked my two fingers across my palm, then gestured toward the store behind him.

"You don't want to go in there, miss. You want a tourist shop. See these books?" He tapped on the glass display window. "They're all in English. *Eng-lish*. Although, if you're looking for book lights, they do have a nice selection."

I shook my head again and stabbed my finger at the doorway, but at that moment a woman passing by decided we needed her input, too. "Maybe she wants that atlas, Joe. She probably needs a map for directions. Do you need directions, honey?"

Never had I realized how hard it was to keep my mouth shut. Now other passersby were stopping to stare, too, so I gave up trying to be nice and simply charged into the store flanked by my interpreters, who took it upon themselves to call ahead to the store personnel, "We have a lost foreigner here! Someone get us a map!"

And I'd feared no one would be fooled by my disguise. Unfortunately, I'd also thought I would be able to slip into the store without attracting attention. But no, that was not to be. As the two owners scrambled to produce a map, and customers stepped from the aisles to gape, I felt as if I had just vaulted off a spaceship on all seven thumbs.

It was time to take matters into my own hands—or thumbs, as it were. "No map!" I exclaimed, channeling Nikki's grandmother once again. "Olga ees looking for book to read."

Everyone froze, and for a second I felt like I was caught in a time warp. Then Joe tipped his hat and said, "Enjoy your stay in town." The woman with him hurriedly backed out of the shop; the customers resumed their browsing; and the owners informed me—through a mixture of careful pronunciation and slow hand gestures—that the foreign-language books were all the way at the back near the unisex washroom, which I supposed would be helpful for non-natives with weak bladders and sexual identity problems.

"Olga tanks you," I said. Then, with dignity befitting a monarch, I held my turbaned head high and made my royal way down the aisle, pausing to check each row for Jocelyn Puffer.

Books of Olde occupied the main floor of a three-story, white frame building that hadn't seen much remodeling in the past century of its life. As a result, the interior walls had been covered over by layers of mustard yellow paint that had bubbled and blistered in many spots, the wood trim was nearly black with age, and the ancient oak floors groaned with every step, eliminating any last chance of me quietly making my way through the shop.

I knew the store well. Having had little money in my college years to spend on items such as new books and CDs, I had become familiar with the library, used book shops, and even the Goodwill store, where bargains abounded. I'd found Books of Olde to be a cozy place to spend a few hours hunting for rare, out-of-print works, treasures that filled the crammed shelves. The scents of vanilla and cinnamon wafted from bowls of potpourri set all around the shop (to cover the mustiness of the old tomes, I suspected); an odd assortment of upholstered chairs occupied various nooks; a coffee bar and a few tall tables filled a bump-out on one side wall, and tall, multipaned windows furnished the store with ample light and a plethora of dust motes.

I found Jocelyn in the second to the last row seated on a low stool, a feather duster in her hand, carefully cleaning the books she was removing from a box on the floor and placing them on the shelf in front of her. She was looking her usual colorless self, sporting a dark brown cotton knit skirt and top, and was so completely engrossed in her work that she didn't notice when I stopped beside her, which explained why she hadn't been one of the gapers earlier.

"Mrs. Puffer?"

She looked up with a startled expression. "Yes?"

I knelt beside her and said quietly, "I need to talk to you about Professor Reed's murder."

Her expression instantly grew guarded. "I'm not giving any statements," she said, then resumed her dusting.

Oops. The disguise. "I'm not a reporter, Mrs. Puffer. I'm

Abby Knight. I own Bloomers Flower Shop. See?" I lifted a bit of the tightly wound scarf so she could see my hair.

She took another look at me, but her expression didn't soften, which surprised me since she'd always been cordial before. "I didn't recognize you, Abby."

"Considering that I'm in disguise, that's actually a good thing." Hoping to win her over, I leaned closer to confide, "I don't know about you, but the reporters are driving me nuts. They're at my shop, they follow me around town—and now they're making me out to be some sort of vengeful killer. Even the police are treating me like a suspect, which is why I'm here. I need to convince them I'm innocent. Is there anything you can tell me about what you saw at the law school Tuesday that might help me?"

"I don't know any more than you do. Probably less, since you were on the second floor before I was." She gave the book in her hand a last swipe and put it on the shelf. She apparently thought she was done talking. Too bad she didn't know me better.

"Maybe there's one thing you can tell me, Mrs. Puffer. When you entered the law school, did you see anyone get off the elevator?"

"Since I used the elevator, I can say for sure that no one was on it."

"That helps. Thanks. Oh, and one more thing. If you got to the school shortly before noon, why did you wait almost an hour to go upstairs?"

"You must be mistaken," she said stiffly. "I was running errands until well past twelve thirty. Besides, my husband wasn't supposed to be in his office until one o'clock, so why would I have gone up there early?"

Exactly what I wanted to know. I put my purse strap on my shoulder and stood up, then paused, as if another thought had just occurred to me. "So the police didn't stop you from coming into the building?"

For a second she seemed taken aback, but she recovered her poise quickly. "I didn't say they didn't stop me."

"I see. Then they *did* stop you."

She shelved another book. "I had to identify myself, naturally. Now, if you don't mind, I'd like to finish my work."

"Sure." I paused again, purposely looking confused. "You still drive a white Saab, right?"

For a normally washed-out-looking woman, she certainly developed high color in her cheeks when she heard my question. "Why?"

"Because I'm sure I saw you at the school before noon."

She bolted to her feet and said in a furious whisper, "You have a lot of nerve questioning me. I have nothing more to say to you." Then she marched through the employee door in the back and that was the end of that.

Yeah, right. Like a dramatic exit would deter me.

CHAPTER SIXTEEN

I glanced around to see whether anyone had witnessed our conversation, then strolled nonchalantly through the store toward the door.

"Didn't find anything to read?" one of the owners called with a smile.

"Tank you, no. Luffly shop, though." I exited the building, glanced right and left, then hurried around the corner before anyone else decided I was lost in translation. As soon as I got to Nikki's car, I called Marco.

"I take back what I said about Jocelyn. Puffer. I'm definitely *not* crossing her off the list. She said the police let her inside after she identified herself. Ha! And did she ever have an angry reaction when I asked her to account for that hour gap."

"That's not surprising. Would you give an accounting of your actions if one of your customers asked for it?"

"If I had nothing to hide I would."

"I'm not so sure about that, but in any case, I'll call

Reilly and see what he'll tell me about her. Be ready at noon for the service. I'll pick you up in front of your apartment building."

"Better make that in the alley behind my building. I think I'm turning into a rodent."

At twelve o'clock that afternoon I cautiously exited the back door of my apartment building and stepped into the alley that separated the building from the garages belonging to homes on the next street. I didn't see any reporters or Marco's dark green car, only a black and silver Toyota Prius with tinted windows parked beside a garage door farther down the alley. I waited five minutes, checked my watch, waited another minute, then called his cell phone. "Where are you?"

"In the alley behind your apartment building. Where are you?"

"In the alley behind my apartment building." I eyed the Toyota, idling quietly two garages away. "Marco, are you driving a Prius, by any chance?"

Spinning its wheels in the gravel, the car spurted toward me, causing me to jump back in alarm. It jerked to a stop, then a window rolled down, and inside I could see a familiar dark head. I slid into the passenger side, arranged the silk kimono over a bared thigh, fastened my seat belt, and glanced at my chauffeur. "I hope you know you just took five years off my life."

"I don't know who you are," Marco said, "but I'll take you wherever you want to go."

Now, there was an offer I couldn't refuse. Marco's black suit and royal blue shirt and tie really set off his dark hair and eyes—and set me off, too, making me want to lurch across the console to nibble his neck. Apparently I was ringing a few bells for him, as well. His gaze had moved to my cleavage and was inching downward.

I crossed one booted leg over the other. "What do you think? This is one of Jillian's designer outfits from her new home-shopping venture." I patted the turban. "Isn't this cool? It hides my hair and changes the whole shape of my face."

His throat bobbed as he swallowed. His gaze had locked on my bare knees. "It's . . . hot."

"Really? So you like it?" (A question all women are compelled to ask. It's built into our genetic code.)

"Let's just say you'd better uncross those legs and cover your knees or we may not make it to the chapel on time."

Oh, yeah. He liked it. What a power trip that was.

"There's one problem," he added. "Every male at the university is going to have the same reaction I did."

A *maximum* power trip. I batted my mascara-coated eyelashes and tilted my head playfully. "And the bad thing about that is . . ."

"You're conspicuous. An investigator never wants to draw attention to herself."

Power off.

As I shifted to cover conspicuous body parts, Marco pulled out of the alley and headed for the university. "How do you like my new wheels?"

"This is *your* car? Wow. It's very cool."

Marco slid his hands over the steering wheel's leather cover. "The green beater was totaled, and this one won't eat up gas, so I thought I'd do my part for ecology."

That was one of the things I liked about Marco. He was a hunk with a conscience.

We pulled into the law school parking lot at twelve thirty and found it already more than half full. Good thing Marco had suggested coming early. As we walked across campus toward the big tower that housed the chapel, I pointed out both Professor Puffer's big black sedan and his wife's Saab. Typically, they had not come together.

Inside the building, Marco ushered me to the staircase that led up to the semicircular balcony overlooking the beautiful chapel. Only a handful of people were upstairs, and they all appeared to be students. Marco positioned us in the front row center, and I scooted to the edge of the wooden pew to peer over the glass railing. Below me was the wide, carpeted center aisle separating the many long rows of light oak benches. At the front was the pulpit on a light oak stage, with a magnificent, soaring, stained-glass window as a backdrop.

"There's Professor Reed's mother," I whispered as a woman in a wide-brimmed black hat adorned with ostrich feathers swept up the aisle, followed by a withered little man in a gray suit, carrying a box of tissues. "Her name is Hepzibah, and she's Reed's only living relative. His father died after joining a religious order in Nepal and falling off a mountain, and his brother moved to Paris to become a street mime and was never heard from again. No pun intended."

Marco said quietly, "His mother looks like an actress from the 1940s."

Hepzibah wore a dress with a long, full skirt that bounced as though she had on layers of petticoats. When she reached the first row she turned to gaze at the crowd, the back of one hand pressed to her forehead, and cried dramatically, "Thank you, good people, for coming." Then she sank onto the pew with a sigh, blocking the view of everyone behind her enormous hat.

"Why do I want to clap?" Marco murmured.

Next, I pointed out Professor Puffer, who was speaking to several dark-suited men at the front of the chapel. His shoulders were back and his hands were clasped behind him as though he were addressing a platoon. When Jocelyn came up the aisle, he left the group to direct her to the second row. She slid in but put her purse on the space beside her, obviously to keep him from sitting too close. I watched as he leaned toward her and spoke. She never glanced his way.

"Jocelyn doesn't seem happy to be here," Marco whispered in my ear, his warm, minty breath sending shivers of pleasure down my spine.

"My guess is that she's not happy to be here with *him*," I whispered back, hoping those shivers were skipping along Marco's vertebrae, too. "Puffer probably forced her to come as a show of support."

Suddenly I caught sight of Beatrice taking a seat at the end of a pew on the left side, near the front. She wore a flowing skirt and blouse in a gauzy navy fabric shot through with threads of gold, a spidery navy and gold shawl, and gold chandelier earrings. She had gathered her long, graying hair into a loose bun, Katherine Hepburn style, and stuck gold chopsticks through it.

"There's Bea," I whispered, pointing her out.

Marco raised his eyebrows. "That's not how I'd pictured her."

Now three out of our four suspects had arrived. The only one missing was Kenny.

To my surprise, at ten minutes before one o'clock, Beatrice's niece Hannah Boyd walked in and looked around, probably searching for her aunt. I'd met Hannah at a luncheon Bea had given in the spring, but I would have recognized her anyway from the photo on Bea's desk. Hannah was a pretty girl with long waves of honey-colored hair that flowed around her heart-shaped face. She had on a short black skirt that hugged her curves and a long-sleeved cotton T-shirt that ended just below her navel, with a chunky black bead choker around her slender neck. To my surprise, she took a seat on the opposite side of the chapel, toward the back. She couldn't have missed seeing Bea with those shiny chopsticks. Why hadn't she sat with her aunt?

"There's Bea's niece, Hannah," I told Marco.

"Odd that they're not sitting together," he remarked, echoing my thought.

Moments before the service started, Kenny and a buddy hurried up a side aisle and sat down. "Kenny Lipinski is here," I whispered to Marco. "He's the dark-haired guy in the brown sport coat beside the tall blond guy in the navy jacket."

"He looks like a younger version of his father."

"Don't say that in Kenny's presence. I suspect he has father issues."

"If Kent Lipinski were my dad, I would, too."

As the university chaplain took his place at the lectern, Kenny and his buddy kept turning around, as though searching for someone. The chaplain started the service with a prayer and a few personal anecdotes, then introduced the speaker for the first eulogy—Professor Z. Archibald Puffer. I nearly gagged when the Dragon strode up to the dais. Judging by the grumbling from the students around me, I wasn't the only one who felt that way.

"Puffer is going out of his way to make people think he and Reed were friends," I whispered to Marco. I had to grit my teeth through the speech, but when Puffer called Reed a humanitarian, it was all I could do not to yell, "What a load of bull!"

Marco must have sensed my emotions, because he casually slid an arm around my shoulders and held on. When Puffer finished, we were instructed to rise for the hymn "Amazing Grace." Afterward, as we all took our seats and the next speaker strode toward the dais, I saw Bea glance around and catch sight of Hannah. A look of dismay flashed across her face, then she picked up her purse and slipped out of the chapel. Hannah must have noticed her leave, because she instantly got up and left, too.

"Did you see that?" I asked Marco.

"Stay here and keep an eye on the others. I'll check it out."

He quietly got up and left the balcony, moving in that smooth, pantherlike gait that was so fascinating to watch. So I did. And as I turned back I happened to glance at the person seated around the curve of the balcony to my right—Connor Mackay.

A small shock went through me and I instantly spun away, holding up my hand to shield my face. I had to get out before he saw me. I glanced quickly in the other direction, wondering whether I could sneak out by pretending to look for something on the floor, then simply crawl away.

Oh, wait. I was in disguise. He wouldn't recognize me. Never mind, then.

I peeked at Connor, noting that he had donned a nice-looking black pinstripe blazer and white shirt, which he paired with—casual khaki pants? Good thing Jillian wasn't there. She'd either slap him silly or swoon in horror. I chuckled at the thought of her fainting and dropping over the balcony onto an unsuspecting person below, then noticed that Connor was smiling at me. He couldn't know me, so what was he up to? Was he flirting with a stranger?

He pointed to his hair. Was that some new come-on? *Hey, baby, I'm not bald.* Okay, so he had hair. And?

Then he pointed to my turbaned head. Aha! He thought *I* was the baldie.

Then he winked and made the okay sign. I stared at him, dumbfounded. He knew me.

CHAPTER SEVENTEEN

Connor had directed his attention back to the service, so I tried to do the same, but instead found myself darting angry glances his way. After turning my life upside down, he had some nerve to sit there so innocently. And how did he end up in the balcony not three yards away . . . unless he'd been following me.

Of course! He wouldn't have recognized me otherwise.

I got up and slid into the next row back, scooting around the curve until I was behind him. He had his reporter's notebook in one hand and a pen in the other, but he closed it as I drew near. Was he hiding something? Had he written about me again?

"How's it going, Olga?" he said quietly, laying an arm over the back of the pew, half turning toward me, but keeping an eye on the chapel below.

"How did you know I'd be up here?" I whispered furiously.

"You know, you might want to get some therapy for that

paranoia of yours. I'm not following you, if that's what you're implying. I came here to report on the memorial service and happened to notice a pretty lady sitting nearby."

He thought I was pretty? *Focus, Abby. Remember why you're here.* "So you didn't know who I was until I came over here just now?"

"Hell, no. I recognized you right away."

I shoved his arm off the top of the pew. "You're evil, you know that?"

"For recognizing you?"

"No, for believing those lies Puffer fed you and putting them in your stories."

"Then why don't you feed me something new?" He turned to give me a look that could only be described as beguiling, and I really didn't want to describe anyone's gaze but Marco's as beguiling. So I was doubly angry.

"Because I can't feed you anything new, that's why," I hissed in his ear.

"Says who?"

"My lawyer."

"Off the record, then. You can be my unnamed source."

I sat back, thinking about that one. If I could stay anonymous, what would be the harm in talking to him? But could I trust this reporter? Why take the chance? "Look, you don't need information from me. Ask around at the law school. Ask any of his students what kind of man Puffer is, and whether they think he's responsible for Reed's . . ." I halted that sentence as soon as I realized where it was heading.

Connor swivelled to look at me. "Are you saying Professor Puffer is involved in the murder?"

Apparently I hadn't killed that sentence soon enough. "Where did you get that idea?"

"So he's not involved? Then why *shouldn't* I believe what he tells me?"

"I didn't say he wasn't involved. Or was involved. I'm just saying . . ." *Why hadn't I kept my mouth shut?*

He flipped open his notebook. "Is this on the record or off?"

"Off! No, wait. It's neither. I'm not saying one more word."

"Not even to tell me why you're running around in that Halloween costume?"

I glanced around to make sure no one was trying to eavesdrop. "It's haute couture, not Halloween, and here's something off the record for you. I don't know who's involved in the murder, but I'd really *like* to know because I don't appreciate having angry mobs show up at Bloomers wanting to lynch me. And FYI, they're angry because of *your* story."

"So you've decided to do a little private investigating of your own?"

I sat back. Oh, that was bad. Marco would *so* not want that to get around. "What makes you think I'm investigating?"

"Besides the fact that you're masquerading as a gypsy? For one thing, you're sitting up in the balcony."

"Well, so are you! And *you're* not investi—" Well, yes he was investigating—for a story. "Anyway, this disguise is for my own safety. I call it my antiterrorism look."

"Is Marco Salvare part of that look, too, assisting your investigation?"

"Marco is merely my—" I started to say *boyfriend*, but stumbled on the *boy* part and only got out *friend*. I wondered what kind of therapy I'd need for that Freudian slip.

"So you and Marco aren't an item?"

"No comment. And how is that important to your story?"

"That wasn't for the story. It was for me."

He *was* flirting. And although I hated to admit it, I kind of liked his flirting. But what did that say about me? I mean, Marco and I were *almost* an item. We'd never discussed our relationship, but I was operating under the assumption that we were exclusive.

Never assume, dear, Grace always said. Maybe it was time Marco and I had that discussion. "Anyway, how do you know Marco?"

"A good reporter never reveals his sources." Connor turned fully to face me. "Are you going to give me your story and put an end to the angry mob scene?"

"Not on your life."

He blinked in surprise. "Why not?"

"Because," I said, rising, "a good florist never reveals her roots."

As I returned to my seat, the speaker was just wrapping up. Puffer, his wife, and Kenny were still there, but Bea hadn't returned, and neither had Hannah or Marco, so when the chaplain had us stand for the final prayer, I headed downstairs, glancing over my shoulder to make sure Connor wasn't following me. He wasn't. Maybe he was right about that paranoia.

Marco met me at the bottom of the stairs and ushered me out the door. "I moved my car to the street across from the chapel so we can sit inside and observe people coming out."

"What happened with Bea?"

"She followed Hannah out here, they argued, Bea watched her head toward the dorm, then she took off in the opposite direction." He pointed off campus.

"Bea's apartment is that way. Did you hear what they were arguing about?"

"I couldn't get that close, but I know Bea wasn't happy about Hannah being there."

"If Bea is anything like my mother, it probably had to do with what Hannah was wearing—or should have been wearing. Or should have eaten. Or how much sleep she got." I saw

Marco's eyes start to glaze over, so I stopped. That list could go on forever.

We settled in the car and Marco readied his camera. "What do you know about Hannah?"

"Not much. Why?"

"If she's in Bea's life, then we'll need to check her out, especially since she took the time to come to Reed's service."

I pondered that for a moment. Marco had a good point. Why would Hannah come unless she knew Reed? And how would she know Reed? She wasn't a law student. But she *was* young and pretty. "Marco, are you thinking what I'm thinking?"

"Unless it has something to do with that silky dress you're wearing, I doubt it."

I glanced down at the kimono, which had come undraped at one side, revealing a thigh and knee. "You devil," I said, covering the thigh but leaving the knee exposed, just to torture him. "Maybe Reed had something going with Hannah, and maybe Bea found out and . . ." I dropped that line of thought because I knew Bea better than that.

Marco picked up on it immediately. "Maybe she confronted Reed about Hannah and ended up stabbing him in anger."

"It's a logical theory, but it simply isn't Bea. She wouldn't hurt a fly."

"Have you ever seen a sparrow attack a predatory hawk to protect its nest?"

"I see where you're going with that, but I don't accept it in Bea's case."

"A PI has to keep an open mind, Sunshine."

"The problem with being open-minded is that your brains tend to fall out."

"I'm not even going to respond to that." Marco aimed his camera toward the chapel entrance. "Here they come. Keep your eyes peeled."

The first out the door was Jocelyn Puffer, who hurried toward the parking lot as if she'd just been sprung from prison. "Looks like her show of support for her husband is over," I said.

"If she came here to support him, it doesn't make sense that she would so obviously draw away from him in the pew and escape at the first opportunity," Marco replied.

"Well, then, maybe she came out of respect for Carson Reed. I mean, he was one of Puffer's colleagues. As the wife of a professor she might think it's the proper thing to do, and she is a very proper person."

Marco gave a noncommittal grunt.

The next one of our suspects out the door was Kenny, who cut through the throng gathering outside, with his blond buddy close behind him. Moments later the Dragon came marching from the chapel in his usual military manner, ignoring everyone until suddenly Connor Mackay broke through the crowd and trotted after him, calling his name. Puffer paused long enough for Connor to catch up, then they walked together toward the parking lot.

"That weasel," I muttered.

"I thought he was a dragon," Marco said, taking photos.

"The reporter is the weasel. That's Connor Mackay, from the *News*. He tried to get me to talk to him again, but I told him no way. It really frosts me how the press can take even the simplest statement and make something totally absurd out of it. Look what they did with that comment I made about delivering flowers."

"Which is exactly why you should never give them so much as one word."

I had a sudden recollection of saying to Connor not ten minutes earlier, *"I don't know who's involved in the murder, but I'd really* like *to know because I don't appreciate having angry mobs show up at Bloomers wanting to lynch me."* Oh, man. I didn't even want to think of how he could twist that one. I felt a headache coming on.

"Who's the old dude with Kenny?" Marco asked, clicking away.

I squinted across the sunny lawn to where Kenny and his friend stood talking with a distinguished-looking man with white sideburns, a close-cropped goatee, and a crisp gray suit. "That's Marvin Y. Brown, the head of Dermacol Labs. He was with Reed the night I was arrested. You probably saw his picture in the paper."

I watched the three huddle in conversation, then shake hands and part, the two guys headed toward the dormitories and Brown for the parking lot. Was that who Kenny had been watching for earlier? But why? Aha! I had it. "Marco, I have a sneaking suspicion Marvin Brown is trying to recruit Kenny as his legal assistant. He wouldn't have to pay him nearly as much as he paid Reed, yet he'd have access to all the law information he needed."

Marco put the camera away and started the engine. "That's not ethical."

"He tortures animals for profit. There's nothing ethical about him. I'm going to have to warn Kenny. He shouldn't get involved with a man like that."

"Abby," Marco said, tossing me a warning glance, "one problem at a time, okay?"

When we reached the alley behind my apartment building, Marco cut the engine, then turned to face me. "We've got to question Puffer next, but we're going to need a strategy. Where does he hang out? The VFW hall? Firing range?"

"He has a gun collection, so the firing range would be a safe bet . . . well, probably not safe for me." I scratched an itchy spot at the back of my head. "He plays golf at the country club on Friday afternoons."

"So you're saying we should take up golf so we can talk to him?"

"Funny. Ha-ha. I was going to say he always has drinks afterward in the bar." I wiggled a finger under the scarf above my forehead.

"And you know this because?"

"Jillian's mom is a regular there—on the golf course, not in the bar. Well, actually, there are times when she—"

Marco glanced at his watch. "How about making a long story short—and would you please take off the scarf before your scalp starts to bleed?"

I yanked it off and shook out my hair. Boy, did that feel good. I obviously wasn't cut out for haute couture. "Here's an idea. Tomorrow is the Knight family dinner at the country club, so if we arrive early, we can corner Puffer in the bar after he's put away a few drinks."

"Country clubs," Marco grunted. "Not a fan."

Actually, I wasn't either. I attended the Friday ritual for my mom's sake. For a girl raised on a farm like she was, being a member of an exclusive club had been a fantasy. For the wife of a cop, it had been an impossible dream—until my older brothers, Jonathan and Jordan, both doctors, had become members. Now she was in hog heaven.

"It would be the perfect opportunity to talk to him, Marco. Mention your Army Ranger training and Puffer will talk your leg off. And as an additional benefit for coming with me, you'll get a nice meal afterward."

"But the drawback is I'll have to have that meal with your family—not that there's anything wrong with them that a few counseling sessions couldn't fix."

"Name a family that doesn't have things wrong with it."

"My family."

Okay, then. "But don't the benefits of being with me for the evening outweigh the drawbacks of being with my family?"

His gaze traveled the length of my kimono, which wasn't much of a length at all. "Wear that and it's a deal."

"Marco, if I show up in this, my parents won't let us sit anywhere near each other. You'd be at one end of the table and I'd be in the restroom with my mother, a stack of linen napkins, and a handful of safety pins. But, hey, I'm wearing it now, and the day is still young."

Marco gave me an apologetic look. "I can't, Abby. Chris is off tonight and I'm shorthanded on waitstaff, too."

"This bar business really cuts into our personal time," I said with a sigh.

"I've only owned the place for six months. Once I get settled in, things will improve."

Somehow I didn't see that happening. Marco loved being at the bar, not that I could blame him, because I loved being at the flower shop. But where did that leave me? Hanging around the bar until the wee hours? I didn't think so, not when I needed to be up at six a.m.

"Tell you what," Marco said. "Tomorrow night we'll tackle Puffer at the country club, dine with your family, and then have time to ourselves afterward. How does that sound?"

"Fine, but let's not wait until Monday to interview the other suspects. In fact, what are you doing this afternoon?"

"Meeting with liquor distributors."

"Tomorrow, then."

"No good. I'll be tied up all day. Don't frown, Sunshine. If you were in immediate danger of being arrested, Reilly would give me a heads-up."

"Well, that's reassuring," I muttered crossly.

Marco crooked his index finger at me. I leaned across the console and he did the same, our lips meeting in a long, hot kiss that left me wanting more. "I won't let anything happen to you, Abby," he whispered.

Oh, how I wanted to believe him. The problem was, I was too much of a realist. I knew that there was only so much one person could control. At that moment, however, I didn't want to think about reality. I pulled back my head to gaze into those dreamy eyes. "Are you positive you have to work this evening?"

"Yes." He kissed me again, and I nearly climbed across the gearshift to get closer. But just because I was in an alley didn't mean I was an alley *cat,* so we ended it before the windows steamed up completely.

I got out and walked around to his side to lean in for one last, lingering kiss. "See you tomorrow evening," I said in a sexy purr. Then I straightened, gave him an over-the-shoulder smolder of a glance, and walked away—no, make that sashayed away, shaking my booty for all it was worth. If he couldn't see me tonight, at least I could make him wish he could.

But as I trudged up the steps to the second floor in those high-heeled torture chambers Jillian called boots, I started thinking about all the hours between now and tomorrow evening. It was only two thirty in the afternoon. I couldn't go to work. I couldn't sit at home watching TV all day, wondering whether the police were about to show up with an arrest warrant. So what was I going to do? Hunt for the killer myself?

Why not?

CHAPTER EIGHTEEN

There wasn't a single reason in the world why I couldn't hunt for the killer myself. I had a brain. I knew how to use tact. And I'd start by talking with Bea. She'd be an easy one to check off the list. As Grace liked to say, why put off till tomorrow what you could do today?

My cell phone rang, so I reached into my purse and glanced at the screen. "What's up?" I asked Jillian, not bothering with the niceties.

"Where are you?"

"In the hallway, just about to step into my apartment."

I heard a door hit the wall and turned to see Jillian shoot out of her new place and come hurrying toward me. "Abby, I don't know what to do," she said, following me inside as Simon, who had come to greet me, took off for parts unknown. "I haven't had any luck finding Peewee, and when I called the police, they told me there's been a rash of pet thefts over the past month and they haven't found any traces of the animals. They've just vanished. Poof! Also, I just told

Mrs. Sample that Peewee was dognapped and she didn't take it well."

She flopped down on my sofa. "You should have seen Mrs. Sample's face, Abby. It was awful. It was like someone cut out her heart. I've never felt this bad in my entire life."

"You jilted four men at the altar. *That* didn't make you feel bad?"

She shot me a scowl.

"Okay," I said with a sigh. "I'll go talk to Mrs. Sample and try to console her."

"Um . . . that's probably not a good idea. In fact, you'd better stay away from her for a while. Maybe you should even consider moving."

"Jillian, what are you talking about?"

"She thinks the dognapping is your fault."

"You didn't explain that *you* were in charge of Peewee?"

"And have her think I'm irresponsible?"

"You *are* irresponsible, Jillian. You lost her dog!"

"And you are a judgmental snot."

"You better believe I'm judging you. I'm also finding you guilty and sentencing you to go talk to *Mr.* Sample to explain what you did. He'll know how to calm his wife."

Jillian wrinkled her nose.

"What?" I asked her. "Did you already talk to him?"

"Mr. Sample is in the hospital. They had to take out his appendix in an emergency operation. He's fine, but now Mrs. Sample is in her apartment all alone and, well . . ." She stopped talking and cupped a hand to her ear. "Can you hear her sobbing?"

I heard her. I'm sure people in the next county heard her, too. On top of everything else, I now had a good neighbor angry with me. I took Jillian's hand and led her toward the doorway.

"Where are we going?"

"Not we. *You,* Jillian. You're going to apologize to Mrs.

Sample for losing her dog and promise to continue searching for him."

Ignoring my cousin's protests, I knocked on the Samples' door. Before I could push Jillian to the front, Mrs. Sample opened the door, saw me, and crushed me to her bounteous bosom, wailing so loud I feared my ears would bleed. "I knew you'd come," she sobbed. "I forgive you for losing him, Abby! Just, please, find my baby."

"Me?"

"The police aren't of any help," she continued, "and the animal shelter doesn't have him. But he can't have just disappeared. He has to be somewhere. With my husband in the hospital, I don't have anywhere else to turn."

"I'd love to help, but the thing is—"

Hiccuping, she gazed at me forlornly, and the rest of my sentence died. "Do you have a photo of Peewee?" I asked. As she ran off to find one, I turned to glare at Jillian. *Now* there was a reason why I couldn't start interviewing suspects.

Wearing a short, curly, blond wig from Jillian's collection, a pair of tan cargo pants, and a white blouse, trying to look as bland and harmless as possible, I dragged my cousin with me on a trip around the neighborhood to canvass everyone who'd had a pet stolen in the past month. Jillian, too, donned a disguise—a cropped black wig, a white T-shirt, and farmer's overalls. She claimed it was to protect her image, but I had my doubts. Jillian always had ulterior motives.

In a four-block area, we discovered that no one had seen Peewee, and twelve pets had gone missing, too many to be a coincidence. Everyone agreed someone was stealing the animals, but no one had seen the thieves at work. However, several people remembered seeing a gray minivan parked on the street, its engine idling. My guess was that the guys

Jillian had asked for help had been the thieves. They must have gotten a kick out of pretending to look for Peewee.

At six o'clock we called it quits and went home, mainly because Jillian's platform sandals were giving her blisters and she was overheating. She'd tolerate blisters for the sake of fashion, but she refused to perspire. At least we had one thing to go on—the gray minivan—so the next step would be to track down that van. I'd have to enlist Reilly's help for that job.

Back home, we ate buttered toast and omelets with salsa on top, then at seven o'clock Jillian left to meet with a client at her new apartment. I tried to reach Bea but got an answering machine, and I didn't know how to reach Kenny, so I sat there tossing a rubber band for Simon and watching a rerun of *That '70s Show,* which I never liked when it was new. I needed to find the killer, but since I couldn't tackle that until tomorrow, what was I going to do?

Lottie and Grace were taking care of everything at Bloomers. According to Lottie, customers were still pouring in, but with her cousin Pearl's help, they were managing just fine. All that business and they didn't need me? Was Pearl that efficient? Or had I been that slow?

I moped around for another half hour, then at eight o'clock I decided that if I went to the shop and simply sat in the workroom and breathed in all that good air, maybe I'd have an inspiration as to how to solve the case. So, wearing the blond wig and the bland outfit that went with it, I snuck out to my car and headed toward the town square.

Half a mile from my apartment, driving along Glendale Boulevard, I glanced up a side street and spotted a gray van double-parked with its headlights off, facing in the opposite direction. Immediately, my inner alarm kicked in—was it the pet thieves at work?—so I made a quick right and headed toward the van. As I drew up behind it, I could see that two people were inside. The license plate was the temporary kind, handwritten on cardboard and taped to the back window, as if the vehicle had recently been purchased.

Just as I pulled out my notebook to copy the numbers, the van drove off, continuing up the street and around the corner. Had I made them nervous? A quick survey of the houses on the block showed that fences enclosed the backyards, making them safer for pets. Maybe that was why they hadn't stuck around. Following their lead, I turned at the next corner and went a few blocks farther, and there was the van again. This time I killed my headlights and pulled over.

Moments later, a figure dressed in dark clothing, wearing a hooded sweatshirt, darted out from between houses carrying a bundle in his arms. He jumped in the van's side door and slammed it, and they took off. Damn! They stole a pet right before my eyes. I flipped open my phone and punched in 911 as I sped after the van.

"I want to report a possible petnapping," I told the dispatcher, making a right turn onto Concord.

"A *possible* petnapping?"

"I didn't actually see the pet, but I did see what looked like an animal in a sack."

"You didn't see the animal. Just a sack."

"And the van—a gray Chrysler minivan with a temporary plate in the back window. I'm following the suspects now." Ahead, the vehicle turned left on Lincoln and headed east. "Look, it's a long story and I'm running out of time because they'll be at the highway in a matter of minutes and then I'll lose them. Could you please send a squad?"

"Your name please."

Did she not understand that time was critical? "Abby Knight," I said, and rattled off my cell phone number. "Is Sgt. Reilly on duty?"

"I'll check. Hold please."

The van sped up the ramp and got on the interstate, heading north, with me in hot pursuit. But when it began veering around cars, weaving dangerously from lane to lane, I gave up the chase. I was willing to sacrifice my time for an animal, but not my life.

"Sgt. Reilly said he will contact you, Abby," the dispatch operator said.

"Tell him never mind. It's too late. They're gone."

Frustrated, I drove back to the neighborhood where I'd seen the van. Just as I had feared, in front of a small, yellow frame house I saw an elderly, gray-haired couple searching behind their shrubs with flashlights. "Sparky!" they called in turn. "Sparky! Here, boy."

Poor people. I couldn't stand the thought of them searching for hours in vain. "Are you looking for your dog?" I asked, stepping out of my car.

The woman put a hand to her heart. "Yes. He was in our backyard. Now he's gone and the fence is open. Have you seen him?" So much for the safety of fences.

"I saw somebody take him. They drove off in a gray minivan and I tried to follow, but they lost me on the highway. I think they're the same people who took my neighbor's Chihuahua. Anyway, I just came back to let you know."

"Our friend's cat went missing a week ago," the elderly gentleman told me as his wife turned to sob against his shoulder.

"There's been a rash of petnappings lately," I said. "Spread the word to your neighbors not to let their pets out without supervision. And please call me if you see a gray Chrysler minivan in your area." I dug out one of my business cards and handed it to him.

"You own Bloomers?" he asked, which made his wife stop sniffling and turn to look at me. "Are you the one that was in the newspaper the other day?"

"That's me, and please don't believe everything you read. All I did was deliver a flower. I didn't kill anyone."

"You don't look like the girl that was in the papers," the woman said, studying my blond curls.

"This is a wig," I said, giving a tug on a curl. "I'm not the most popular person in town right now. I thought it would be better to go incognito for awhile."

"You don't need to hide your identity around us." The man stuck out his hand to shake mine vigorously. "I'm Digger Johnson. This is my wife, Helen. We're very pleased to meet you, Abby. We marched at the protest rally and saw how you stood up to those bastards at Dermacol. You're a hero in our book."

"A heroine, Digger, not a hero," his wife said, giving me a tearful smile even as she corrected him—another trait that all women inherited. "We admire you for standing up for those poor animals, Abby. We'd love to see that lab closed down."

Wow. Someone *was* on my side.

Suddenly Helen looked at her husband with a gasp of horror. "What if the thefts are related to the testing at the lab, Digger? What if they took our Sparky for their research?"

I didn't want to alarm her further, but that thought had crossed my mind, too. I'd read about such cases before. Dermacol had to get their animals somewhere, and stealing them would be a whole lot cheaper than buying them. But why had the van headed north toward Lake Michigan instead of south, to the laboratory?

Duh. To throw me off the trail. "Please call the police and file a report," I said, backing toward my car. "If I come across any information about Sparky, I'll let you know."

I hopped in the Vette and headed straight for Dermacol Labs. If my hunch was right, the thieves would show up soon to drop off the animals. But what was I going to do if I caught them? Make a citizen's arrest? Yeah, right. I could call the police again, but even if they did buy my story, by the time they arrived, the animals would be tucked away inside, and the cops couldn't search the lab without a warrant. And to get a warrant, they'd need proof.

So I detoured to Walgreens drugstore to buy a disposable camera.

Hurrying through the automatic doors, I nearly collided with Kenny Lipinski, his arms loaded with bags of chips and liters of Coke.

"Sorry," he muttered, giving me a quick glance. Then he did a double take. "Abby?"

"Yeah, it's me, trying to avoid the press."

"No kidding. It seems like someone is working hard to make you look guilty."

"Yeah, and I have a strong hunch who that someone is."

"Are you talking about the Dragon?"

"Who else?"

At that moment the doors swished open and a customer came out, so Kenny stepped off to the side and motioned for me to join him. "Just so you know," he said quietly, "Puffer wasn't the only one who had a beef with Professor Reed."

"Kenny, if you know anything that will help me clear my name, please tell me."

He pursed his lips, as though debating what to say. "I'm not sure if this will help, so take it for what it's worth. Professor Reed came in Monday morning in a foul mood. He'd just ended an affair with a woman who wanted to leave her husband for him. I don't know who she was, but she didn't take the breakup well and even made a few threats about his job."

Another one of Reed's conquests. Poor woman. How many other victims had he left behind? "What did he expect you to do about it, Kenny?"

"Nothing. He was just venting. He never takes threats seriously . . . never *took* them seriously, I mean. Sorry. It's still setting in that he's gone." Kenny looked down at his shoes briefly, then cleared his throat. "Anyway, I did tell the police about the woman."

"And yet they keep focusing on me," I said with a sigh. "But thanks for the tip."

"No problem," Kenny said, shifting his goods. "I'd better go. I've got a huge exam to study for and never enough time."

I was about to add that at least he didn't have Reed's research to worry about anymore, but decided that would be tacky. However, it did jog my memory. "Kenny, very quickly, do you know Marvin Y. Brown?"

"The name sounds familiar. . . . Isn't he the head of Dermacol Labs?"

"That's him."

"Sure, I met him today at the memorial service. Seems like a nice enough guy. Professor Reed spoke well of him."

"I'll bet he did."

Before I could say more, a car full of guys came to a screeching stop in front of us. "Hey, Ken," one of them called from the window, "let's go, man. Pizza's getting cold."

"I'm coming." He gave me a sheepish shrug. "Sorry."

"That's okay. I'll talk to you some other time. Good luck with your test."

So there was a jilted married woman in town with an ax to grind. Hmm. I turned over that possibility as I shopped for the camera. If that woman was the killer, she would have been at the law school, but the only woman I saw was Jocelyn. Even if I accepted the idea that Reed would have had an affair with her, the big question was, would she dare cheat on Puffer? I couldn't imagine her running the risk of his finding out. He'd go nuts. He'd be furious enough—to kill.

Maybe Puffer had found out.

*   *   *

Armed with a disposable camera, I drove to the neighborhood that housed the lab, parked the car a block away, and hoofed it to Dermacol's modern, barnlike building. Staying low to the ground—not hard for a short person—I circled the chainlink fence protecting the employee parking lot at the rear of the building and found a spot under a tree that afforded me a direct view of a huge garage door in the building's rear wall. Then I readied the camera and waited.

Fifteen mosquito bites later, with no moon to light up the area, I heard the whir of a motor and saw headlights shine on the big gate as it slid open. Then an engine revved and a dark van glided through, driving around to the garage door, which was on its way up. As the van turned, I saw the wide headlight beam swing my way and quickly flattened myself on the scrubby grass. Seconds before the light reached me I remembered the wig, tugged it off, and shoved it under my stomach. My red hair wouldn't be the beacon the yellow wig would.

As the van swung toward the open garage bay, I got to my knees and aimed the camera, snapping a number of shots in the hope that I could get at least one clear view of the paper license plate.

Suddenly, the van's brake lights went on, doors slammed, and a man shouted, "I saw camera flashes coming from behind the fence. Someone's taking photos."

"We're on it," another male replied.

I grabbed the wig and scrambled away, hugging my purse to my body, keeping low, until I was past the fenced area. Then I fled east, darting between houses until I reached the western edge of the university campus three blocks away. Students were still out at that hour, walking home from the library, congregating with friends at the student union, or heading toward Starbucks for a late-night latte, so it was easy to blend in.

Stopping to wrestle the wig over my hair, I stowed the

camera in my purse and strolled casually along the sidewalk. I checked over my shoulder several times, but no one appeared to be tailing me. As I passed the library I spotted Hannah Boyd sitting glumly on the wide steps, chin in hand, looking like she could use a friend. Or maybe that was just wishful thinking on my part, since I needed to talk to her anyway. Being a shameless opportunist, I changed direction and walked up to where she sat. "Hi, Hannah. How's it going?"

She raised her head to look me over. "Do I know you?"

"Abby Knight," I said, taking a seat beside her. I wasn't sure how willing she'd be to talk to me, so I decided to beat around the bush for a bit and see where that led. "We met at a luncheon your aunt put on for one of the secretaries. I also attended law school here for awhile, but that's a story best shared over a beer and a box of tissues. Anyway, I wanted you to know that your aunt's kindness and moral support helped me through some really rough times."

Hannah sank her chin back onto her hand and muttered, "Lucky you."

"Not exactly. I flunked out of school."

"Like I said, lucky you."

Okay, *that* tactic wasn't working. I'd have to go for something a bit bolder. "My luck really isn't so good, Hannah. I'm the one who found Professor Reed's body."

She turned to stare at me with huge eyes. "You're the florist?"

I put a finger against my lips to caution her to be quiet, then I whispered, "I'm trying to keep a low profile."

She clutched my wrist with surprising strength and in a voice that was definitely *not* quiet cried, "Was my aunt there when you delivered the flower?"

"She was just leaving. She said she was late for an appointment."

At once Hannah burst into tears and ran off, sobbing

noisily, which prompted other students to turn to stare at me. Thank goodness I still had on the wig. I resumed my stroll, trying to figure out what it was about her aunt's appointment that had upset her. Was Bea ill? Was she hiding something from Hannah about her health?

I made it back to my car without incident, drove to Walgreens, and turned in the camera. "Could I have that developed right away?" I asked the college-aged clerk. "There are only a few prints on it, and I'm in a rush." I gave him a smile that I hoped was bewitching yet anxious.

Looking bored, he glanced at the clock on the wall. "They'll be done at eleven." Fifteen minutes. Obviously, I'd have to perfect that smile.

I wandered through the store and stopped at the magazine section to peruse the latest home-and-garden journals, then browsed the hair-care aisle. My shampoo was missing from the bathroom and I suspected my cousin had nipped it. I finally located the brand I liked, which I was relieved to see had been improved—again. *Now with hayseed oil!* Hi-yo, Silver. Hand me my spurs.

I picked up my prints and slipped them out of the envelope. The license number was still hard to see, so I upped the wattage on my smile and asked the clerk if he would mind enlarging them. Making me feel as though I'd just stepped out of the Ice Age, he led me to the easy-to-use photo station and showed me how to enlarge them myself.

"I'm a florist," I said lamely. "I'm not so good with gadg—" He ambled off, yawning.

As soon as the first one came sliding out, I grabbed it for a look. There it was—45 PC 7788. Or was that 2288? It didn't matter. With a magnifying glass I'd be able to read those numbers perfectly. I paid for everything, thanked the clerk for my Photo Enlarging for Dummies lesson, and drove home.

As I turned into the apartment complex's parking lot, I spotted a gray minivan parked down the street, facing my way. My heart began to race. Were the thieves back? I pulled into my assigned spot, got out, and quietly shut the door, then circled the lot on foot, ducking behind cars as I snuck toward the van. The engine was idling, but no one appeared to be inside, making me suspect they were out scouting for pets.

There was one way to tell for sure: look in the back of the van.

CHAPTER NINETEEN

Abby. Hello-o-o. This is your cerebrum calling. I need an ice pack here. Wake up. I'm in pain. I opened my eyes and blinked several times, wondering why I was seeing stars—the real kind—in the inky sky above. Was that prickly grass beneath me? And, *ew,* did I smell worms?

I turned my head to see where I was and instantly clutched my skull as a blinding pain ripped through it. A search of my scalp found a lump forming on top. With a groan, I rolled onto my side, then pushed up to a sitting position. I was on the lawn beside the curb, a short distance from my apartment building, with the blond wig beside me and my purse several yards away. How did that happen?

As I sat there trying to get my bearings, Nikki pulled into the lot, saw me on the grass, jumped out of her car, and came running over. "Abby, what are you doing? Are you okay?"

"I have a lump on my head and I don't have a clue as to why. The last thing I remember is pulling into the parking lot."

"I'll call for an ambulance," she said, opening her purse. "You might have a concussion."

"Wait. I remember now. I was trying to get a look inside a gray van. Then a door opened and knocked me to the ground, and before I could get up, someone came at me. Nikki, don't make that call! All I need is for a reporter listening to a police scanner to hear my name. We can watch for a concussion ourselves. Just hand me my purse and the wig and help me up."

"But you still have to file an assault report."

"Not on the 911 line. I'll try to catch Reilly on his cell phone when we get inside."

"What's his number? I'll call right now." She punched in what I gave her—I'd called it often enough to know it by heart—and waited a few rings. "Um, hi. This is Abby Knight's roommate, Nikki. I'd like to report an assault on Abby. She was hit on the head outside the apartment building." Nikki covered the phone and whispered, "He sounds a little testy." She thanked him and hung up. "He's on his way. Let's get you upstairs."

She put her arm around me and maneuvered me to my feet. With a few rest stops and one near-tumble down the steps—the elevator was out of service, as usual—we finally made it to the apartment. While she packed a plastic bag with ice cubes, I dropped the wig and purse on the floor and eased my body onto the sofa.

In a few minutes, Nikki brought in the ice pack, along with two aspirin and a glass of chocolate soy milk. "You have to stay awake all night, you know."

"With this pain, it won't be a problem. Would you get that photo envelope from Walgreens out of my purse? I need to give the pictures to Reilly."

Nikki rummaged through my bag, then emptied the contents onto the floor. "Don't you ever clean this out? You've got receipts in here from two months ago—but no photos.

Maybe they fell out onto the grass." She grabbed my keys and headed for the door. "I'll go look."

"If you don't see them on the ground, check my car. And, Nik?"

She paused to glance back at me. "What?"

"Sorry to keep you up so late."

"You'd do the same for me. Let's just not make this a habit, okay?"

While she was gone, I did a visual inspection of my purse's contents to see whether anything else was missing, like my wallet. Nope, the wallet was there and everything else seemed to be intact, as well. With any luck, the photos had merely tumbled out.

Nikki returned five minutes later with Reilly right behind her. "No photos anywhere, Abby," she reported. "Sorry."

It wasn't possible that the thieves had known about those prints—unless they'd followed me to Walgreens. But I'd checked carefully to be sure I wasn't followed. Maybe the guy at the camera counter was part of the theft ring and had alerted them. Or . . . I suddenly noticed Reilly gazing down at me with a scowl, so I tried my bewitching-yet-anxious smile on him, hoping for better results than I'd had the last time I used it. Unfortunately, stretching my mouth made my head hurt, so it came out more like a grimace. "Hey, Sarge. Thanks for coming over."

"I hear you were mugged." He picked up the blond wig and dangled it in front of me as though it were roadkill. "Were you wearing this at the time?"

"Don't joke. A disguise is preferable to being lynched by an angry mob."

Reilly lifted the ice pack to take a look at the top of my head. "Jaysus, Abby. Why aren't you in the ER?"

"You know reporters listen to police scanners. Can I afford more publicity? No. Besides, it's just a lump—no big deal. Nikki is monitoring my condition."

"Does anyone want ice cream?" she called from the kitchen.

Reilly gave me a look that said, *She's your monitor?* "No, thanks," he called, patting his gut. "I'm on a diet."

His stomach looked flat to me, but then uniforms made everyone look trimmer. "If you eat after midnight, the calories don't count. Hey, Nikki, put chocolate syrup on mine. Ow." I had to stop moving my head.

"Tell me what happened," he said, pulling out his notepad.

"You'd better sit down. It's a long story and I don't want your feet to go numb."

He made a rolling motion with his hand. "Just get on with it."

I told him about Peewee's disappearance, the rash of petnappings, my pursuit of the gray minivan, the missing photos, and my conk on the head, then I waited for him to catch up.

"Let me get this straight," he said, looking over his notes. "You followed the van through town onto the highway going north. Then you circled back to Dermacol, and the van turned up there soon after. You took pictures, had them developed, then drove home, where the van's occupants waylaid you. Correct?" At my nod, he said, "Is there any way they'd know who you are, or where you live?"

"Only if they'd managed to follow me, and I checked carefully for a tail."

"Did you get a look at the men's faces?"

"No."

"Are you certain they were men?"

"No, but yesterday I saw someone from a gray van run across a yard, and he sure moved like a man. And the voices I heard at the Dermacol garage were men's, too."

"Did you get a license plate number?"

"Part of it. It was a temporary plate and the handwriting

wasn't great. Damn. I wish I had those photos." I gave him the numbers I remembered and he wrote them down.

"What about negatives?"

"I used a disposable camera. No negatives. I can check with the drugstore to see if they still have it lying around in a trash can somewhere."

"If you don't mind, *I'll* do the checking. Anything else you remember about the van?"

"It wasn't a new model, maybe five years old, but I'd bet any money it's registered to Dermacol. Who else would want to steal pets? If it is a Dermacol van, can you get a warrant to search the lab for the missing animals?"

"Not without probable cause."

"Hmm. Then we need to find a way to get inside with a camera. My neighbor would be able to identify her Chihuahua from a photograph, and I'm sure the other owners—"

"Stop right there," he said. "There's no *we* in this. *You* are out of it."

"But I can help, Reilly—ouch—once my head stops throbbing. Think about it. If anyone from Dermacol sees a cop snooping around, they might destroy the animals to hide the evidence."

"Give me a little credit, Abby. I'm not a rookie. Besides, if you were caught sneaking around the premises, what do you suppose the DA would do to you?"

I shifted the ice pack to a more comfortable position. "I'll concede the point. Then promise me you won't forget about this case, Reilly. It's hugely important to me."

He tucked the notepad into his shirt pocket. "I'm not going to forget about it."

"I just remembered something else. Dermacol has a fence that wraps around the parking lot, so if you want to do a stake-out . . ." I noticed Reilly's eyebrows drawing together, a sure sign he was running low on patience. "I'm only trying to help."

"Sure. How about if I stop by Bloomers to help you arrange flowers?"

I heard Nikki chuckling in the kitchen.

"Fine. Another point for your side." I heaved a frustrated sigh.

"If it'll help you sleep tonight, I'll put two men on it tomorrow, and I'll personally search the DMV records for a newly licensed used minivan that matches your description. In the meantime, stay away from Dermacol. You don't want trespassing charges brought against you, not with everything else going on."

"Such as my being the number one murder suspect? After the way Melvin Darnell and Al Corbison went after me, I'm surprised I'm still a free woman."

His gaze flickered away from my face, as though he knew more about that subject. I gave him a probing glance. "Are you keeping something from me, Sean Reilly?"

"Now she's my mother," he muttered, casting his gaze heavenward.

"Be straight with me, Sarge. I'm serious. Am I about to be arrested?"

CHAPTER TWENTY

"I didn't say anything about you being arrested," Reilly protested, but he still wouldn't meet my gaze.

Now I was truly concerned and starting to feel a rising panic, which made my head throb harder. "They're ready to haul me off in handcuffs again, aren't they?"

"You're going to be arrested?" Nikki cried, running out from the kitchen.

"Whoa," Reilly said, making a T with his hands. "Time out. I don't know what the prosecutor's plans are. All I know is that he's getting calls from parents of the college students, demanding that an arrest be made so their kids will be safe again." He picked up the wig and handed it to me. "People are up in arms, Abby, and that makes the DA nervous. So stick with your disguises until the case gets resolved. And for heaven's sake, stay away from Dermacol."

"The case isn't going to get resolved in *my* favor unless I find the killer. So if you can just give me a little information—"

He pointed his index finger at me and said sternly, "Keep your nose out of it, Abby. I'm working the case. Besides, you know I can't tell you anything."

"But you can answer with a simple nod or shake of your head, just to make me feel better, okay? Good. Now, was anyone allowed to enter the law school after the police arrived?"

He scowled at me for a long moment, but finally shook his head. No one had been allowed to enter.

"What about letting someone in who could identify him-or herself?"

Again he shook his head. That meant Jocelyn Puffer had lied to me. She'd been in the law school before the police arrived. However, that didn't mean she killed Reed. What I needed was a credible motive; otherwise, naming her as a suspect made no sense. I recalled what Kenny had told me about Reed having just ended an affair with a married woman, but I still couldn't imagine that woman being Jocelyn. Yet I couldn't ignore that she had lied, either. Somehow I had to find out what she was doing at the school during that hour.

"One more question," I said as he turned to go. "Did you find out who ordered that funeral rose?"

"I suppose there's no harm in telling you. We traced the call to one of Professor Puffer's students. It was nothing more than a stupid prank. No connection to the murder."

A dead end. "That's what I figured. Thanks for your help, Reilly."

Nikki showed him out, locked the door, then came back with two bowls of ice cream. I ate my dessert, set the bowl aside, and closed my eyes. It had been a trying day.

"You have to stay awake, Abby."

"No problem. I'm just resting my eyes." Right. No way would I be able to stay awake.

"Let's play a game." She opened the end-table drawer and removed a pack of cards. "Rummy or go fish? Don't wrinkle your nose. How about a movie, then?" She found the *TV Guide* and read off our choices. "*One Flew Over the Cuckoo's Nest, Texas Chain Saw Massacre,* or *Animal House*?"

"In other words, demented, deranged, or disgusting." I thought a moment. "Let's go for demented."

Nikki brought out her sleeping bag and pillow and made a bed for herself beside the sofa. Then we turned on the television and watched *One Flew Over the Cuckoo's Nest*. When it was over, I glanced down at Nikki and saw that she was sound asleep. Simon, too, was in dreamland, curled into a furry white ball between her feet. I switched to a shopping channel and watched Susan Lucci tout her hair products for awhile but, despite my best intentions, I, too, dozed off.

The next thing I knew, the apartment was filled with light and Nikki was shaking my shoulder. "Abby, wake up. You weren't supposed to sleep. You'd better not be in a coma."

I stretched my arms over my head, then winced as pain radiated through my skull so severely that even my teeth hurt. "Not in a coma," I gasped. "Need aspirin."

Nikki pressed gentle fingers along the top of my head. "The lump is smaller. I'll turn on the coffeemaker and be right back with aspirin."

"What time is it?"

"Eight o'clock in the morning."

At least I'd gotten some rest—and hadn't expired. Two good things. Did good luck come in threes?

"I'll make oatmeal," Nikki said. "Do you want today's newspaper?"

"Yes. I want to see if Connor wrote about the memorial service." Or wrote about me *at* the memorial service.

She handed me the paper. I unrolled it, tossed the rubber band to Simon, who was waiting patiently beside the sofa, then glanced down the front page. In the lower right quadrant I spotted the headline: PROFESSOR REMEMBERED. I skimmed the article, then let out a sigh of relief. Connor hadn't written anything about seeing me in the balcony.

But I was mentioned on the next page, in the Letters to the Editor section.

"Why does Abby Knight, the owner of Bloomers Flower Shop, feel the need to go about town in a disguise? Is she hiding a guilty conscience?" It was signed John Q. Public. Thanks, John Q. Now everyone in town would be on the alert for me in disguise. There were other letters ranting about my guilt, too, but I refused to read them, so I dropped the paper on the floor.

Give Connor a call, that little voice inside told me. *Defend yourself.* But what could I tell him that would prove my innocence? That Jocelyn had been at the law school at the time of the murder? So had her husband. So had Kenny. So had I.

The telephone rang and Nikki picked it up in the kitchen. "Hello, Mrs. Knight," she chirped. "How are you?"

Oh, no! Mom had seen the newspaper.

Nikki came across the living room toward me, listening as my mother talked. I shook my head at her, shut my eyes, and started to snore.

"Yes, she's right here." She handed me the phone and whispered, "Sorry. I froze."

"Hi, Mom. How are you? Yes, I saw the letters in the paper. Yes, I know everyone thinks I'm guilty. Yes, I *am* wearing disguises as self-protection. Yes, I promise I will be very careful. You've made a new piece of art for Bloomers? Great. Can't wait to see it. Okay, tonight then. I love you, too. Hug Dad for me. Bye."

Nikki came in with a glass of soy milk and two aspirin. "Oatmeal is coming up," she said, handing me the pills. "Did I hear you say the word *surprise*?"

"Aspirin first." I downed the medicine. "Mom has a new piece of art for me to sell. She says it will cheer me up and she's bringing it to dinner at the country club tonight. I wonder if I should alert the staff. They may want to put us in a room by ourselves."

Nikki snickered. "Maybe you can hang her artwork around your neck to ward off the reporters."

By the time I had finished my bowl of oatmeal, the aspirin had kicked in and the coffee had perked me up, so I was able to get up and take a shower without too much pain. Then I stood in front of my closet looking over the various outfits Jillian had created, trying to decide who I was going to be today.

"What do you think?" I asked Nikki ten minutes later, strutting before her.

She took one look at the short, spiked black wig, the zebra-striped chiffon blouse with sleeves that hung four inches beyond my fingertips, the thick silver chains that dangled in my cleavage, the yellow linen pants with sequined flowers on the thighs, and the faux snakeskin open-toed, high-heeled shoes—and burst out laughing. "You're a high-class punk rocker."

"Would you recognize me?"

"Never." She studied me for a moment, then shook her head. "Someone would actually pay Jillian money for that outfit?"

"Let's hope so. The last thing we want is for her to go belly-up and move back in with us. Speaking of Jill, I wonder why she hasn't barged in yet this morning."

"Sh-h-h. You'll jinx us. Isn't that wig uncomfortable with that lump on your head?"

"Only when I breathe." I picked up my purse and car keys, then let the keys swing from my fingers as I pondered how to get around town. Kind of pointless to wear a disguise if I was going to drive the Vette. "Hey, Nik. How about switching cars with me again today?"

"Hmm. Do I want to give up my bland subcompact for a bright yellow convertible? Let me think . . ."

It was always best to ask. We switched keys, then I left the apartment and walked up the hallway toward the stairway exit. As I passed Jillian's apartment I stopped to listen. All was quiet. She must have been sleeping. I took it as a sign that Jillian's life was returning to normal.

But as I walked away, she stuck her head out, looked in both directions, then whispered, "What did you want?"

"How did you know I was out here?"

"I saw you through the peephole."

"Okay, then my next question is, why were you looking through the peephole?"

"Because I heard someone out here and wanted to see who it was."

"Were you expecting someone?"

"Absolutely not."

"Why are you whispering?"

"My throat is dry. That happens when I sleep with the air conditioner on. Silly me. I should have remembered to open my bedroom window."

Yeah, right. Jillian hadn't slept near an open window since she was seven years old, when she saw the movie *Peter Pan* and had been frightened by Tinker Bell. "Jillian, what's going on? Is someone harassing you?"

"Nothing is going on. I have to go now." She shot a quick glance both ways, then shut the door. I heard the sound of the chain and bolt being slid into place.

Something was definitely going on. I just didn't want to know what it was.

Using Nikki's white Corolla, I drove to Bea's four-flat apartment building half a mile from the campus, found a parking space along the curb a few houses down, and shut off the engine. Before I could get out of the car, my cell phone chirped, and it was Marco.

"Are you all right?" he asked immediately.

I glanced at my watch. It was only nine thirty in the morning. He couldn't possibly have heard about what happened last night. And frankly, I was so embarrassed that I wasn't inclined to fill him in. I was still asking myself why I had approached that van along its side instead of from the rear. I knew better than that. And Marco knew I knew better than that. Morever, he would *tell* me I knew better than that.

"By *all right,* do you mean my health in general or are you referring to my spirits, because my spirits could use a boost. So if you have anything that would cheer me up, tell me."

"Don't give me that innocent act. I talked to Reilly. How the hell do you get yourself into these situations?"

"It takes a certain amount of natural ability combined with a proclivity for adventure."

"I don't want to hear about your proclivities. Why were you following that minivan around town alone?"

"Because no one was in the car with me. It was a spur-of-the-moment decision."

"That decision could have cost you a lot more than a goose egg on the head. You were damn lucky they didn't run over you in the street."

"But now the police know for sure what kind of vehicle to look for. Anyway, that's over and done with, and we can change subjects because I have some news for you. Reilly verified that no one was allowed into the law school after the body was discovered, so that means Jocelyn lied. Another thing: Kenny told me Professor Reed had just ended an affair with a married woman, and although I doubt Jocelyn was the woman, I thought I'd mention it because, as you say, you never know when some little piece of information will be important."

"You're learning, Sunshine."

I lived for that man's praise. Well, not really, but it did make me feel good. "My next step is to find out if Jocelyn has a motive—although you might want to try your hand at questioning her, because I doubt she'll talk to me again. She got kind of huffy there at the end."

"Remind me to give you a lesson in tact. In the meantime, I'll visit the bookstore before lunch and see what I can get her to tell me."

"I can be tactful." If I tried really, really hard. "In fact, I'm just pulling up to Bea's flat now. I have my list of questions and I'll be as tactful as I know how."

"Good. Let's reconnoiter at three o'clock. Can you make it to the bar without jeopardizing your life, or do you want me to meet you in the alley again?"

The alley was sounding way too appealing. "I'll see you at the bar. But you won't see *me* unless I want you to."

"A new disguise?"

"You bet."

"You're turning me on."

"That's the idea. See you later." I locked the Corolla, walked up the front stoop, stepped into the small entranceway, and rang the buzzer for Bea's first-floor flat.

"Hello," she sang out.

"Hi, Bea. It's Abby Knight. Do you have a few minutes to talk?"

In the long silence that followed, I thought maybe she hadn't heard me. Then the buzzer sounded and I let myself inside, puzzling over her hesitation. Up the hallway, she opened her door, took one look at my wig and outfit, and clapped her hands to her face in surprise. "What are you doing in that getup?"

"Protecting myself," I said as she ushered me inside. "Not only have the police made me their prime suspect, but also I've become a very unpopular person in town. This is the only way I can get around safely."

"I'm sorry to hear you're having so much trouble."

I expected a hug followed by an offer of organic bean curd cookies and chai tea—or at least some kind of display of sympathy, since it was what she did best—but she simply stood there shaking her head in commiseration. She didn't even invite me to sit. Obviously she wasn't *that* sorry to hear about my troubles.

"Tell me what I can do for you, Abby."

That was my opening. "Actually, since I've decided to conduct my own investigation, I was hoping I could ask you about your recollection of the day of the murder."

Bea hesitated, then said with noticeable reluctance, "Have a seat. I'll get you some tea."

"Please don't go to all that trouble. I'll only take a few minutes of your time."

She led me into the small sitting room done in shades of lilac and green. Her decor had a 1960s feeling to it, with sofa and chairs covered in a tie-dyed pink and purple cotton, hanging beads in her doorways, a collection of oddly shaped mirrors framed in dark purple satin, and a self-contained waterfall in one corner that trickled down stone ledges into a pebble-filled basin.

Beside a lava lamp on a drum table were silver-framed photos of Hannah at various stages of her life. Seeing them, I felt unexpectedly sorry for Bea. With no children of her own, she had found a substitute daughter in Hannah.

I took a pen and notepad from my purse. "I hope you don't mind if I take notes."

"Of course not." She sat in a chair adjacent to the sofa, her hands in her lap, her back straight, as though ready to take dictation.

I referred to the list of questions Marco and I had made.

"Before you left for your appointment on Tuesday at noon, did you see Jocelyn Puffer in the building?"

Bea thought for a moment. "No. However, I did see her car in the parking lot."

"Have you seen Jocelyn at the school at all in the past few weeks?"

She shook her head, so I asked, "Have you heard any gossip about Professor Reed seeing a married woman?"

She looked down at her hands. "I make it a policy not to listen to or repeat gossip."

I figured as much. "Did you see Kenny Lipinski in the building that morning?"

"Kenny came in around ten o'clock, as usual, to work in the computer lab."

"So he's normally at the school at that time?"

"For the past week or so he has been. You can check the log for the exact time he arrived that day."

"Did you know that Kenny had been chosen for a federal clerkship?"

"I hadn't heard yet, but I'm not surprised. Kenny is a bright young man and has been an invaluable assistant to Professor Reed."

"What about the other students who applied for the clerkship?"

"Professor Reed kept that information to himself, along with their applications."

"Can you tell me how students are notified of the results?"

"By letter. I don't have a copy of that, either. Professor Reed always handwrote those himself. He felt a personal note would make the rejections a little easier to handle."

"He was kind of a control freak, wasn't he? Do you know when he sent the letters?"

"I'm not aware that they *were* sent, or that he'd even

written them, but one of the other secretaries might have done the mailing for him."

"Did Carson Reed have any enemies at the school that you knew of?"

"No one comes to mind."

"Professor Puffer is claiming that he and Professor Reed were close friends, but I never saw that when I was attending school there. In fact, they seemed more like adversaries to me. Had their relationship changed in the last year?"

"Not that I am aware of."

"Would you say they were cordial toward each other?"

Another glance down at her hands. "I couldn't say."

What she meant was that she *wouldn't* say. As a loyal employee, it probably went against the grain to say anything negative about her bosses. I had to push harder. "Do you know if Professor Reed was dating anyone new?"

Once again, she wouldn't meet my gaze, but I caught a grimace of dislike in the downward curve of her lips. "Other than working for him, I really didn't know the man, so I doubt I could be of help in that department."

I had a feeling she was finished with that topic, so I asked, "How is Hannah doing in school?"

Bea lifted her gaze, her eyes wary. "She's doing fine. Why?"

"I ran into her on campus yesterday evening and she seemed distraught. I thought perhaps she was struggling with her classes, or had just broken up with a boyfriend."

Judging by the sudden clasping of her hands in her lap, I knew she wasn't pleased by the news. "What did Hannah say?"

"She told me I was lucky to have been kicked out of law school."

Bea looked away, her fingers still twisting against each other, clearly not wanting to share her thoughts. I put my hand on hers and summoned up all the tact I'd promised

Marco I had. "Hannah also seemed concerned about you, Bea. She asked me if you were at the school when I made my flower delivery. When I mentioned that you had been on your way to an appointment, she began to cry. Are you all right? Is there anything I can do to help?"

"I don't know why Hannah would react like that. I'm perfectly fine." Bea eased her hand out from under mine. "Now, if you'll excuse me, I have to get over to the law school and catch up on my work. One of the secretaries is on vacation, and it's all I can do to keep up with my own dictation, let alone hers. I hope you understand."

I understood that she wanted me to leave. She was good at tact, too. I also understood that she was hiding something, for which Hannah was the key. For my own peace of mind, I decided to follow Bea to see whether she was at least telling the truth about her work.

CHAPTER TWENTY-ONE

I sat low in the Corolla, my gaze fixed on Bea's front door, praying that she had been honest with me. Within minutes she came out, turned right, and headed toward the university. *So far, so good.*

Keeping my distance, I followed her to the campus, where, instead of entering the law school, she turned left toward Simpson Hall. *Damn. She'd lied after all.* I pulled into a nearby parking lot and watched as she went inside the dorm. There was only one reason Bea would enter that building—to see Hannah. So much for catching up on her work. I wondered what else she had lied about.

Five minutes later Bea came hurrying out, and I could tell by her expression that she was in distress. What had caused it? An argument with Hannah? My curiosity was too strong not to investigate, so as soon as Bea was out of sight, I strolled into Simpson Hall and asked the student volunteer behind the check-in counter to ring Hannah Boyd's room.

"She's popular today," the volunteer said, barely giving

me or my punk-rocker costume a second look. Then again, she had yellow and green striped hair, a silver stud in each nostril, and a dog collar around her neck. She checked a list, punched in a few numbers, spoke into the phone, then asked me for my name.

"Just tell Hannah I'm a friend of Professor Reed's."

The girl repeated my message, then hung up. "Put your name on the sign-in sheet at the end of the counter. Hannah's on the third floor, room three fifteen."

Pretty lax as far as security went. I signed in as Jane Smith, then had a brainstorm. "Excuse me," I said to the girl. "Do you have a register that shows visitors from this past Tuesday?"

I was fully prepared to give her a reason, but she merely shrugged, then pulled out a loose-leaf notebook and slid it down to me. I flipped back a few pages and checked the names. No Beatrice Boyd listed, but she wouldn't have signed in if Hannah hadn't been in her room. Then where had Bea gone instead?

"Thanks," I said and slid the notebook back, then took the stairs to the third floor. At my knock Hannah opened the door a crack to peer out at me.

"Hi," I said cheerily. "It's me again. Abby Knight."

"You're not a friend of Professor Reed's," Hannah said accusingly. "Did my aunt send you up here?"

"No. Please don't shut the door. I actually came to talk to you *about* your aunt. I'm very concerned about her. Is her health okay?"

Hannah snorted. "There's nothing wrong with my aunt's health. Go ask her if you want to know what's going on."

"I did ask her, but she didn't want to share."

"Then why should I tell you anything?"

She started the shut the door again, so I blurted, "Why did your aunt lie about having an appointment at the time Professor Reed was murdered?"

Hannah stuck her head out and looked down the hallway, then said in a harsh whisper, "Would you go away?"

Time for a bluff. "I'm sorry to keep hounding you, Hannah, but I'm trying to find out who killed Professor Reed, and right now your aunt's behavior is looking highly suspicious. I'm betting you don't want to see Bea accused of murder any more than I do."

"Sh-h-h!" Hannah grabbed my arm, dragged me inside, and shut the door. "Look, I don't know where my aunt went for her appointment Tuesday. She said she came here to talk to me, but since I was at the library, I don't know if it's true."

"Did you ask her where she went after she came here and found you gone?"

"No, and I don't care, either."

Yeah, right. "Okay, then. Next question. Why did you go to the memorial service?"

She immediately bristled. "What does that have to do with my aunt?"

"You didn't sit with her, so it made me wonder. Did you know Carson Reed well?"

"I was *acquainted* with him," Hannah said warily.

"You weren't seeing him?"

"You're insane." She reached for the doorknob. "You need to go now."

"Then you *were* seeing him. Otherwise you would have denied it."

"Leave now, or I'll call security."

She was jittery. With a bit more of a push, I knew she'd crack. "Your aunt must have raised quite a stink when she found out. I'll bet you told her to bug off, then Reed was murdered, and now you're afraid she did it because you know how protective she is of you."

Bingo. The dam burst and tears flowed down her cheeks. Hannah collapsed onto her bed, sobbing into her hands. "We were in love! What's so wrong with that?"

"Other than the fact that he was twice your age and a player, I can't think of a thing."

"Now you sound like Aunt Bea." Hannah grabbed a tissue from her desk and blew her nose. "Neither one of you knew the real Carson Reed. He was sweet and romantic. . . . He even wrote me poems. We were going to be married." At that, she cried harder.

"Married?" My jaw nearly hit the floor.

"Yes, in H-Hawaii, d-during semester break." She plucked a new tissue and blew noisily. "Carson knew Aunt Bea would have a fit, so he asked me to keep our relationship a secret until after we had married."

Oh, brother. I didn't even want to imagine how often Reed had used that excuse on gullible women. "How did your aunt find out?"

"She overheard him in his office talking to me on the phone. She called me afterward and demanded to know what was going on, but I pretended I didn't know what she was talking about. Then she said she was going to confront Carson, so I had to tell her about our plans."

I could only imagine Bea's horror. "When did this take place?"

"Tuesday morning."

"The day Professor Reed was murdered?"

She nodded, more tears filling her eyes. "After I told her, she got really quiet—I thought she'd hung up—but then in this calm voice she thanked me for being straight with her and said she would handle it. I told her there was nothing for her to handle and that she needed to stay out of it or I'd never speak to her again. Then she got all emotional and begged me to meet with her so we could discuss it. But I said no. I was really angry, you know? I'm an adult. She can't tell me what to do."

"She wanted to meet you Tuesday at noon?"

Hannah sniffled as fresh tears filled her eyes. "Yes. But I was too angry to talk to her so I went to the library."

My heart took a dive. I hated to admit it, but Hannah had just given Bea a motive. Still, I had to ask myself to what extreme Bea would go to keep her niece safe from a predator like Reed. Would she be so enraged, so frightened for Hannah, that she would commit murder? The little bird defending its nest against the hawk? It didn't sound like the Bea I knew. But did I really know her?

I decided to ask Hannah nothing more until I had talked to Marco. I put my arm around her and gave her a gentle squeeze. "I'm sorry for your loss. I'll be in touch."

Just before I went out the door, Hannah called, "What would happen to my aunt if she did kill him?"

"She'd go to prison."

I left to the sound of Hannah sobbing.

I stopped at the student union to get a bottle of water from the soft-drink vending machine, then checked the time. Since it was only eleven o'clock, and I was near the law school anyway, I decided to examine the log at the computer lab to verify Kenny's alibi. Fortunately, although classes had been canceled, the building remained open to students and faculty who wished to use the facilities, so I had no trouble getting inside.

I tucked the water bottle in my purse, climbed the stairs to the second floor, and looked around. None of the secretaries had come in to work and no lights showed through the glass door panes of the professors' offices—except for Puffer's. Seeing that glow, I felt a *gi-normous* shiver go up my spine and I nearly headed back down the stairs when that little voice of reason in my head whispered, *So what if he sees you? You're in disguise, remember?*

Right. Whew.

The computer lab was locked, but someone had posted a

sticky note on the door that read: *If you need entry, call Dustin.* His dorm phone number was listed beneath, and he answered on the first ring, promising to be there in ten minutes. Translated into college time, that could mean anywhere up to an hour. So, after first checking to be sure Puffer wasn't on the move, I snuck over to Bea's desk for a quick look around. I wasn't sure what I was looking for, but it never hurt to take a peek.

Usually her desk was tidy, with not even a stray pencil out of its cup. But today it was heaped with files, letters needing signatures, and envelopes waiting to be stamped and taken to the mail drop. At least she'd told me the truth about her workload.

From the corner of my eye I caught a quick flash of light. I glanced at Puffer's door, but the glow through the glass panes was steady. Reed's office was dark, as was Myra Baumgarten's, so I chalked it up to my imagination. Then a light flickered again, like a flashlight beam. Keeping low to the ground, I crept over to the glass and peered inside, where I saw Puffer rooting through Reed's desk. Snapdragon was on a hunt.

At once he glanced toward the door, as though he sensed someone watching. I ducked down and held my breath, praying he hadn't seen me. When nothing happened I raised my head for another look. This time Puffer was sitting in Reed's chair, rifling through an open filing-cabinet drawer. I watched as he pulled out a long, manila folder, leafed through it, and removed what appeared to be a letter. As he read it, his thin lips curled into a look of pure hatred. Then he jammed the paper back into the file, fighting with a bent corner so he could close the cover. He stuck the folder into the drawer, shut it, then rose.

Instantly, I dropped to the carpet and crawled over to hide behind Bea's desk, fearing he would leave through the front exit. A moment later I heard the faint sound of a door closing, so I raised my head for a look. Reed's window was dark, and Puffer was nowhere in sight. Obviously, he'd completed his mission and left through the back. Now if only I dared sneak into Reed's office to see whether I could find that letter, but the thought of Puffer catching me there was enough to stop that idea in its tracks.

Puffer's light went out, followed moments later by the ding of the elevator. If that wasn't a sign I should do a little snooping, nothing was. I moved quietly across to Reed's office, tried the door, and found it locked. Damn. Did I dare take the elevator up to the back door? What if Puffer hadn't left the building? Hmm. Maybe Bea had a key.

I searched inside her desk drawers, then felt beneath the desk. Nothing. I looked around, tapping my fingers on the desktop. On a hunch, I grabbed Hannah's photo in its rosewood frame, removed the backing—and a key fell into my hand. Wow. Another sign. My karma was in top form today.

Moving swiftly, I unlocked the door and slipped inside Reed's office. It was stuffy from being closed up for so long, and smelled of his musky aftershave. I put his green glass lamp on the floor behind the desk before switching it on, hoping the glow wouldn't be noticeable from outside. Then I crouched in front of the desk and opened the file-cabinet drawer—only to have my long silver necklaces bang into the metal cabinet. Yikes. I grabbed the chains and held my breath. When nothing happened, I tucked them inside my blouse, shivering as the metal touched my perspiring skin.

All the file folders were neatly labeled, with headings such as *Supreme Court Decisions, Federal Court Decisions, Research, Law Reviews*—nothing that looked particularly damning. With minutes ticking by, I flipped through the folders again, until there was only one possibility left—a file marked *Tenure Committee,* of which Reed was the chair. Since Puffer had been seeking tenure, I hoped there was a connection.

Inside the folder I found copies of recent correspondence between committee members, along with a short list of professors being considered. I ran my finger down the entries and a tingle of excitement shot through me. The last name on the list was Z. Archibald Puffer.

All the papers in the file were neatly aligned but one. I pulled it out and found a letter from Carson Reed dated the previous Friday, four days before the murder, addressed to the other committee members. In it, Reed strongly recommended that Puffer be denied tenure for reasons he'd previously outlined. A final decision would be made the following Monday.

Hmm. The very next day, Reed had been murdered. Coincidence? Or had I found Puffer's motive?

I tried to picture what might have transpired after I'd rushed out of the building that day. Seeing that Puffer was already in a temper from my visit, Reed might have sauntered into his office, hinting that he had news on Puffer's bid for tenure, just to see him squirm. He would have come around the desk to stand eyeball-to-eyeball with Puffer. Reed might have taken a seat in Puffer's chair, put up his feet, and smugly dropped the bomb—no tenure—provoking Puffer into a rage. I could easily picture him knocking Reed out cold, then, in a panic, realizing that he'd be fired once Reed came to and reported him. So Puffer had finished the job, then fled out the back door and down the elevator.

"Hello? Anyone here?"

I nearly toppled over in my reach for the lamp's off switch. Replacing the folder, I quietly closed the drawer, repositioned the lamp, then crawled to the front door to peer out the glass window. To my left I saw a tall, blond man walking toward the computer lab. It had to be Dustin. I crawled to the rear door, slipped out, and eased the door shut behind me.

But once I was in the back hallway, I had another problem.

Other than leaving through one of the professors' offices, which I couldn't do without a good explanation, the only exit was the elevator, which meant I'd have to go down to the first floor, then come up the stairway. But as I reached for the Down button, the hydraulic lift kicked in and the elevator began to rise.

Someone was coming up. And I had a strong hunch it was Puffer.

CHAPTER TWENTY-TWO

I glanced wildly in both directions, then darted down the hall to Myra Baumgarten's office. Locked! My heart pounded as I sped back to Reed's door, but before I could slip inside, the elevator dinged, the door opened—and the Dragon emerged. Puffer took one look at me, my hand on Reed's doorknob, and flames practically shot from his nostrils. "What are you doing in this hallway? Students are forbidden up here."

He hadn't recognized me! "I—I—" I didn't have a clue as to how to answer that, and the elevator door had just shut, leaving me no escape hatch.

"Wait there!" he ordered. "I'm calling security."

That was all I needed. "Please don't call. I came up by mistake. See? I'm leaving now." I ran to the elevator and pounded the Down button with the heel of my hand, and the door slid open.

Before I could jump inside, Puffer made a grab for me. I ducked and he latched on to the wig, only to have it come off in his hands. For a moment he stared at it, then he took in my costume, saw my red hair, and went ballistic. "You!"

"I can explain, Professor. Wait."

He burst into his office, flipped on the light, and lunged for the phone on his desk. My brain went into overdrive as I desperately searched for a way to talk myself out of the situation. I couldn't let him make that call. Prosecutor Mel would have me arrested in five minutes flat.

Remember what your dad told you, that little voice of reason whispered in my mind. *The best defense is a good offense.* If ever there was a time to test that theory, it was now.

"Call the cops," I said, following him inside. "I have nothing to hide. I came here to use the computer lab. Besides, I'd like to tell them about your rifling through Professor Reed's files. And while I'm at it, I'll clue them in on your motive for wanting him dead."

Puffer slammed the phone onto the base, the vein at his temple throbbing so hard I thought it would burst. With my luck, he'd drop dead from a stroke and I'd be accused of killing him, too. I could just see the headline in tomorrow's newspaper: MS. BLOOM-AND-DOOM STRIKES AGAIN.

"What the hell are you babbling about?" he snapped.

"I saw you in Professor Reed's office. I know what you were looking for—and found—and I'd be happy to share that information with the police."

Puffer's eyes narrowed, a sure sign of an impending blast of fury. What had I been thinking? I was alone with a man who most likely had murdered his associate—in that very room. Trying not to show fear, I started edging toward the front door, hoping Dustin was near enough to hear me if I had to shout for help.

But there was no blast, just a sly smile that was more unnerving than his anger. "Tell me, Betty Boob," he said, folding his arms across his poplin shirt as though he were doing a cross-examination, "how did you end up in the back hall-way?"

"I took the elevator—b-by mistake." We both knew it was no mistake.

"I was in the lobby downstairs getting coffee. No one got on the elevator. Are you sure you want to stick with that story?"

I drew a deep breath and said bravely, "I don't need to explain anything to you. I'll save my story for the cops."

Puffer made a temple of his fingers, tapping them against his chin as he eyed me. "So you came here to use the computer lab. Why? You're not in law school anymore. But you *are* in disguise. What does that mean, I wonder, that you're sneaking around here wearing a disguise?"

Time to use Dad's method again. "It means that, thanks to your insinuations, everyone in town thinks I killed Professor Reed. I can't step outside without being hounded by the press or fearing for my life. Now, are you going to make that call or shall we just forget the whole thing and let the detective draw his own conclusions about your motive?"

There. I had given him a way to save face—and save my own skin while I was at it.

His cold eyes studied me for a long moment, then he said evenly, "Let's forget it."

I didn't trust him, but I had given him the option, so now I had to live with it. "Okay, then. It's forgotten."

"Have a nice day," he said with a sneer, "Betty Boob." He tossed the wig onto his desk, picked up his phone to make a call, and turned his chairback to me, so I hurried toward the front door.

Oops. The wig. I wasn't about to lose it and have Jillian after my hide, too. I darted back for it, tucked it under my arm, then stopped dead in my tracks.

The phone. That was what I'd been trying to remember. When I'd found Reed's body, a black handset had been in his lap. But Puffer was holding an ivory receiver. Where had the old phone gone?

At that moment, the Dragon spun around to see why I hadn't left, so I quickly stepped out and pulled the door shut. My legs were still quivering like wet spaghetti, so I paused to draw a few steadying breaths, then caught sight of a blond guy striding toward me—the same guy I'd seen with Kenny at Professor Reed's memorial service. I made a mental note to ask Reilly about the black telephone, then smiled as though I didn't have a care in the world. "You're Dustin?"

"Yeah. And you're—?"

"Abby. I need to use the computer lab for five minutes, so if you could just let me in?"

He glanced at the wig in my hands, then at my hair, which was probably a twisted pile of red straw by now, then gave me a skeptical look. "Do you have a student ID?"

"Not anymore. I wrote a resume on this computer and I just need to print a copy. I'd download it onto a disk but, stupid me, I forgot to bring the disk." It wasn't a total lie. I did write a resume once. "If you don't trust me, call Kenny. He'll vouch for me."

Dustin hesitated, still unsure, then finally unlocked the door and turned on the light. "You have to sign in," he said and pointed to a clipboard hanging on a nail by the door.

I signed my name to the top sheet, already dated for that day. There were two squares after the signature line where I was to mark the time I logged in and out, so I checked my watch and wrote *11:30 a.m.* Now I needed to find Kenny's entries for the day of the murder, but I didn't want to start flipping through the pages in front of Dustin because he'd surely want to know why. So I returned the clipboard to the nail, trying to come up with another way to get a peek.

"Sit wherever you want," he said.

There were five computer stations in the room, so I went to the farthest one. Dustin plunked down next to the door, logged on, and started playing a game. I opened the word-processing program and typed whatever came to mind, which turned out to be *Who killed Professor Reed and why?* Followed by, *Abby Knight + Marco Salvare = Abby Salvare. Mrs. Abigail Salvare. Mr. and Mrs. Marco Salvare . . .* Wonderful. I was regressing to a seventh-grade mentality.

I sent the page to the printer, retrieved it, and sat back down, pretending to study it while I cast surreptitious glances at Dustin, who seemed engrossed in the game. I dug in my purse for my Evian water and took a swig. *Think, Abby. How can you get him out of the room? What can you use as a diversion?* My gaze landed on the bottle in my hands. *Voila!*

I set the Evian beside the keyboard, put my hands on the keys, and gave the bottle a little nudge with my elbow. But instead of tipping neatly over the edge of the desk, it tipped into my lap, the water soaking my pants and the seat of the chair, *then* spilling onto the tiles beneath. *Note to self: Never cut down a tree; it will fall on you.* With a yelp of surprise, I jumped up and looked around for something to absorb the water.

"I'll get paper towels from the restroom," Dustin said and took off.

Shutting my mind to the huge wet spot on the crotch and rear of the expensive, dry-clean-only pants, I stuffed the printed page into my purse, ran for the clipboard, turned back the pages until I found Tuesday, and skimmed the names. There was Kenny's signature, logged in at ten o'clock, just as Bea had said, but there was nothing to indicate that he had left the lab in answer to my call for help, and nothing to indicate that he had returned. Given the emergency nature of the situation, it wasn't surprising. It also wasn't helpful. In other words, I'd gone through this silly charade for nothing.

I hung the clipboard up and was hurrying back to the computer station when I heard "Hey, Abby. What are you doing here?"

Startled, I spun to see Kenny standing in the doorway. "Oh, hi, Kenny. I had to print out something I'd left on the computer." Noticing that he was staring at the huge wet spot on the front of my slacks, I casually crossed my hands over it. "So, what are you up to?"

"Research." He spotted the puddle under my shoes. "Drink too much coffee today?"

"Ha. Funny. No, it was just me being a klutz with my water. Dustin went to get some paper towels."

At that moment Dustin loped in with a wad of towels and both guys helped me sop up the spill. "Thanks for the help," I told them as I started for the door. "I've got to get home. These slacks are dry clean only. See you around, Kenny."

"Hey," Dustin said. "You have to log out."

I took a quick look at my watch, scribbled the time next to my name, and headed for the staircase.

"Abby, hold up a minute," Kenny called, striding after me. "Any word on how the police are coming with the murder investigation?"

"As far as I know, they're still focusing on me."

"I thought of something this morning that might help you. When I was in Professor Reed's office Monday morning, organizing his files for the day, his phone rang, so I answered as I always did, 'Carson Reed's office, Kenny speaking,' and the caller hung up. Just out of curiosity I did a call-back search on the number and it went to the Books of Olde bookstore. I figured someone had dialed wrong and didn't think anything more of it, but it happened again Tuesday morning, before Professor Reed arrived. I did the call-back again and—same thing. The bookstore. It might be nothing, but I thought it was worth mentioning."

Books of Olde—where Jocelyn Puffer worked. Hmm. Were the calls mere coincidences, a case of two misdialed numbers? Was it someone from the bookstore phoning about a book Reed had ordered? But if that were the case, why not leave a message? Or . . . was it possible that Reed and Jocelyn *were* having an affair?

As unlikely as that seemed, in light of those phone calls, I had to consider that Reed might have been dallying with Jocelyn *and* Hannah. It probably wouldn't have been the first time he'd had two on the line. But I was betting it was the first time he'd plonked someone's wife while trying to ruin her husband's career.

"Kenny, can you tell me anything about the status of Professor Puffer's bid for tenure?"

"I really can't, Abby. I don't have the authority."

Damn. "Okay, then, how about this? Can you think of a reason Professor Reed might have recommended that Puffer be denied tenure—hypothetically speaking, of course?"

"Everyone knew the two men didn't get along. Other than that, I couldn't say."

"When Professor Reed made a recommendation to the committee, did they usually follow it?"

"From what I've seen so far, yes."

"How do you think Puffer would react if he were turned down?"

Kenny imitated the sound of a bomb dropping. "I wouldn't want to be around to witness the explosion."

"Okay, suppose Reed *did* recommend that Puffer be denied tenure. Do you think he would tell Puffer to his face?"

"And risk provoking the Dragon? Why would he do that?"

"It would be ultimate power trip, wouldn't it? I know you thought highly of Professor Reed, but I can attest to the fact that he was in a taunting mood that day. He was essentially holding Puffer's future in his hands. He might have enjoyed goading him into a rage."

"Giving Puffer a reason to kill him." Kenny rubbed his chin as the attorney-in-training began to muse. "With the Dragon's history of violent outbursts, I could see that working as a legal defense for him. Diminished capacity . . . temporary insanity . . . it's a plausible theory. How will you prove Puffer's the killer?"

"I'm still working on that. Plus I still have a few other suspects to check out."

"If I can help in any way, let me know."

"Ditto, if you remember anything else." I turned to go down the steps, then remembered one other question. "Hey, about that clerkship? Can you think of any applicant who might be so angry at not being selected that he or she would go ballistic?"

"Not really. It's so difficult to snag a clerkship with a federal appellate judge that most students don't even aspire to it. Many of them would rather stay close to home and get jobs in local law firms than be absorbed into the huge Seventh Circuit Court. Besides, none of the applicants had been notified about the selection because Professor Reed never had a chance to write their letters. He told me privately on Monday afternoon only so I could begin to make plans for next year."

I crossed that theory off my list. "Okay, Kenny. Thanks for your help."

On my way back to the car, I pulled out my phone and called Marco, hoping to catch him before he left to talk to Jocelyn so I could tell him about the bookstore calls, but all I got was his voice mail. I phoned the bar next and learned Marco had just left, so I parked the car on a side street and headed for Books of Olde. I had no sooner stepped onto Lincoln when I caught sight of Uncle Sam heading my way, handing out his little flags. Afraid he would think I was yet another new face in town, I opened my phone and pretended I was having a conversation.

"So, like, I heard the new Coldplay album? And it's, like, totally stratospheric? Do you have it? Awesome! Play it for me." I began snapping my fingers and bobbing my entire body, causing everyone nearby to give me wide berth. My plan was working perfectly until my phone actually *did* ring. "Hey, dog," I answered, smiling sheepishly at the people around me.

"Halloo?" Grace said. "Good heavens, Lottie, I think someone has nicked Abby's cell phone. You'd better ring the police."

"Wait, Grace," I cried. Catching startled looks, I tried to make it sound like I was rapping. "Stay cool, dude. It's, like, totally me. I'm walking down Lincoln, glad to be free."

"You're under too much stress, dear. You're simply not sounding yourself. Go home and put menthol rub on your forehead."

Menthol rub? I waited until Joe had passed, then I whispered, "I'm fine, Grace, but I'm in disguise and people are around. Is everything okay there?"

"Everything is fine, but we've been worried about you. You haven't called today."

"I promise I'll call you later and fill you in, and I'll be in this evening, too, but right now I gotta go."

Inside the bookstore, the clerk at the counter eyed me warily, forgoing her usual cheerful greeting, reminding me how much a person's appearance affected other people's reactions. I gave her a pleasant smile, then took the center aisle toward the back, checking each row, but I didn't see Marco or Jocelyn. Had he completed his mission, or had he failed?

Then I remembered the little coffee nook on the opposite side of the store, so I strolled up an aisle, peered around a corner, and there they were, sitting on stools at a tall table, mugs of steaming beverages in front of them. I wandered along the row, pretending to search for a title, but I couldn't get close without being obvious. Marco glanced my way briefly but apparently didn't recognize me, because he turned his full attention back to Jocelyn, who was gazing at him as if he were the whipped cream on her latte.

I plucked a book from the shelf, took it to one of the over-stuffed reading chairs near the coffee nook, and settled in to read—*advanced calculus?* A shudder of revulsion shook me. Math and I were not friends. We weren't even strong acquaintances. Sure, I knew the basics—how to balance a checkbook, tally an order, calculate sales tax, and leave a tip that wouldn't have the waitress chasing me down with a butter knife—but beyond that it was all hieroglyphics. That was one of the many reasons I valued Lottie's help. She was an excellent bookkeeper.

I flipped through the pages looking for something recognizable as I tuned in to Marco's conversation. His voice was a low, indistinct murmur, but Jocelyn's was easy to hear.

"I wish I could offer more help but I really didn't know Carson Reed all that well." She paused, staring into the contents of the mug she held in her hands. "I can tell you there has always been an intense rivalry between Carson and my husband."

Marco spoke to her again, probably trying to get more information about the rivalry, to which she looked him in the eye and replied, "Because my husband is a jealous, bitter man who resented Carson's higher status and greater income."

Wow. That was quite a slam. Marco spoke to her again, his deep voice a low, soothing hum, prompting her to reply, "He didn't leave JAG voluntarily. He was asked to resign. My husband has a knack for making enemies wherever he goes."

Slam number two. Yay, Marco. There was nothing like witnessing a genius at work. He suddenly leaned toward her, putting a hand over hers, and I saw a blush color her pale cheeks, as if, at a man's touch, the plain Jane blossomed. She dropped her gaze and said in a voice so quiet I almost didn't catch it, "Yes, I believe he is capable of murder."

What an admission! Score a major victory for Marco. Now Puffer was a sure fit for Reed's killer. I was so excited, it was all I could do not to jump for joy. But Jocelyn's response to Marco's next question put a damper on that.

"No, that's wrong," she said in a tight voice, as though her throat muscles had gone rigid. "I entered the building shortly before one o'clock."

Marco must have pointed out that he had it on good authority the police hadn't let anyone in after twelve thirty, because she suddenly leaned toward him and said in a harsh whisper, "What are you implying? That I had something to do with Carson's murder? What possible reason could I have to kill him?"

Marco talked to her until she calmed down, then he gave her his card, thanked her, and left. I waited until Jocelyn had moved to another section, then I put the book back on the shelf and took off. When I stepped outside, Marco was already halfway across the courthouse lawn, heading back to his bar. It was only half past twelve, and our meeting wasn't until three o'clock, but since I was eager to share my news with him, and hungry besides, I followed.

When I arrived several minutes later, the place was jammed with lunch customers and Marco was pouring drinks, so I found an empty table and put in an order for a turkey on rye with a side of potato salad. Gert didn't recognize me, so to have a bit of fun, when the food came I said to her in my best Valley girl voice, "This place is like totally trashy? So I was thinking maybe my dad could rent it out for my birthday? That would be so awesome and I could, like, totally freak out my friends? So, like, who do I have to talk to?"

"Mr. Salvare," Gert grumbled, huffing over the insults I had just heaped on the place that had employed her for most of her life. "I'll get him."

I forked a bite of potato salad and slid it into my mouth, smiling to myself. I was getting pretty good at this disguise bit. Then I saw Marco saunter toward me in that way males have perfected when meeting an unknown female, and my mouth went dry. Had I been a college girl, I would have, like, totally drooled all over myself.

Like, totally? Had the black wig cut off circulation to my brain?

"Hi, I'm Marco Salvare," he said, offering a hand.

I quickly wiped mine on a napkin and stuck it out while I polled my brain for a name other than the highly unimaginative Jane Smith. My gaze lit on the rows of bottles behind the bar. "I'm Rye Daniels," I said in a high, breathy voice.

"Rye. Interesting name," Marco said, clasping my hand. He gave it a low-key shake, holding it a moment too long. What was that about?

Watching me with those sexy bedroom eyes, he turned a chair backward and sat across from me, his arms resting on the seatback. "I understand you have questions about renting the bar for a party. One thing you should know up front: I only rent to friends." His gaze raked over me, causing tingles of excitement to career around inside my stomach and various other organs. Then he added suggestively, "Close friends."

The tingles turned to cinders. So this was how he behaved around other women? How dare he come on to a stranger! Or was he pulling my leg? "So how do I become your close friend?" I asked on an exhale that left me slightly light-headed.

His mouth curved up at the corners—the famous Marco smile—making me burn with jealousy over . . . myself? He rose and wiggled an index finger, signaling for me to follow, then headed toward his office.

One of us was going to get a surprise.

CHAPTER TWENTY-THREE

Marco shut the door behind us and locked it. Why hadn't he ever done that with me? The real me, anyway. He stepped up close, put his hands on my shoulders, and said huskily, "You're sure you want to be my close friend?"

At my nod, he slid his hands down my back and gazed lustily into my heavily smudged, black-rimmed eyes. He was too close not to recognize me, because if he seriously didn't know who I was, I would have to kill him.

All at once, he pressed me up against the door and leaned into me for one long, wanton, mind-blowing kiss. I mean a straight-from-the-movies, too-hot-to-handle melding of the lips that made me consider wearing that wig permanently. Wow! I finally understood the meaning of the word *swoon*.

His kiss deepened, intensified, leaving me so weak-kneed I wrapped my arms around his neck to hold myself up—and to make it easier to kiss him back. Our tongues fenced, swirled, and teased until I was nothing but melted taffy inside. Then, suddenly, it was over, and all I could do was try to sound sultry, not stupefied, when I asked, "Was that close enough?"

"Not quite." With one sly quirk of his mouth, he put a hand on the back of my neck, prompting me to close my eyes and pucker up for the next one. But he merely plucked the wig off my head and tossed it over his shoulder. "Hello, Sunshine."

"You tricked me!" I cried.

"Says who? Rye Daniels?"

"It was the best I could come up with on the spur of the moment."

With a wicked grin, Marco pulled me into his arms again, his lips moving down my throat and up along my jaw to the tender point in front of my ear, sending ripples of pleasure up my spine and banishing all traces of huffiness. "You were one hot number in that wig."

With those teasing nibbles on my nape, I was so completely into the moment that his words didn't register—at first. But like most females, I eventually registered every word a man uttered, and not usually in his favor. So when Marco said I was sexy *in* the wig, what I heard was that I wasn't sexy *without* the wig. And hadn't he made that same comment when I wore the scarf? So, basically, what he was telling me was that the regular Abby was *boring*. Was that why our relationship had stalled?

Marco broke the kiss. "What is it? You've lost your concentration."

I couldn't admit to this mouthwatering male that I knew he thought I was boring. How *boring* would that be? So I resorted to another typically female response. "It's nothing."

He gazed down at me with lowered eyebrows. "Now I'm worried."

"No, really. There's so much going on, it's hard to keep my focus."

That killed his mood. "Thanks," he muttered and went to sit at his desk. The male ego was so fragile.

"Trust me, Marco. It's not you." *It's just boring old me.* "Besides, I've got so much to tell you—new information on Puffer and his wife, and Bea and Hannah—and I'm dying to know what Jocelyn said."

"You mean you didn't overhear enough?"

"You recognized me at the bookstore, too? What gave me away?"

"Your perky little nose—among other attributes." He wiggled an eyebrow. Marco was the only male who could get away with making a comment about my bra size, only because he was one of the few men who looked me in the eye when we talked, and not in the boobs.

"You go first," he said, pulling out his legal pad.

"One second. I left a sandwich out front." I had my priorities, after all. I darted out of his office, picked up my plate, and hurried back, settling into one of the sling-back chairs. In between bites I told him about Hannah Boyd's affair with, and alleged engagement to, Carson Reed, and how Bea had learned of it on the morning of the murder.

Marco was stunned. "Hannah and Reed? I'll be damned."

I gave him a full account of my conversation with both Hannah and Bea, then paused for a bite of potato salad while Marco digested the information.

"So, prior to Reed's death, Bea found out her beloved niece was not only involved with a playboy, but believed she was going to elope with him. That smells like a motive to me."

"The thing is, I still can't imagine Bea committing a murder. She's a kind person, Marco, and she's always in control."

"You said yourself she's very protective. Put yourself in her shoes. What if Hannah were your niece and you thought some playboy was about to ruin her life? What if you believed there was no way to stop him? Isn't it possible that you might lose control?"

"Me? No way."

Marco gave me a scowl. "She stays on the list."

"Okay, fine. She stays—with much reluctance. Write that down. Now here's what else I learned today." I gave him my report about finding Puffer digging in Reed's office, and about the letter recommending he be turned down for tenure. I described my meeting with Puffer afterward, and how he'd reacted when I told him I knew what he'd found in Reed's files.

Marco rubbed his forehead, gazing at me from beneath his brows. "You *told* him you saw him going through Reed's desk?"

"Okay, I probably shouldn't have done that, in case he is the killer, but here I am, safe and sound, so let's move on to the part about Puffer being denied tenure—again. You have to admit, that's a strong motive."

"It doesn't hold up, Abby. Puffer found the letter *after* Reed died, not before."

"But Reed could have *told* him before."

"Then why did Puffer look for the letter?"

"To find out if Reed had told him the truth."

"Pure speculation on your part. We need solid facts. Puffer is still in the mix, obviously, but I'm not as convinced of his guilt as you are."

"But why would he keep pointing to me as the murderer if not to take the heat off himself?"

"Maybe because he doesn't like you. Or maybe he thinks you *are* the killer."

I was still sure Puffer was our man, but there was no sense arguing about it, so I moved on, telling Marco about the mysterious phone calls from Books of Olde. "It might have been nothing more than misdialed numbers—*or* it might have been the married woman with whom Reed had an affair. And what married woman works at Books of Olde? Jocelyn, for one."

"My gut feeling from the start was that Jocelyn and Reed were having an affair, and after talking to her I can tell you she would be an easy target for a smooth player like Reed. She's starving for male affection and Reed is a predator. He'd spot her neediness in a second. But again, this is all conjecture."

"You're right," I said with a frustrated sigh. "Plus, I'm still having a hard time imagining the two of them together. She's so not his type."

"If Reed had a reason to use her, type wouldn't matter. Maybe he just wanted to cuckold his rival—his private joke on Puffer."

"Not to mention the tenure issue. A double whammy. I could see Reed doing that. So let's suppose that was his intent. And let's suppose Jocelyn fell hard for him and assumed he felt the same. Can you imagine how his ending it would devastate her? Finally, someone is kind to her, pays attention to her, then suddenly it's bye-bye, baby. Maybe she called him at the office to beg him to come back, and when he said no, she decided to try to talk to him in person, and that's why she came to the law school on Tuesday."

Marco didn't look convinced. "She'd go see Reed with her husband right next door? That's awfully risky."

"She'd be distraught; she wouldn't be thinking straight." I was on a roll now. "Besides, Puffer is always out of his office over the noon hour. What better time to visit the school? If she confronted Reed and he rejected her, I'll bet she'd snap like a twig."

"Don't forget, the murder happened in her husband's office. Would she be so distraught she wouldn't think how that might implicate her husband?"

"Obviously," I said with a heavy sigh, "you've never been dumped."

"Or maybe," Marco said, ignoring my comment, "she *wanted* her husband to be blamed."

"I hadn't thought of that. Did Jocelyn stick with her alibi about going to the school to have lunch with Puffer?"

"Yes, but she wouldn't look me in the eye when she said it. Another point. She kept referring to Reed by his first name, as though she knew him personally."

"She's older than Reed. It would sound kind of formal to call him Professor."

"Not if she didn't know him well. And once I told her I was investigating everyone who'd been at the scene, she suddenly became more than willing to talk about her husband."

"If Jocelyn *is* the murderer, it would make sense to steer us toward Puffer."

"Jocelyn was definitely going through some kind of inner turmoil, like there was this boil of resentment just beneath the surface that only needed to be probed a little to burst— and I think I know how to do it."

I put down the last bite of my sandwich. The boil image had killed that for me.

Marco sat forward and began to write. "We'll need a record of calls made to Reed's office and to his mobile number. If they show what I think they will, I'll need to have another chat with Jocelyn."

I gasped, startling Marco. "I almost forgot to tell you. When I found Reed's body in the chair, there was a black handset in his lap, as if he'd been talking to someone when he was murdered. When Reilly interviewed me, it completely slipped my mind, and now it might be too late for him to check it out, because Puffer has a new phone."

"I wonder what happened to the old one?" Marco mused as he jotted down the information. "I need to touch base with Reilly anyway, so I'll tell him about it."

"Ask him about his search for the petnappers, while you're at it."

"Let's just stick with the murder for now." He glanced over his notes. "The only suspect we haven't discussed is Kenny Lipinski."

"I thought about his being the killer, but there's no motive. I asked Kenny if any of the other applicants might have gone off the deep end because they'd been turned down for the federal clerkship, but he said no one else had been informed. Bea basically told me the same thing."

"She knew for sure that Kenny had been chosen?"

"Well, no. She said she wasn't surprised that he'd been chosen. Apparently Reed thought highly of Kenny."

"So everything we know about Reed bestowing this clerkship on Kenny comes from Kenny."

"That's true, but it should be easy to verify. I'll check with Bea on that."

Marco tapped his pen against his lips. "On the day of the murder, you said he came right away when you called for help. How do you know he was in the computer lab?"

"I checked the computer log and it showed he had signed in at ten o'clock that morning but hadn't signed out. Once the police arrived, we had to stay in the secretarial pool area, so he wouldn't have had a chance to log out. But the monitor should be able to confirm it."

"Are you sure there was a monitor that morning?"

"I'll check it out."

"As it stands," Marco said, looking over his notes, "we have solid motives for Bea, Puffer, and Jocelyn, with a question mark by Kenny."

"Can we cross Hannah off our list?"

"From what you learned today, I'd say so."

"That's still three strong suspects, Marco. Who do we focus on first?"

"Puffer. I'm still supposed to ambush him at the country

club tonight, before that wonderful dinner with your family, right?"

Yikes. How could I have forgotten the Friday Knight dinner? Oh, right. I'd blocked it.

"I'll pick you up at six." Marco held up a hand. "Don't say it. I know. In the alley."

He was not dumb, that man.

"What am I going to wear?" I whined as I stood in front of my closet at four o'clock that afternoon. "I need something classy but not boring. Whatever else it is, it can't be boring."

Jillian sat on my bed, combing her fingers through the black wig. "How did you get this so tangled?"

"It's a long story. Never mind that. Help me."

"How about a peasant look? It's very hot right now."

"I'll be at the country club, Jillian, and this is Marco's first time there. I want to look like a confident, exciting *babe,* not a fortune-teller."

With an impatient sigh, Jillian left, returning minutes later with an outfit. "Here you go."

An off-white suit with loads of pizzazz. And best of all, it wasn't boring. "It's perfect."

"Of course it's perfect. Clothes are my business. Now you have to do me a favor."

I felt my stomach preparing to tie itself into a tiny knot of stress. The last time Jillian asked me for a favor, I had to watch her fiancé's ninety-year-old grandmother during their wedding reception, which wouldn't have been all that terrible if Grandma Osborne hadn't managed to lose me long enough to find a dead body. It was a wedding no one would ever forget.

I swallowed my fear. "What's the favor?"

"If anyone tries to leave papers for me, don't take them.

And just a reminder, if Claymore calls, you are not to speak to him about me or divulge my whereabouts."

"First of all, you've been reminding me of that for almost two months. I'm sure he's gotten the message. Second, if someone came to serve you papers, they wouldn't leave them with me. And third, what papers are you talking about?"

She flapped her hands impatiently against her sides. "I don't know. Maybe divorce papers."

"So take the papers. Remember, Claymore *left* you, Jill. Why wouldn't you want to give him a divorce?"

"Abby, Abby, Abby." She gazed at me with an expression of pity. "You still haven't gotten over Pryce dumping you, have you? You have to let these things go, Abs. Carrying grudges just isn't healthy."

"I *have* let it go. You're the one who brings it up all the time. Anyway, are you telling me you're not even a smidgen angry about Pryce's little brother dumping you?"

"My motto is to forgive and forget. Live and let live. Besides, why go through a messy divorce when we can just live separate but happy lives?" She picked up the wig and walked out, calling back, "Learn from my example, Abby. You'll be a better woman for it."

At two minutes before six o'clock, as I was putting the final touches on my eye makeup, the phone rang. I dashed from the bathroom, grabbed the handset in the living room, and said, "I'll be down in a minute, Marco."

There was a pause, and then a male voice said, "Abby? It's Claymore. Is Jillian there?"

Claymore Osborne was a nerdy perfectionist with a thin, jittery voice. In fact, he reminded me a lot of Niles Crane, from the old television show *Frasier*. But this Claymore sounded anything but jittery. He was downright subdued.

"Claymore, you know I can't tell you. Why are you calling?"

"I've tried every means I can think of to reach her, Abby. I'm at the end of my rope. Please help me."

"Why?" I said rather sourly. "You left her." Okay, so I was still a *little* bitter over Pryce dumping me.

He sighed wearily. "I know you think you're protecting Jillian from her evil husband, but I can't let this farce continue any longer. I didn't leave her, Abby. She left me. In the middle of the night. In the middle of our honeymoon. In the middle of Oahu."

I was speechless—and outraged. Jillian had let me feel sorry for her! And now she wanted me to shield her from her own shallowness, from her own fear of commitment. Well, no deal. She wasn't going to use me any longer. "Claymore," I began. Then I stopped. I couldn't betray my own kin, my own flesh and blood. "I'm sorry. I can't help you."

He sighed dejectedly. "I kept hoping she'd miss me. I really thought she loved me. It seems I was nothing more than notch number five on her belt."

There was no way I could harden my heart against that. "Look, I have to be someplace in ten minutes, but don't give up hope. Jillian hasn't filed for divorce or an annulment"— that I knew of, anyway—"and that tells me that she does love you. She's just afraid she'll be a lousy wife."

"If there's any way to let her know I still want to work this out, would you try?"

It was my turn to sigh. He was right about me not wanting to get involved, yet here I was, smack in the middle. "Where are you staying, Claymore?"

"At my folks' house."

"Okay, let me get back to you."

"You have the phone number, right?"

"I have it." More than that, I now had Jillian's number.

*   *   *

At three minutes after six o'clock in the growing dusk of a mild September eve, wearing a fitted, short-waisted jacket over a sexy little bustier, slim slacks, a stunning, cloche-type hat with little seed pearls knitted into the yarn, and a pair of Jillian's stylish, strappy silver sandals (unfortunately, a half size too large), I slid into Marco's car and turned to face him. "What do you think?"

He gave me a long, slow once-over with those hooded eyes, heating my blood to such a degree that my feet swelled, making the sandals suddenly a bit snug. But all he said was, "Nice."

He had to do better than that. Casting him a lascivious glance, I ran my palm across the little embedded pearls in the cloche, then trailed my fingers down my bare throat, leaned toward him, and said in a husky purr, "What do you think of the hat?"

His gaze flickered to my head. "Well, it certainly covers your hair."

I sat back with a huff. "Don't you find my outfit the least bit sexy?"

"The outfit, yes. But not the hat."

"Well, okay, then, Tommy Bahama, I guess you'll just have to put up with me for the evening."

Marco's mouth twitched in mirth as he pulled onto the street and headed toward the club. "Or you could just take off the hat. You don't have to hide that gorgeous red hair tonight, do you?"

I whipped off that hat before he'd even put the question mark at the end of his sentence. He'd called my red hair gorgeous! All was forgiven.

As I combed my fingers through my bob, I glanced at Marco, who was looking incredibly sexy in black slacks, a very spiffy gray sport coat, a pearl gray shirt, and a multicolored silk tie. He seemed in a good mood for someone who was going to spend the next few hours with a bunch of redheaded crazy people. Too good. He knew something.

"Okay, out with it, buster. What did you learn?"

"It's about time you asked. For one thing, over twenty calls were made to Reed's office and mobile phone from the Books of Olde shop over a period of three weeks, including the morning of the murder. Guess who made the calls?"

"It had to be Jocelyn."

"You got it. I also learned that Jocelyn had been leaving the bookstore every day to go out to lunch, something new for her, according to her coworkers."

"Phone calls, lunch dates, probably a rosy glow to her cheeks. Puffer could have picked up on those signs, Marco. Maybe he found out about Jocelyn's affair and *that's* why he killed him."

Marco looked doubtful. "I didn't get the impression from Jocelyn that Puffer cares that much about her. If he killed Reed, I'd bet it wasn't over her."

"But he cares about his reputation, Marco. How would it look if people found out his rival was bonking his wife? Put that with his suspicion that Reed was behind his not getting tenure, and you have a very strong motive. What better revenge against both Jocelyn and Reed than to kill Reed? And by blaming me, he protected himself and kept his control over her."

Marco was silent as he turned onto Country Club Road. Then suddenly his attention snapped to his rearview mirror. "Did you say that gray minivan had a temporary plate in the back window?"

"Yes, why?" I said, twisting to look behind me.

"We just passed one fitting that description." He pulled over, waited for traffic to pass, then made a U-turn and doubled back. "What do you say we try to catch a couple of thieves?"

CHAPTER TWENTY-FOUR

"Marco, I'm in an off-white suit. This isn't how I should be dressed to follow someone. Besides, it's not totally dark yet."

"Sometimes you have to go with the flow." He took a corner on two wheels, then abruptly braked, sending me scrambling for a grip on the dashboard. The gray van was a block ahead, cruising along a residential street as though casing the houses. Marco parked alongside the curb, took his camera and telescopic lens from the glove compartment, and snapped a few pictures as the van cruised slowly forward.

I checked my watch. It was 6:20. "Maybe we should call Reilly and let him take over. He did warn me about staying out of this case, and we do have to get to the club before the Dragon leaves."

"Since when did you ever want to turn anything over to the cops? Besides, this is good training."

"But Puffer will be gone by seven o'clock."

"Here we go," he said and pulled away from the curb, creeping up the block, then onto the next one, until the van was just ahead. "I'm going to pull around it and slow up alongside so you can take pictures. Maybe we can get one the police can use to ID the driver."

Before I could ready the camera, another car came up the street behind us, its headlights illuminating the interior of Marco's car. He swore under his breath, drove around the van, and continued up the block.

"Let's just head for the club," I said. "Like you said, we should stick to one case at a time." Also, that lump on my head was starting to throb, not that I wanted to remind Marco of it.

My suggestion fell on deaf ears. In typical male fashion, Marco's complete focus was on getting those photos. He turned the corner at the next intersection and pulled over, killing the motor.

"Plan B," he said, pulling a black knit cap out of the console. "I'm going back on foot. You man the driver's seat and be ready to take off when I jump in."

We'd never make it to the club in time to see Puffer. But it was no use arguing that point now. Marco had tossed his coat in the backseat and tugged a black sweatshirt over his shirt, and had the cap on his head. I handed him the camera, then, as he jogged off, I scrambled around the car and into the driver's side. As I strapped on the seat belt, I glanced over at the passenger side and saw the telescopic lens lying there. Yikes. When had it come off? Had I twisted it loose? I had to get it to Marco.

I tucked the lens in my jacket pocket, put my purse under the seat, took the keys from the ignition, and got out, then glanced down at my suit. There was no way I could sneak around in off-white. In a panic, I opened the trunk and rooted around to see if Marco had any spare clothing. All I found was a black plastic trash bag, giant-sized. It would have to do.

I used the car key to tear a hole in the bottom of the bag for my head, and one on each side for my arms, then I tugged it down over my clothes. Because the bottom reached only to midcalf, I had to roll up my pant cuffs. The silver sandals had to go, too. I found Marco's spare black hat and pulled it over my hair, then quietly shut the trunk and took off, the grass prickly beneath my bare feet as I cut through a yard and came out on the other block.

Darkness had finally fallen, but by the light of a street-lamp I could see the van half a block ahead. Moving carefully so as not to make the plastic crinkle, I hid behind a large viburnum in a front yard two houses away from the van and peered out from around the spreading branches, trying to spot Marco. A dog began to bark from someone's backyard. Suddenly, there was a *yelp* and then silence. My heart stopped. Had the thieves just napped another pet?

Almost at once a shadowy figure emerged from the far corner of the house behind me. I made a quick dive for the ground and rolled beneath the branches of the big shrub, hoping I hadn't been spotted. Something crawled across my bare foot and I had to bite my lower lip to keep from panicking. I held my breath as the figure passed not three yards away, then stopped with a whispered curse as something slipped from his arms and fell to the grass.

I heard the muffled whines of a frightened dog, and a white-hot fury burst inside me. There was no way that creep was taking that animal. I tumbled out of the bush and lunged at the person's ankles—thick, male ankles—tripping him. While he scrambled upright, I grabbed the wiggling sack and took off, cradling the animal against me as I yelled at the top of my lungs, "Marco, call the cops! I have the dog!"

With my heart drumming in my ears and a headache thumping in my skull, I raced around the corner and saw

Marco's Prius just ahead. But as I bore down on it I heard someone behind me. Afraid I was about to be attacked, I spun around and took a defensive stance, the dog still clutched against me, prepared to use my foot to kick someone's groin. "Stay back!" I cried.

"It's me," Marco said, breathing hard. "The thieves took off. Unlock the car and let's go get them."

I almost collapsed against him in relief, but he had the cell phone to his ear and was barking instructions to someone. Oh, no. What had I done with the car key? I thrust the wiggling bundle at Marco and tugged the plastic bag over my hip so I could get to my pocket. Then I unlocked his door and ran around to the passenger side, slid in, took the bundle from him, and strapped myself in as he tore away.

Too late. The van was nowhere in sight. "Damn," he muttered and made a U-turn.

"At least we saved the dog." I opened the burlap bag and released a very frightened dachshund, who gazed up at me with terrified eyes. "You're okay, buddy," I murmured, stroking his head and scratching behind his soft ears. The dog jumped up and licked my chin.

"At least I snapped some photos," Marco said, "although for some reason my camera was missing the telephoto lens. . . . Are you wearing a garbage bag?"

"I found it in your trunk. I am *so* sorry about the lens, Marco. I must have twisted it loose. But look at this little guy. Isn't he worth all the trouble?" I cuddled the animal against me. "We didn't let those bad guys get you, did we?"

"Let's get him back to his owner."

I pointed out the house and Marco pulled up in front just as a squad car came from the opposite direction. I quickly handed the dog to Marco, removed the plastic bag, and was slipping on the silver sandals as Reilly strode toward us, shaking his head. "You just couldn't keep out of it, could you?" he asked me. *Me,* not Marco, who was standing four inches away.

I pointed to my silent sidekick. "This was his idea." Sometimes you just had to rat people out.

Marco gave Reilly the details of our encounter and promised to get him copies of whatever he was able to catch on film. He handed the dog to Reilly, who took him to the front door and rang the doorbell. As we pulled away, a young woman stepped out and hugged the dog against her, crying. I had to blink as tears filled my eyes.

"It's seven thirty," Marco said. "Too late to catch Puffer. What do you want to do?"

I glanced down at my dirty feet and grass-stained pants. "I can't show up at the country club like this, and I've got to get these slacks off before Jillian sees them, so I'd better go home."

"I've got some things to do, too, so why don't I take you home, then pick you up in, say, an hour. We'll grab dinner at the bar and figure out our next move."

I pulled my purse from beneath the seat. "Sounds like a plan to me."

That was the problem with plans. They never worked out the way you, well, planned.

As soon as I was in the door, I popped two aspirins for my headache, downed a glass of chocolate soy milk, and fed Simon, who was doing his best to trip me. I had just removed the soiled suit, washed my face, and changed into jeans and a button-down shirt when the doorbell buzzed, followed by a furious pounding. Before I could get to the door I heard, "Abigail, it's Mom. Are you there? Please be there, otherwise I'll have to believe you are lying in a ditch on the side of a deserted road."

Why was it always a *deserted* road? Didn't busy roads have ditches? "I'm here," I said, opening the door. "I'm sorry I didn't call to let you know about dinner. We had an unfortunate incident—"

"I knew it! I told your brothers you'd had an accident."

"An *incident,* Mom," I said, grabbing her shoulders so she couldn't leap for the telephone, "not an accident. *In,* not *ac.* I didn't call you sooner because it happened on our way to the club, and things got crazy. Marco and I were chasing pet thieves and—"

She clutched my arms so tightly, my fingertips went numb. "You were chasing thieves? What have I told you about putting yourself in danger! I am *so* glad I didn't bring your father over here. Do you know what this would do to him?"

She followed that up by engulfing me in a hug and smothering me with kisses. "If anything had happened to you," she said as I mouthed the familiar words along with her, "they'd have to put me in a padded room and feed me tranquilizers all day."

I untangled her arms and smiled up at her. I had no choice but to smile *up* at people, even my own mother. "But see? I didn't get hurt. Look at me. I'm fine. Besides, Marco was with me. Again, Mom, I apologize for not letting you know sooner. I had to wash and change and then I was going to phone, I swear. Now, how about a glass of water—or better yet, wine?"

"Water would be nice." She sank down in a chair while I trotted off to the kitchen. "I had a cabernet with dinner."

"Water it is," I called, reaching into a cabinet for a glass.

"Oh, Abigail. I almost forgot. I brought your surprise with me."

The glass nearly slipped from my hand. Not a *surprise.* Not after the day I'd had! On second thought, how bad could it be? I hadn't seen her carrying it, so she must have tucked it into her purse. At least it was a small surprise. "Great, Mom."

"I left it in the hallway. Would you get it? It's rather heavy."

Oh, no. Her naked-dancing-monkey table had been heavy. Her human-footed footstool had been heavy. Her coatrack palm tree, with its lifelike human palms? Also heavy. I handed her the water, took a determined breath, and marched toward the door. How worried had she really been about my being in that ditch if she'd toted a heavy art piece up a flight of stairs?

Just outside the door sat a huge shopping bag. I stooped to pick it up and almost wrenched my back. I pulled it inside instead, stopping in front of her chair.

"Open it," she instructed excitedly.

Peeling back layers of green tissue paper, I uncovered a gardener's hand spade, a trowel, and a watering can, which shouldn't have been that heavy, except that these were completely covered in small mirrored squares, making each object weigh in at around fifteen pounds. I could see the ad for them now: *Build muscle while you garden.* "Wow. They're really—different, Mom."

She hugged me. "I knew you'd like them. We have the same taste."

Someone, shoot me now.

She picked up the spade, turning it so it reflected light off its plethora of shiny squares. I had to squint to see her face. "What do you think they'll sell for?" she asked.

The phone rang, saving me from giving her an answer. In truth, I had no idea. As far as I knew, these were the only mirrored garden tools in existence. The good thing was that they'd be hard to lose. The bad thing was that they'd be hard to lose. I excused myself to take the call in the kitchen, leaving my mother to carefully fold the tissue paper and shopping bag and stow them in her bowling-bag purse to be used another day.

"There's been another change in plans," Marco said quietly when I answered. "Jocelyn is here, and she's ready to talk about Tuesday."

CHAPTER TWENTY-FIVE

"Marco, this could be the breakthrough we needed. Should I come down?"

"I think it would be better if I spoke with her alone. She's sloshed and weepy. I'll call you when she leaves."

I returned to the living room to see my mom waving an envelope at me. "I brought you something else. You know how I always cut out newspaper clippings about you and your brothers? Well, these are yours. I saved them for you."

The first two articles were on Reed's murder, and the third was on the protest march, with the grainy black-and-white photo of me in handcuffs shouting at Professor Reed, with Marvin Y. Brown at his side. Just what I wanted for my scrapbook. If I ever had kids, they would *not* be seeing these. "Thanks, Mom."

I started to put them back in the envelope, then I took a closer look at the two blurry faces behind Reed and Brown. One was a lanky blond who reminded me a whole lot of Dustin. The other—hmm. It kind of looked like Kenny. But

surely it wasn't either one of them. Kenny had said he'd
only just met Marvin Brown at the memorial service, and
why would he lie about that? . . . Unless there was something about their relationship he didn't want me to know.

*Okay, let's not jump to conclusions, here. There could be
a perfectly innocent explanation.* What I needed was a clear
photo to see whether it really *was* Kenny in the picture.
Then I'd worry about why he lied. Maybe I could tap Connor Mackay for a copy of the original.

As soon as my mother was out the door, I rummaged
through my purse looking for Connor's card. Nikki was
right. There were way too many receipts in there. I found it
at last, and three rings later I heard, "Connor Mackay here."

"Hey, Connor, this is Abby Knight."

"Well, what do you know? How are you, Abby?"

I hated that perky tone in his voice, as if he knew I'd call
eventually. "I need a favor, Connor. I need a glossy of that
photo of me at the protest march a couple weeks ago."

"The one of you in handcuffs?"

I could almost hear the snicker in his voice. "You took
great delight in saying that, didn't you? Yes, that one. Can
you get one for me?"

"I think I can manage that. What's the date on that photo?"

I gave it to him. "How soon can I have it?"

"Do you want me to e-mail it to you?"

"Me, download a JPEG file? Thanks, but I'd rather have
a hard copy."

"Computer illiterate, huh? I can give you lessons."

"Just the photo, Connor."

"Then you'll have to wait until tomorrow."

"Good enough. Where can I pick it up?"

"Hold on there, Olga. I want something in exchange." He
was all business now. "How about an interview?"

"You know what? I'll get the photo from someone else."

"I think you should talk to me, Abby."

"I don't like that threatening tone in your voice, Mackay."

"Then you're really going to hate the piece that's set to run tomorrow. If you thought you looked guilty before, oh, baby. So why don't you meet me in thirty minutes at the Daily Grind coffee shop and tell your side of the story?"

Was it blackmail or was he doing me a favor? If I didn't talk to him, I wasn't sure what would happen if a more damaging article came out. If I did talk to him, I could mitigate the damage and also get my hands on that photo. I glanced at my watch. It was eight o'clock. I wanted to get down to Bloomers to check things out there, but this was a bit more important. "Are you sure you can get a story in tomorrow's paper?"

"Hey, we're living in the computer age, remember?"

"Will you have the photo with you?"

"Tonight?"

"Hey, we're living in the computer age, remember?"

There was a pause, then he grumbled, "Fine. I'll see you then."

At eight thirty, I pulled into one of the public parking lots on the outer fringe of the town square and checked my appearance in the rearview mirror. To remain incognito, I had donned the blond wig and put on a T-shirt with a pair of beat-up blue jeans so I'd blend in with the clientele, which, in the evenings, was mostly college students. I was having second thoughts about meeting Connor, knowing how Marco and Dave would react, but I reassured myself that it was for a good cause. Me.

With one last adjustment of the wig, I got out of the car and by habit looked around to see whether anyone had noticed me, then I hurried across the street and up Lincoln Avenue two blocks east to the Daily Grind, a small, eclectically decorated coffee shop with soft lighting and jazz playing in the background. I walked in and glanced around. Most of the small wooden tables were occupied, and at my entrance, everyone looked up, decided they didn't know me, and resumed what they'd been doing.

Connor was way in the back at a table for two. He gazed at me quizzically as I pulled out a chair and sat down. "How's it going, Mackay?"

"So, it's you, Olga. Or can I call you Abby tonight? You're still in disguise, I see."

"Yeah, no thanks to you."

He tried to look sheepish but I knew he didn't feel it. "I'm glad you decided to talk to me."

"Can I get you anything?" a young waitress asked, giving Connor the eye. He did look sort of appealing in his crumpled white shirt rolled up to his elbows and a pair of slim-fitting jeans. His hair was a little too shaggy, but it was clean and shiny.

"Espresso with milk on the side, please," I told her.

"Plain coffee." As the waitress bustled off, Connor flipped open his reporter's notepad and pulled a pen from his shirt pocket. "Okay, what would you like to talk about first?"

"The weather. What do you think, Connor?"

He gave me that great big smile that was so darned charming. "Okay, then. Let's get right down to it. Tell me your side of the story."

"Photograph first, Mackay."

He rubbed his eyebrow. "There was a slight hitch."

I slipped my purse strap over my shoulder and rose. "See you around."

"Wait, Abby." He pulled a tiny disk from his pants pocket and slipped it onto the table. "The photo is on this. I won't be able to get you a glossy until tomorrow."

"And I'm supposed to take your word on that?"

He held up his hand. "My word as a journalist, and I take that very seriously. Look, if you don't believe me, I'll give you my editor's home phone number. You can tell him what our deal is, so I'll have to abide by it. Or you can take the disk to the office supply store tomorrow and have them print the photo. Or you can trust me to get it to you."

I studied him a moment and decided I believed him. I sat down again as the waitress set beverage napkins and green cups and saucers in front of us. "I've never done this before. Why don't you ask me some questions?"

"It's better to simply start from the beginning and let it all out. Remember, this is your chance to correct any misinformation."

"There's plenty of that out there, believe me." I drew in a breath, let it out again, forming in my mind what I wanted him to know. Then I began my tale from when Puffer crossed in front of my car while he was on his cell phone to when I walked back into Puffer's office to get my flower and found Reed's body. Connor had been writing rapidly as I spoke, and unlike Marco, he waited until I'd stopped to ask his questions.

He recapped what I'd given him, reading from his notepad, then asked, "So when the body was discovered, you were the only person there?"

"That's what the phrase 'I discovered his body' usually means, Connor."

He rubbed his forehead, ignoring my little jab. "I'm having a hard time understanding why you're number one on the police list of suspects, other than that you do have a history with Carson Reed."

"Exactly what I keep saying. I have a history with Professor Puffer, too, but I didn't kill him. Then again, if I hadn't slammed on my brakes in time, I probably *would* have killed him, but that's another story." The waitress came by to fill our cups, so I stopped to add milk to my coffee and take a sip.

Connor tapped his pen on the notepad. "It doesn't add up.

Just because you found the body and had some previous run-ins with the professor—"

"One previous run-in, at the protest march."

"And then again when you ran into him after you left Professor Puffer's office."

"Right. Like I said, I hadn't expected to see him. He stepped out of his office as I came out of Puffer's office and we literally ran into each other. We exchanged a few barbs and I left. And here's a fact you can check. I made a call to Marco while I was sitting in my car, before I went back inside. He'll tell you my only concern was to retrieve my flower."

Connor shook his head, puzzled. "I still don't get it. To make you their prime suspect . . . the police must have more on you than that." He leaned across the table, searching my face. "What aren't you telling me, Abby? You're holding something back."

Like I would admit to him that my fingerprints were on the murder weapon? Fat chance. "Why would you say that, Connor?"

"For one thing, you're tense as hell. You've torn your napkin into tiny pieces."

Yikes. He was right. I must have shredded it while I was talking. Great. Now my face was getting warm, too, which meant it was turning red. In a few moments I'd look like a giant pickled beet. It was time to backpedal. "Well, it's no secret I was dismayed that Reed was defending Dermacol. But my issue wasn't with him as much as it was with Dermacol's policy of testing products on animals. That's why I was at the protest march."

Connor's left eyebrow lifted skeptically, so I went at him with both barrels. "Do you know about Dermacol's policy? Do you know that animals are poisoned and killed simply to test the toxicity of beauty-product ingredients? The animals are force-fed makeup, Connor. Their lungs are pumped with hair spray until it eats away at the lining. Hair dyes are rubbed into their eyes and skin until they bleed. Are you sick yet? Because this is what Dermacol does, and will continue to do, unless we consumers speak up."

"Do you really want me to put this in the article?"

"Sure. Why not? It's the truth."

"First of all, what does this have to do with your innocence or guilt? Second, are you aware that the FBI has put animal rights extremists under their microscope? Do you really want that to happen to you?"

That took me aback. "I'm not an extremist. I realize that it's sometimes necessary to perform tests on animals for health reasons, but there are humane ways of doing that, and in fact, many labs *are* doing it. I'm simply trying to do my part to save helpless animals from being tortured by an unscrupulous company right here in our town. That doesn't mean I would blow up people or buildings to do so. I mean, that's a little extreme, wouldn't you say?"

"That's why they're called extremists."

I downed my coffee and signaled for more. No milk this time. I wanted it as strong as I could get it. Somehow I had to change the direction the interview had taken, because it was not going the way I had planned. Then again, what did?

"Okay, let's forget about Dermacol for now," I said. "I can't tell you why the police are so focused on me, but I can say that there are people connected with Carson Reed who not only had the opportunity but also a reason for wanting him dead. And reason, Connor, translates into motive."

He was interested now. "Who are these people? Can you be more specific?"

"I don't want to name names, and this is totally between you and me, but I'm this close to figuring out which one of them is the murderer."

"Can you give me a hint?"

"Not yet. Trust me, though, when I have it nailed down, it'll be a huge headline."

"Have you shared this with the police?"

"When they start sharing with me, I'll be more than happy to share with them."

He scribbled furiously, then flipped the notepad closed and put away his pen. "Great stuff, Abby. Now, I've got to run. The paper gets put to bed in an hour. I'll submit my story tonight and it should be in tomorrow's edition."

The Sunday paper. My stomach grew jittery thinking about it. I put a five-dollar bill on the table and stood up, scattering tiny napkin scraps in all directions. "When will you have that photo?"

"Not until Sunday. How about around three o'clock Sunday afternoon? I'll drop it off at your apartment."

"Fine. Let me give you the address."

"I already have it."

"How do you know my address?"

"I'm a reporter, remember?"

Sometimes it was better not to know. I pointed down the street to the public lot. "I'm parked down there. How about you?"

"Me, too. I'll walk with you. So, tell me, off the record, is Marco still involved?"

"With the murder investigation?" I paused, wondering whether Marco would mind him knowing, then decided to hedge my bets. "He's helping me with it."

Connor was silent as we headed across the parking lot to my car. I put the key in the lock, then turned to say good-bye, only to find him very close. "Actually," he said, "I meant involved with you."

Connor was putting a move on me. I gazed into those vivid eyes and wondered why I wasn't outraged, or at least appalled, but I wasn't either of those things. What was wrong with me? "Look, Connor, Marco and I are very good friends. No, better than good. Close. Yes, close friends. Dear, close friends." What a wimp I was.

"So was that a yes?"

I gave a light shrug, leaving it to him to interpret. I felt bad for being so wishy-washy about the matter, but the truth was that I didn't know how to answer. Were we involved or not? I thought we were, but Marco had never said what he thought.

Connor placed a hand on the car on one side of my body, and I knew what was coming. Clearly his interpretation was that Marco and I were not involved, and I made no attempt to correct him. In fact, I even let him dip his head down and press his lips against mine, liking that he tasted of coffee and smelled of citrus. I was so bad.

Would you want Marco to behave like this with other women? Well, no, but what was to stop him? We'd never agreed not to see anyone else, although I would if he would. Why was that, anyway? Was Marco afraid to commit? Was I afraid to bring up the subject? Were we both wimps?

Connor broke the kiss and gazed down at me, but I turned my head so I didn't have to look into those gorgeous green eyes and feel even more doubts. "I have to go, Connor."

He stepped back as if I'd just told him I never wanted to see him again. "Okay. Sure. I understand. Hey, thanks for the interview. I'll drop the photo off tomorrow."

I opened the door and slid inside, then tried to insert the key to start the engine. Why was I shaking? It wasn't like I had never kissed anyone but Marco before.

Maybe because you liked it a little too much. Maybe because you feel like a heel.

My headache was coming back. I sat there for a moment watching Connor drive out of the lot, then I got out and walked briskly to Bloomers. I felt a strong need to see Marco, but I didn't want to interrupt his meeting with Jocelyn, so I let myself into Bloomers and went straight back to my place of peace.

Sitting at my desk, I swivelled the chair to take it all in—colors, aromas, the sweetly pungent fragrance of a fresh batch of eucalypti, and spicy paperwhites. . . . I stretched to reach a leaf that had fallen on the floor and hold it to my nose. Ah-h, mint. Damn, I missed Bloomers. I felt tears sting my eyes and scrubbed them away. Would I ever clear my name so I could come back here without having to slink in like a rat?

Suddenly I noticed an envelope propped next to the computer monitor. Inside was a note from Lottie.

Dear Abby,

An order came in just before we locked up for the day. If you have time, would you do it? Also, take a look at our bank account. I think you'll be very pleased.

Big hugs, Lottie.

I rummaged in the bottom desk drawer and pulled out the ledger. Lottie did everything the old-fashioned way, including the bookkeeping, which was fine with me since I knew nothing about accounting software anyway. To me, spreadsheets was what I did on Saturday mornings after washing my bed linen.

In a neat column under the heading *September Receipts,* Lottie had recorded all the deposits, leaving a big, fat, in-the-black total at the bottom. We were not only solvent, we were making a generous profit! Now, there was something to celebrate.

With renewed enthusiasm I wrote a note of my own.

Dear Lottie,

Thanks for the terrific news. Once this case is resolved I'm taking you and Grace out for a celebration dinner.

Love, Abby.

Then I tackled the order: a twenty-first-birthday arrangement from a best friend.

I practically skipped across the room to the giant cooler. Stepping inside, I gazed with delight at the choices in front of me, then spotted a giant amaryllis—a Grand Trumpet Candy Cane amaryllis with three blooms on it. Perfect. I nestled it in a squat, white ceramic vase and put sphagnum moss over the top. Then I hot-glued a row of red and white candy canes all the way around the pot, added a scattering of brightly colored, cellophane-wrapped candies on top of the canes, and finished it with a rainbow-colored bow.

I was about to wrap it when my cell phone rang. I answered to hear Marco's incredibly sexy, husky voice. "Hey, Sunshine. Do I have news for you."

CHAPTER TWENTY-SIX

"Did Jocelyn confess?"

"Can you come down?" he said over the din in the bar. "I'd rather tell you in person."

It had to be good news. He sounded too upbeat for it to be otherwise. "I'm at Bloomers. Give me ten minutes to finish what I'm doing here. Oh, Marco, do me a favor, please. Call Reilly and let him know I'm here so I don't walk into a SWAT team ambush."

I finished the arrangement, put it in the cooler, and locked up. No surprise ambushes awaited outside, so I hurried down the street and into the bar, threading my way through the heavy, Friday-night crowd. Marco was pouring beers behind the bar, casting quick glances around as though searching for me, but he wasn't watching for a blonde, so for a moment I just watched him, soaking in that swarthy Italian countenance. I raised a hand to catch his eye, and he motioned for me to meet him in his office.

As soon as I was inside, I pulled off the itchy wig and

shook out my hair, smoothing it away from my face. The door opened and I swung around as Marco strode in, and for the life of me I couldn't remember why I had thought Connor attractive. I rushed forward and Marco obliged by opening his arms, which is exactly what I'd hoped he'd do. I slipped my arms around his ribs and squeezed hard.

"What's this about?" he asked, gazing down at me in bafflement.

I knew this was not the time to start a relationship discussion, so all I could say was, "I'm happy to see you."

"I'm happy to see you, too."

"Good." I smiled up at him, but he only gave me a questioning glance.

"You seem a little flushed. Do you want something cold to drink?"

"Maybe later. So tell me what Jocelyn said. Did she kill Reed?

"I don't think so."

"Does she know who did?"

"No, but she suspects her husband."

I gazed up in bewilderment. "We already knew that."

He *tsk*ed me. "You're so impatient." He led me to the two sling-back chairs and we sat facing each other. "When Jocelyn came in with a snoot full of liquor I knew she had something big to unload. Turns out she'd been working up the nerve for a few hours. Anyway, she confirmed that she and Reed had been having an affair."

So Marco had been right after all. I should have trusted his instincts. "How long had it been going on?"

"About three weeks. He instigated it, by the way. Apparently they'd been meeting for noon trysts, but the sneaking around wasn't sitting well with Jocelyn. Naturally, she was head over heels for the guy and assumed he was the same, and since she wanted out of her marriage anyway, she decided the right thing to do was to divorce her husband so she and Reed could be together. She told Reed about her decision on Monday morning."

I shook my head in wonder. Another naive woman. Reed sure knew how to pick them. "I can imagine how Reed took that news."

"He told her to hold off until after the tenure issue had been settled, claiming it would make him look bad. But on Tuesday morning Puffer made a nasty little comment to Jocelyn that led her to believe he knew about the affair. So she phoned Reed in a panic and told him she thought they should confront Puffer together right away. That's when Reed told her they had to break it off."

"Poor Jocelyn. That must have destroyed her."

"Yes, but not for the reason you'd expect. She thought Reed was trying to protect her from Puffer's abuse, so she took matters into her own hands and set up a three-way meeting for twelve forty-five Tuesday afternoon."

"So that's why Puffer showed up then."

"Jocelyn then phoned Reed on his mobile to let him know what she'd done, and he told her in no uncertain terms that they were finished. She was so upset that she left the bookstore and drove straight to the school, hoping to convince Reed to change his mind. She got there a little before noon."

"That's when I saw her."

"But once she was inside the law school, she lost her nerve, ran to the women's restroom, and was violently ill. When she finally went upstairs, Reed was dead."

"It sounds plausible, but what makes you think she's telling the truth this time? She lied before."

"For one thing, the cops found the janitor who cleaned up after her. Besides that, there's zero evidence linking her to the crime scene. I can usually tell when someone is lying. Jocelyn is hurt and angry and frightened, but I'd bet my last dollar she's not lying. It took a lot of courage for her to tell me such a humiliating story."

"Haven't you ever heard the saying 'Hell hath no fury like a woman scorned?' Jocelyn was scorned."

"Maybe, but think about it, Sunshine. She didn't have to tell me anything. I'm not the police. Also, I didn't tell her I had the phone records. She volunteered that information."

"So why did she come to see you?"

"Because she found something that puts her husband's alibi in doubt, but she's afraid to go to the police herself for fear that word of her affair will get out and ruin her good name, not to mention her husband's reputation—if he isn't guilty, of course."

"Get to the good part. What did she find?"

"Let's start with the alibi. Puffer's statement was that he was having lunch in the cafeteria from shortly after twelve noon until he arrived back at his office at twelve forty-five. According to Reilly, the cops checked with the cafeteria personnel, they confirmed he was there, and that was good enough for them. But two days ago Jocelyn came across a cafeteria receipt that showed Puffer purchased a sandwich at twelve thirty-five that day. Not exactly shortly after noon, is it?"

"So Puffer could have killed Reed in between my two visits, stopped at the cafeteria to establish his alibi, snuck back into the law school, and waited for someone to discover the body." I clapped my hands together. "Wait till the prosecutor hears about this. Won't he be sorry I was ever on that list."

"Don't get ahead of yourself. A receipt isn't proof. Puffer could come up with any number of reasons for buying his lunch late."

I sank back against the chair, feeling like someone had just let the air out of my tires. "It's been almost a week since the murder, Marco. The cops are going to have to make an arrest soon, and we still haven't figured this thing out. I'm worried."

Marco reached over and took my hands, squeezing them in his big, strong ones. "Come on, Sunshine. It's not that bad. We'll find proof."

"Yeah, right. I'm beginning to think there isn't any out there."

He knelt in front of me and lifted my chin so I'd have to meet his earnest gaze. "We're going to get you out of this."

I gazed into those pools of chocolate and wished I could just fall in and be done with it. But I knew neither one of us was the type to give up without a good fight, so I shook off the negative feelings and sighed. "You're right. We'll find proof. So what do we do next?"

He put a hand on the back of my head and gave me a slow, gentle kiss that said more about how much he cared than any words ever could. Then, with his nose against mine, he said softly, "For starters, don't ever doubt yourself—or me. We're a team, remember?"

Then he sat back in his chair, while I just blinked at him, wondering what he meant. He had to be talking about solving the case. He couldn't know about that quick kiss I shared with Mackay. Could he?

"Now, onto our next suspect—Bea," he said. "When I went over the phone records, I discovered something interesting. A call was made from Puffer's office to Hannah Boyd's dorm room at twelve twenty-two p.m., Tuesday afternoon, the approximate time Carson Reed was killed. So we have to consider that Bea might have overheard him talking to her niece and confronted him about it afterward."

"I could see her confronting Reed, but not killing him. Besides, Reed couldn't have been talking to Hannah in her dorm room. She was in the library."

"Do you know that for sure? Could she have just not answered her door?"

"Bea's name wasn't in the dorm's register. If she'd gone up to see Hannah, she would have had to sign in."

"I think you should meet with Bea again, and this time see if she knew about Reed's relationship with Jocelyn. If she did, that could have further impacted her reaction to finding out about Hannah's affair with Reed."

"What do we do about Puffer?"

"For now, let's try to eliminate the others. Do you want to talk to Kenny?"

"Sure. That reminds me, my mother dropped off some newspaper clippings and one was of me at the protest march with Reed and Marvin Brown. Behind them were two guys that I swear looked like Kenny and his friend Dustin. But you know how grainy those black-and-white news photos can be, so I arranged to get a glossy print of the photo from Connor Mackay. I don't know if there's any connection to the murder, but Kenny told me he'd never met Marvin Brown until Reed's memorial service. If that *is* him in the photo, then he lied to me. I know it's thin, but because of the connection with Professor Reed I thought I'd check it out."

Marco's eyebrows lifted in acknowledgment. "Good thinking, Sunshine."

I beamed with pride until he clasped his hands behind his head and peered at me through half-closed eyes. "So tell me. How did you get Mackay to agree to get you the glossy?"

"I agreed to give him an interview."

"You don't need the photo that badly. I'll talk to a friend of mine who works at the paper."

I gave him a sheepish shrug. "Too late."

"You didn't."

I checked my watch. "I did. About forty minutes ago."

Marco made no reply, so I sincerely hoped that was the end of that discussion, because my head was killing me. But when he began to massage his temples, I figured I should try to minimize the damage. "Before you say anything, I gave

Connor only the information I wanted him to have. I even got a plug in for animal rights. It'll be okay, Marco. I had everything under control—most of the time."

"Most of the time?" He jumped to his feet and headed for the door. "I need a drink. Do you want anything? A brain transplant, perhaps?"

I cradled my pounding head. "Do you have aspirin handy?"

Saturday could not go by fast enough. Luckily Nikki was off work and willing to help me pass the time. We drove to an outlet mall in a nearby city and spent the day shopping for the perfect pair of jeans, which, as any woman knew, could be an all-day affair if not a lifetime event.

On Sunday I awoke with renewed determination to find the proof I needed to clear my name. I fed Simon, settled at the kitchen counter with a bowl of wheat flakes and toast, and opened the Sunday newspaper to a big, bold headline that read: SUSPECT READY TO NAME PROFESSOR'S KILLER. The byline was Connor Mackay.

A bite of toast nearly stuck in my throat. That headline was about me! *I* was the suspect ready to name the killer. Why had he printed that? I pushed aside the rest of my food. Dave was going to kill me. And if he didn't, Marco would. I didn't even want to think about my parents' reactions. And wouldn't Reed's murderer enjoy waking up to that little gem of information?

Boy, did I want a piece of Connor. But first I had to get the photograph. I read through the article and felt somewhat better. At least the rest of the story was accurate.

Before the calls started pouring in, I switched on the answering machine, then wrote a note to Nikki telling her I had to go to work. I stuck it on the face of the newspaper, then donned my Bogie coat and hat and left. I would have gone to church, but the thought of wearing a disguise and sneaking into a house of worship felt all wrong, not to mention risky, so instead I said a long prayer as I headed for Bloomers and hoped that would cover me.

Only five orders had come in overnight, but that was enough to take my mind off the murder. Surrounded by roses, lilies, mums, sphagnum moss, and wet foam, with Enya playing in the background, I whipped up one gorgeous arrangement after another. I was in seventh heaven—until questions started to creep in, and then my stomach knotted with anxiety.

Was Puffer guilty, or did I just want him to be? Was Jocelyn telling the truth, or was Marco being naive? Was there a connection between Kenny and Marvin Y. Brown, and if so, did it have anything to do with Reed's death? And most of all, would Bea commit murder to protect her niece?

It was that last question that preyed on my mind the most. *"The one you least expect is the one you'll overlook,"* Marco had warned. But would Bea lose all control because her niece thought she was in love with Reed? I decided to be bold and ask her, straight out. Her machine answered on the fifth ring, so I left a message saying that I needed to talk to her as soon as possible and would she please ring my cell phone?

No sooner had I hung up than a call came in. "Why are you at work?" Jillian asked. "It's Sunday morning."

"Because no one expects me to be here so there are no protesters or reporters out front. I suppose you saw the newspaper headline."

"I haven't read the paper yet. I need to get that white suit from you. I have a client coming over tonight, and it'll be perfect for her."

Yikes. I couldn't let Jillian sell her client a grass-stained suit. "Jillian, I—um—want to buy that outfit."

"Abby, hello-o-o. It's fifteen hundred dollars."

I nearly passed out. Fifteen hundred was two months'

rent. The bell over the front door gave a quick jingle, so I said, "Hold on, Jillian, someone just came in."

"You opened the store on a Sunday?"

She was right. I had *locked* the front door.

"Abby, are you there?" Jillian cried.

I swallowed hard, keeping my eyes on the curtain that separated the two rooms. Then, quietly, I whispered, "Jillian, someone is in the shop."

CHAPTER TWENTY-SEVEN

"**D**o you want me to call the cops?" Jillian whispered back, apparently forgetting that her voice couldn't be heard to anyone but me.

I darted a hand across to the worktable and grabbed the floral knife. "Yes. Tell them to hurry."

"Grace?" Lottie boomed out. "Is that you back there?"

My entire body, including the hangnail on my index finger, sagged in relief. "It's Lottie. Never mind, Jillian."

"Oh, good. So what do you want to do about the suit?"

"I'll talk to you about that later." I hung up, then called, "It's me, Lottie. I'm back here."

"Abby?"

I turned to find myself enfolded in a hug that lifted me off my feet. "It's good to see you, sweetie," she cried.

"Likewise," I gasped.

"Is it true what I read in the paper?" she asked, setting me down. "You found the killer?"

"Not exactly. We're getting close, though."

"It can't happen soon enough for me."

"I'll second that. You don't know how much I miss this place."

"Honey, I know exactly how much. When Herman took ill and had to be cared for twenty-four hours a day, it almost broke my heart to leave Bloomers. And then when I had to put her up for sale . . ." Lottie paused to wipe tears from her eyes, unable to continue.

"I came along and here we are." I was getting a little misty-eyed myself, so I picked up the stack of orders and handed them to her. "These are finished and in the cooler. Is there anything else I can do?"

"That'll do it." Lottie put an arm around me and walked me toward the curtain. "Now we can both go home and enjoy the rest of the day."

"If I didn't know better, I'd think you were trying to get rid of me," I joked.

The bell jingled again and then I heard Grace's chipper, "Halloo? Lottie?" A moment later she came in carrying a big plate of muffins. She stopped short when she saw me, then said lightly, "Good heavens, dear. I didn't expect to see you here. How are you?"

I caught a quick exchange between the two, so I said, "Okay, what's going on?"

Grace looked from me to Lottie. "You tell her. I'll start the kettle for tea."

I folded my arms and waited. Giving me a sheepish glance, Lottie opened a cabinet and pulled out a spindle stacked high with orders. "We didn't want you to have any more stress, so we've been coming in on our free time to keep up."

I wasn't slow after all. They needed me! "I love you guys."

Over tea and cranberry muffins, I brought them up to speed on the murder investigation, then we put on our aprons and set to work. With the three of us snipping and clipping and sharing laughs, it felt like old times, until I glanced at the clock and saw that it was two thirty—almost time to meet Connor—and that was the end of our happy reunion.

I raced back to my apartment, shed the coat and hat, and found a note from Nikki saying that she had gone shopping with her mother. Good. She wouldn't be around to witness the debacle, because once I had that photo I intended to give Connor a piece of my mind.

My cell phone chirped softly, so I raced to the bedroom, dug it out of my purse, and flipped it open. "Hello?"

"Abby, this is Bea. You wanted to talk to me?"

I glanced at my watch. Five minutes until Connor was due. "Thanks for returning my call. I really need to see you. Will you be home later this afternoon?"

"Honestly, Abby, I don't have time. I'm at the law school right now trying to finish a stack of dictation. I'm leaving for a week's vacation and my friend will be here in an hour to pick me up."

"I can drop by the school. It won't take long."

"Well . . . I suppose."

"I'll be there in half an hour." The doorbell buzzed, so I ended the conversation, tossed the phone onto the bed, and dashed to the front door.

"Look who I found in the hallway," Jillian gushed. "Connor Mackay! And he has something for you." In a stage whisper he was bound to have heard she said, "Isn't he quixy!"

"Quixy?" I whispered back. That was a new one.

"Quietly sexy," she said in my ear, then turned her beautiful smile on him. I had to admit he looked dashing—in an Indiana Jones kind of way. He had on a mint green button-down shirt that played up his eyes, with a beat-up brown leather bomber jacket, khakis, and brown loafers.

"What are we standing here for?" Jillian asked, threading her hand through his arm. "Let's have a seat in the living room. Would you like something to drink, Connor? We have lite beer, white wine, soda."

I tried to grab her sleeve and drag her back, but she was too quick on her feet.

"No, thanks," Connor told her.

I trailed after them as my cousin steered Connor toward the sofa. "Why don't you have a seat beside him, Abby?" She tried to make it sound like a question, but I recognized that militant spark in her eye.

I sat down and narrowed my gaze on her, seething, but she merely settled in the adjacent chair and folded her hands in her lap. She would pay for this big-time. Not only was I going to tell Claymore where she lived, but I'd personally take him to her door.

"So Abby tells me there was an article about her in the newspaper." Jillian smiled at Connor, as though waiting for him to pick up the thread of conversation.

"Yes, and please tell us about that headline, too," I said dryly.

"That wasn't my headline, Abby." He saw my icy glare and added, "I'll just give you the photo and leave, okay?"

"Photo?" Jillian jumped up from the chair and sat beside him. "Let's see."

Connor glanced at me and I nodded my consent. Was there any use trying to hide it from her? He handed me a manila envelope from which I removed a five-by-seven, glossy, black-and-white print. Jillian leaned across Connor to look at it with me, then covered her mouth and snickered.

There I was in shackles, my mouth open, obviously shouting at Carson Reed, who was speaking into the microphones that had been shoved under his face. Next to him was Marvin Y. Brown. And just behind them were Dustin and Kenny, looking very self-important.

"Hey!" Jillian tapped the print with a long, ice pink fingernail. "Those are the two guys who helped me look for Peewee."

I gazed at her in surprise. "The ones in the gray minivan? Are you sure?"

"I never forget a man's face." She winked at Connor.

Were Kenny and Dustin the petnappers? No wonder Kenny had lied about knowing Marvin Brown. He was working for the man. "I need to make a call. I'll be right back."

I shut myself in the bedroom, opened my cell phone, and hit speed-dial number two. As soon as Marco answered I said, "The two guys in the newspaper photo *were* Kenny and Dustin, so Kenny *did* lie to me. And you'll never believe this. Jillian recognized them as being the same guys she saw in our parking lot in the gray minivan. They could be part of a petnapping ring, Marco!"

"Whoa. Slow down. Did Jillian see them take the dog? Did she get a license plate number? Gray minivans are pretty common."

"No to both questions, but come on, it's a strong coincidence."

"You're right. I'll call Reilly and run it past him. He'll probably want to see the photo."

"I'll keep it in my purse. I'm going to be leaving shortly to talk to Bea."

"Call me afterward."

When I returned to the living room, Jillian was just shutting the front door. I glanced around, puzzled. "Where's Connor?"

"He left. But don't worry, he'll be back at seven thirty this evening."

"You made a *date* for me?"

"No, silly. He's coming to see me."

"You can't do that, Jillian. You're still married to Claymore. If you want to date Connor, you need to file for divorce."

"I don't want to date Connor. I want to sell him new clothes. Did you see those pants he was wearing?"

She started for the door, but this time I did manage to get ahold of her sleeve. "Not so fast. What about Claymore?"

"What *about* Claymore?" she cried, trying to shake me loose.

"You can't keep him twisting in the wind, Jillian. It isn't fair to him."

"It serves him right for leaving me. Would you let go of my sleeve?"

"Claymore didn't leave you. You walked out on him, and don't you dare deny it."

She gasped in outrage. "You talked to him?"

"You love Claymore. How could you break his heart?"

"Better now than later."

"What are you talking about?"

She heaved a sigh and turned to face me. "I left him because I couldn't bear for him to find out what a horrendous wife I'd be. Look at me. I'm silly and selfish and totally inept. I can't cook—not that I'd want to, but what if I did? The only thing I know how to make is Jello. Plain Jello! I don't even know how to add fruit to it."

"Jillian, you are not"—actually, she *was* silly and selfish— "totally inept. You have more fashion sense than anyone I know. Look how you pulled together those outfits for me. If you want to be a better wife, get counseling. If you don't know how to cook, sign up for a class. But for God's sake, knock off the pity party. Beneath your selfish exterior is a gentle, loving woman who just needs to believe in herself a little more and trust in those who love her."

She looked at me in surprise. "Really?"

"You don't think Claymore is an idiot, do you? So why would he choose an inept wife? Listen to me. He married you because he truly loves you, but he won't wait forever. You can't let your selfish side win in this, Jillian. Call him right now and tell him you made a huge mistake and you're sorry."

She gave me an exuberant hug, pressing my forehead against her collarbone. "Little Abs, you are the best. Thank you! I really needed that pep talk."

"So you'll call Claymore?" I asked as she jumped up and headed for the door.

"No." She paused to glance over her shoulder. "But I appreciate all the nice things you said about me."

I grabbed a pillow from the sofa and heaved it at the door as it shut behind her. So she wouldn't see Claymore, hmm? We'd see about that. I threw the dead bolt, looked up Claymore's phone number, and called him. "Hey, it's Abby. You wouldn't happen to need a new suit, would you? You do? Great. Meet me at my apartment at seven this evening."

Fearing I'd missed my chance to talk to Bea, I sped to the law school, where I found her seated at her desk, her fingers flying over the keyboard, her eyes fixed on the monitor. She was dressed in a white peasant blouse and long brown suede skirt, her heavy hair tied at the nape with a leather cord. Silver earrings shaped like feathers dangled from her earlobes, a yellow pencil was tucked behind one ear, and a turquoise-encrusted Native American totem hung on a silver chain around her neck.

I didn't think she'd noticed me, but without turning her head in my direction she said, "I'll be right with you, Abby." She hit a key, then turned to watch the big printer behind her clatter to life.

I wheeled over a chair from another secretary's desk and sat down, taking a quick glance around. None of the other secretaries were there, and all of the office windows were dark—with one exception. The Dragon's. *Damn.* "Professor Puffer is here?" I whispered.

"He came in shortly after I arrived, in quite a temper, too."

Great. He'd probably seen the newspaper. I crossed my fingers and hoped he'd stay put for the five minutes I needed to be there. "This won't take long, I promise. I just need to ask you a few questions about the day of the murder."

She sighed impatiently. "You know I'd like to oblige, but I've already told you everything."

"But some new information has come to light."

She pulled the pencil out from behind her ear and tossed it on her desk. "You'll have to be quick."

Feeling suddenly anxious, I rubbed my hands together. This was the woman who'd been there for me during some of the worst moments of my life. I couldn't grill her like a common criminal. But I couldn't keep beating around the bush, either. Maybe I'd try tact again. "Would it surprise you to learn that Jocelyn Puffer had been seeing Professor Reed?"

Bea gazed at me with her mouth open, clearly at a loss for words. "I'd never dreamed . . . Jocelyn Puffer? I certainly wouldn't have expected that of her."

"But wouldn't you have expected it of Professor Reed—especially in light of Hannah's relationship with him?"

She waved away my question as if it were a gnat. "That silly crush she had on him? It was nothing but a romantic fantasy."

"It wasn't a fantasy to her. Hannah thought they were going to elope. She truly believed he loved her."

"Hannah is a child. I told her Carson Reed had no intention of marrying her, or anyone else for that matter."

"You also told Hannah you'd take care of everything. What did you mean by that?"

"That I'd talk to him. What do you think I meant?"

"Is that all you did?" I asked as kindly as I could. "Talk to him?"

She stared at me for a long moment; then her eyes widened. "So, it was me you were referring to in the newspaper article? You're ready to name me as the killer? Do you truly think I would take another human being's life?"

"I don't want to think so, Bea, but I know how much you love Hannah."

"Which is why I confronted Professor Reed about her Tuesday morning. I may have stepped out of bounds—he was one of my bosses, after all—but my duty to Hannah comes first. I told him in no uncertain terms to stay away from her or I'd report him for sexual harassment. That got his attention, believe me. But I certainly didn't kill the man."

"Did anyone see or hear you talk to him?"

"Professor Puffer did. He called me into his office afterward and asked me what had happened, but I refused to tell him. It was none of his business."

I glanced over at the Dragon's office, where all was quiet, thank God. "Did you tell the police about your confrontation with Reed?"

"My niece is none of their business, either—but, yes, I did tell them."

I was so relieved I wanted to hug her. But there was still another hurdle to get over. "When you left here at noon, where did you go?"

"To see Hannah. When I learned she wasn't in, I went home. My landlady has already verified that for the detectives. I love Hannah as my own child, Abby, and I'd do just about anything to keep her from being hurt, but I would never kill another human being." She took my hands in hers and gazed into my eyes. "Please promise me you won't let this get out. It's been terribly difficult for Hannah and I don't want to see her suffer any further. After all, Carson Reed is dead, and she's safe, so there's really no reason to drag their names through the mud, is there?"

"You're right."

"Thank you," she said, smiling for the first time.

Suddenly, there was a loud crash from Puffer's office. At my gasp, Bea shook her head. "He still throws things when he's upset." She glanced at her watch. "I really must hurry. I still have to get some things ready for mailing."

I wanted to hurry, too—away from Puffer. I thanked Bea for her time, wished her a safe trip, and started for the stairway, satisfied that I could cross her off the list.

"Abby, just a moment," Bea called. "Remember the letters you asked about, the ones Professor Reed was supposed to send out to the clerkship applicants? Surprisingly, they're right here in my dictation."

I hurried back for a look. In front of her was a short stack of handwritten notes with envelopes. "Would you mind if I glanced through them?"

I could tell by the pursing of her lips that she was debating the ethics issue. But I *had* promised to keep Hannah's secret. Surely that was worth a peek. "Tell you what," I said. "I'll even stuff and stamp them for you—I remember how to work the stamp machine—then I'll drop them in the mail on my way home."

She considered my offer for a moment, then smiled. "That would help a lot."

As soon as she was gone, I sat down at her desk and pulled the stack toward me. But before I had a chance to look at them, Puffer's door opened, and from inside his office he yelled, "Boyd! Come in here."

My stomach lurched. I was alone with the Dragon. And I wasn't wearing a disguise. *ZAP.*

CHAPTER TWENTY-EIGHT

"Bea just left," I called nervously. "Sorry."

Puffer stuck his head out and saw me, and his face went purple. "You!" he bellowed, charging toward me. "How dare you show your face around here!"

"I'm just helping Bea," I squeaked, cringing as he came to a stop on the other side of the desk.

"After what you told that reporter, you should be banned from this school for life."

What *I* told the reporter? That did it. I shot to my feet, all five feet two inches of me, sending the chair skittering backward. Fire-breathing dragon or not, he wasn't getting away with that nonsense. "How about what you've been saying about *me,* Professor? You've done everything in your power to make me look guilty, so don't even try to criticize me for defending myself. Talk about nerve!" I huffed loudly and glared at him, hoping he'd back down. Boy, was I an optimist.

Puffer moved slowly around the desk, like a hungry lion

circling a lame gazelle. "You're here to spy on me, aren't you? To collect more nonsense to feed to the press."

His eyes were glittering madly, and I was starting to sweat. "That's not why I'm here."

"Sure it is. You want everyone to think I murdered that son of a bitch Reed."

"Wait a minute. Reed was found in *your* office with *your* pencil in his neck, so it's not a big stretch for people to conclude that you killed him."

"All based on circumstance, not fact," he sneered. "Or can't you tell the difference? Fact. A can of black pencils sits on my desk within easy reach. Fact. Reed came into my office to discuss my tenure application, which, for your information, the police found on the desk. Fact. I was short on time, so we agreed to meet later, as my appointment book shows. What happened afterward is pure conjecture. Is it any wonder you flunked my class?"

That hurt. But since the Dragon was towering above me, looking very ugly and threatening, I kept silent and looked around for a means of escape.

Suddenly, I heard footsteps on the stairs and turned to see Kenny carrying a stack of boxes toward Carson Reed's office. He peered around them and saw us. "I'm supposed to start packing up Professor Reed's office. I hope that's okay."

"It's fine," I called. *Really, really fine*. Whether Kenny was a pet thief or not, it was better than being alone with Puffer.

As he continued into Reed's office, I turned my gaze back to the Dragon, and although my insides were still trembling, I managed to retrieve the chair and sit in it, crossing my arms over my chest and saying nonchalantly, "I think you should leave now."

And the award for Best Actress in a Tense Situation goes to . . . Abby Knight!

I'd get no applause from Puffer. In fact, he looked as

though he would have liked to go for my throat, but he wouldn't dare touch me now, not with Kenny there.

At that very moment Kenny came out of Reed's office and headed for the stairs. My heart sank to the level of my ankle bones. "Leaving so soon?" I called.

"Just going for more boxes. Back in a sec."

"Want some help?"

"I've got it," he called from halfway down the steps. I risked a peek at the Dragon. Dear God.

His eyes were slits of rage, glaring with such intensity that I could feel my skin blistering. He grabbed the back of the chair and spun me around so I couldn't see him, then he leaned down from behind me to snarl in my right ear, "I never did like you, Knight. I knew you were trouble from the moment you first bounced into my lecture hall." He swung the chair in the other direction, whispering into my left ear, "You know what you need?"

Rescuing?

At that moment Kenny came up again, panting slightly. Instantly, Puffer released my chair and stepped back.

"More boxes," Kenny called and disappeared into the office.

I shot out of the chair, ready to flee if Puffer came at me again. But he simply shook his fist and snarled, "I'm not done with you, Betty Boob." Then he stalked back to his office.

Kenny came out again and headed for the steps. "Last trip," he called, then he took a look at me and paused. "Is everything all right?"

I sank into the chair and dropped my head into my hands. "It got a little tense there for a moment but it's okay now. Stick around for awhile, okay?"

"It was that article in today's paper, wasn't it?" Kenny asked as he strolled toward me. "I'll bet the old Dragon was fuming. He's got to be worried, especially if you really *are* close to naming the killer."

"I never should have talked to the reporter," I said with a groan.

Kenny snickered. "They're almost as bad as lawyers when it comes to twisting words. He started to turn away, then noticed the letters on the desk between us. "Is that Professor Reed's stationery?"

"Some of his mail didn't get out last week. I'm taking care of it for Bea."

The news seemed to unsettle him—or maybe he was merely being curious as he craned his neck for a closer look. Whatever the reason for his interest, it had my inner alarm buzzing. When that happens, I don't ask why, I just act. I leaned forward, my hands covering the names on the envelopes. "They're thank-you notes."

"Professor Reed didn't mention anything to me about sending out thank-you notes."

I shrugged, wishing I could get him off the subject. Then I remembered the newspaper photo. "Say, Kenny, I have a question for you. Didn't you tell me you met Marvin Brown for the first time on the day of the memorial service?"

"That's right."

He was still trying to see the names, so I dropped my purse on top of the envelopes and dug out the print. "Take a look at this. Isn't that you standing behind Brown?"

He gave it a cursory glance and tossed it back. "It appears that way."

"So you *did* meet him before the service."

"All right, Abby. You caught me. But give me a break. Everyone knows how you feel about Dermacol. Can you blame me for not wanting you to find out I was doing their legal legwork?"

"I thought Reed was handling it."

"Officially, yes, but *I* did the research," he said proudly, thumping his chest. "*I* wrote the briefs. The only thing he did was sign his name to them."

"Please tell me that's all you were doing for them, Kenny."

"What do you mean?"

"I mean, someone has been stealing pets for their lab."

He burst out with a sharp laugh, as if he couldn't believe what I'd just said. "You're accusing *me* of stealing them? Why would I do something as stupid as that?"

"I don't know. Why does anyone steal? For money?"

"Obviously," he said, looking bemused, "you're forgetting who I am. I *have* money."

Why hadn't I noticed before now how much he resembled his father—right down to the attitude? "You mean your father has money, don't you?"

"Same pocket," he said with a dismissive shrug.

I dangled the black-and-white glossy in front of him. "You and your buddy Dustin were identified from this picture as being the same guys seen in a gray minivan shortly after a Chihuahua disappeared."

"You know what, Abby? I'm betting lots of people ride in gray minivans. All that picture proves is that I was at that protest march."

Damn. He had me there. "We also have photos of a gray minivan driving into the Dermacol facility just after it was used to snatch a dog."

"And that connects me to the thefts how?"

It didn't connect him at all, and I was out of ways to get him to confess. The problem was, I was also more convinced than ever that he was involved. "Then you're flat-out denying you had anything to do with the pet thefts?"

He gave me a look of disgust. "What do you think?" Then he walked away, shaking his head as though he couldn't believe how absurd I was.

Frustrated, I called after him, "I don't believe you, Kenny."

"You know what? I don't care. Try to prove it."

"I will."

At least he'd forgotten about the letters. And how cleverly he had avoided giving straight answers to my questions. He strode back to Reed's office, where I heard him tossing books into boxes. I'd rattled him; that was evident by the noise he was making. Good. There wasn't much I could do about Dermacol's testing policies, but I was going to find a way to connect him to those pet thefts.

I glanced over at Puffer's office, surprised to see that his light was out. He must have left while I was talking to Kenny. Odd that I hadn't heard the elevator ding. *Okay, Abby. Get those letters stuffed before he decides to come back and make good on his threat.*

I started to stuff the top letter into the envelope but couldn't resist taking a peek first.

Dear Ms. Albertson,
I regret to inform you that you were not selected for the clerkship available in the Seventh Circuit Court of Appeals. Please know that this decision was not easy, as all candidates were highly qualified. Good luck in your future endeavors.
Carson Reed.

Poor Ms. Albertson. How disappointing it would be to get that rejection. I slid it into the envelope, then picked up the next one. The name stopped me in surprise.

Dear Mr. Lipinksi,
I regret to inform you that you were not selected for the clerkship available in the Seventh Circuit Court of Appeals. Please know that this decision was not easy,

*as all candidates were highly qualified. Good luck in
your future endeavors.*
　　Carson Reed.

Kenny was rejected?

I got up and walked over to Reed's office, where I found
Kenny pulling file folders from the desk. He looked up with
a scowl. "What now?"

"Professor Reed told you in person that he'd selected you
for the clerkship, right?"

"Yes." He gave the drawer a shove and rose, a distrustful
look in his eyes. "Why?"

My inner alarm was starting to buzz, so all I said was, "I
was just wondering."

He stared at me, not saying a word, so I returned to Bea's
desk to ponder the matter. There had to be a mix-up. Kenny
was arrogant but, as he'd pointed out, he wasn't stupid. He
wouldn't claim something he didn't have, especially something as big as a federal clerkship. Reed must have written
Kenny's letter, then had a change of heart.

Or had he? As Marco had pointed out, everything we
knew about Reed giving the clerkship to Kenny *came* from
Kenny. I thought back to the first time he mentioned what
Reed had done for him: *"He'd just secured a clerkship for
me with a federal appellate judge. I hadn't even had a
chance to thank him."*

But if Reed had told him in person, wouldn't Kenny have
thanked him then?

Too many things weren't adding up. I needed someone to
look at the facts objectively. I turned my back on Reed's office, pulled out my cell phone, and hit speed-dial number
two. "Marco, listen to this," I whispered. "I just found a letter Carson Reed wrote to Kenny telling him he'd been
turned down for the clerkship. The letter was dated Monday,

yet Kenny says Reed informed him Monday afternoon that he'd been selected. Something's not right."

"Where are you?"

"At the law school. Kenny is here packing up Reed's office and Puffer was in earlier, but he left, thank God. So what do you think? Am I right to be suspicious?"

"If Kenny was rejected, then someone else must have been chosen? Any way to check on that?"

I shuffled through the remaining letters. "There's nothing here. Maybe I'm wrong, and Kenny did get the clerkship. Maybe Reed changed his mind and forgot to pull his letter."

"Have you told Kenny about it?"

"Not yet."

"Good. Put it in your purse and come back here. I've got new information."

I glanced at the Dragon's dark window. "About Puffer?"

"About his phone."

"I knew it! He replaced it, didn't he?"

"He probably had to. After I told Reilly what you remembered about the handset lying in Reed's lap, the cops went to his office to confiscate it as evidence. Good thing, too, since the lab tests showed it was used to deliver a blow to Reed's head. But get this. Reilly checked his original notes. When he arrived at the murder scene, the handset was in the base, yet no fingerprints, not even Puffer's, were found on it. Someone wiped it clean and put it back. Luckily, they were able to find traces of scalp on it."

"I'm confused. It couldn't have been Puffer who put it back. He didn't arrive until *after* Reilly got there."

"Are you sure he wasn't up there earlier?"

I thought back to the moment I found Reed's body, then I ran through the events up to when I stepped out of the office for air while Kenny got ready to heave into the wastebasket. If Puffer had returned then, Kenny would have seen him. Besides, Reilly had shown up a few minutes later, so it couldn't have been Puffer.

That left Kenny.

All at once, the hairs on the back of my neck rose. Then I caught the faintest sound near my ear, like an indrawn breath.

Someone was standing behind me.

CHAPTER TWENTY-NINE

Goose bumps covered my skin. It had to be Kenny . . . unless Puffer came back—or had never left.

"Marco," I whispered urgently, but before I could say more, the phone was yanked from my fingers. I turned with a gasp. There stood Kenny, face composed, body relaxed— the picture of calm. He snapped the phone shut, then extended his other hand. "I'll take those letters."

I didn't know how long he'd been standing there, or how much of the conversation he'd heard, but if I'd accidentally tipped him off, I needed to hang on to Reed's letters for evidence. "I told you, Kenny, they're just thank-you notes. Why would you want a bunch of thank-you notes?"

Kenny slammed his fist against the desktop, rattling everything within a five-foot radius—including me, making me jerk back with a gasp. "Don't play games with me, Abby. You're not smart enough to win."

Normally, I'd take exception to that remark, but Kenny was scaring me. I'd never seen him react so violently. "Hey, no problem," I said, holding up my hands. Who would have ever believed that I'd wish Snapdragon had stuck around? I hoped Marco had figured out I was in trouble and called the cops. But if he hadn't . . .

I eyed the silver cell phone in Kenny's hand. An idea was forming, but I wasn't sure if I dared try it. As he reached toward the pile of letters and envelopes, I threw my arms around them and drew them toward me. "Tell you what. I'll trade you these letters for my phone."

It was a long shot, but for some reason Kenny bought it, probably because my demand was unexpected, or maybe because he couldn't hold on to both the phone and the papers. He wiped his prints off the shiny surface with the hem of his shirt, then, holding the phone with his shirttail, he tossed it onto the desk. "Now put it in your purse."

My purse was sitting on the other side of the monitor, the open end facing me. I placed the phone inside. "There you go. All done."

He held out his hand and wiggled his fingers impatiently. "The letters."

"Listen, Kenny," I said, making a neat stack of the envelopes to stall for time, "I'm sorry Professor Reed lied to you about getting the clerkship. I know you had your hopes up, but there are other positions available."

"I don't know what you're talking about. I *got* the clerkship."

I tapped the top letter. "Then this is a mistake?"

"That's right." His gaze narrowed, as if daring me to contradict him. Either I had it figured wrong or there was some major denial going on in his head.

Time to put my plan into action. I eased my chair to the left. "It's lucky we caught the mistake, then, because you damn well deserved that clerkship." As I talked, I slid my left hand into my purse, hidden from his view by the monitor, and used my thumb and index finger to flip open the phone. "Even Bea said you were the obvious choice."

Just as I was feeling for the redial button, Kenny reached for the pencil on the desk. Having a sudden vision of the black stub protruding from Reed's neck, I shrank back with a gasp. Kenny was onto my plan!

But he merely twirled it between his fingers, watching it spin. "Damn right I deserve that position. I worked my ass off for Reed. I did everything he asked, every menial chore, even if it meant staying up all night. So why wouldn't I be his choice?"

My shoulders sagged in relief. Slowly, I felt for the redial button again and pressed it, then eased my hand out of the purse, praying Marco would pick up and realize what was happening. "But even if you hadn't been selected, Kenny," I said loudly as I arranged the letters alongside the envelopes, "you were the one who said this clerkship wasn't a matter of life or death."

"Not for the average law student, perhaps." He leaned toward me, his hands braced on the desk. "But for someone of my caliber, Abby, it's the opportunity of a lifetime, a springboard to a whole new world. Do you think I could let that get away? I mean, think about it. The Justice Department, Washington, D.C., power, prestige, independence—the sky's the limit for a man with my brains and ambition. It's my ticket out of New Chapel, secured without my father's influence or control. I'll be in the federal system and finally be able to say 'To hell with Kent Lipinski.' "

"But not getting the clerkship doesn't stop you from leaving town and taking a position with a firm in, say, New York. Like you said, the sky's the limit."

He wagged his index finger in my face. "In the Lipinksi family, sons don't leave home. They follow in their fathers' footsteps. The name must be carried on, blah, blah, blah.

And if we dare do otherwise, Kent Lipinski will fix that. Ask my brother, the, *quote,* junior partner."

Kenny began to pace in front of the desk. "Let me tell you how it is, Abby. There's an office already waiting for me at my dad's firm, with my name on the door. He's even picked out the furniture and artwork. Oh, and let's not forget the house he bought for me—next door to his, of course. My wife will be his choice, too. I hear he's interviewing candidates next week."

Kenny came around to crouch beside my chair, his pupils fully dilated, giving him a maniacal appearance. "Do you see why I have to have this federal clerkship? I have to be more powerful than he is so I won't ever have to answer to him again." He smacked the pencil on the side of the desk. "Ever!"

He was totally bonkers.

I shot a quick glance toward my purse and froze. Oh, no. If Kenny looked beyond my shoulder he would see my open phone.

Diversionary tactics! that little voice in my head cried. *He's a male. For God's sake, Abby, use your boobs!* I arched my back as though I were stretching, effectively thrusting my breasts in his face. "Kenny, I really do understand," I said, sliding my chair to one side, drawing his bulging eyeballs with me. "This is your future, your freedom. You deserve the best."

For a second, I thought I had him, but then, giving me a canny look, he got to his feet, holding the pencil as though it were a fencing sword. "You're playing games with me again."

"Trust me," I muttered, "the last I feel like doing is playing a game." I shot a quick glance at my phone, praying that someone was on the other end, because I was about to prod Kenny into a confession. "Okay, how about if we strike a bargain? I'll give you the letters if you tell me why Reed rejected you."

"I told you I *got* the position," he snapped.

"Come on, Kenny," I urged gently, trying not to provoke his anger. "We both know you didn't."

"Yes, I did!" he bellowed, pounding the desk with his palm Clearly, I hadn't been gentle enough. "It was *promised* to me. Don't you understand? People can't renege on promises."

Was he delusional? People always reneged on their— At once, the whole picture became clear in my mind. "Reed broke his promise to you, didn't he, Kenny? You went to see him, hoping to get him to change his mind."

"Shut up!" Kenny yelled, clapping his hands over his ears. "Stop talking!"

Right. Like that was a possibility. *I hope you're listening, Marco, because here goes everything.* "I know rejection hurts, Kenny. I've been through it. But did you really think you could kill the professor and get away with it?"

"I said shut up!" he cried, brandishing the pencil inches from my face. "Give me the friggin' letters!"

Being threatened by a man who had recently stabbed someone had the effect of reducing my limbs to the consistency of wet noodles, which wouldn't be too helpful if I had to run for my life. *Take a deep breath, Abby. There you go. Now keep him talking until the cops arrive.*

"Okay, Kenny," I forced myself to say. "The letters are right here. So calm down and think this through. You can't pretend to get a clerkship. If Reed didn't give it to you, he gave it to someone else. Destroying these letters doesn't change that."

"*Wrong,* Abby. Professor Reed told me he was considering two other candidates, but he hadn't notified anyone yet. He wanted to break the news to me first. So all I need to do is get rid of the letters, then it's your word against mine—and let me remind you, *you're* the suspect, Abby. Not me."

At least he hadn't decided he had to get rid of me, as well. I snuck a quick peek at the clock on Bea's desk, wondering how much longer I could stall. Where were the cops? What if my phone call hadn't gone through? Should I make a run for the stairs?

"You're right, Kenny. The cops won't take my word for it. What I still don't get is why Reed didn't pick you, especially after all you did for him."

He snorted contemptuously. "Ironic, isn't it? Kenny Lipinski, the guy with everything—intelligence, ambition, loyalty—fetching, carrying, humbling myself for that *asshole* . . ."

"Stealing pets," I put in.

"Would you give it a rest?" he said irritably.

And lose the chance to play for more time? No way. "Okay, look, I understand that you humbled yourself to get the clerkship, but why would you take people's pets?"

"Because it made me look good. Brown needed animals, I supplied manpower, Reed was grateful."

I stared at him in amazement. A nutcase without a conscience. Just what the world needed more of.

"And after all that, Reed had the nerve to say I wasn't qualified," Kenny continued. "Me! The guy who did all the work for Dermacol while he took all the credit—*I* wasn't qualified. He didn't think I could handle the pressure. Do you believe that? I was doing his work *and* mine and he told me I couldn't handle pressure, that maybe I should see a shrink."

Reed was smarter than I'd thought. "Actually, it wouldn't hurt to talk to someone, Kenny."

He thrust the pointed tip against my throat. "Give me the letters."

"Okay," I whispered, keeping perfectly still. "Could you give me a little room to move?"

We were almost eyeball-to-eyeball, and Kenny glared at me, making me think my minutes on earth were numbered. Then, thank heavens, he lowered the pencil. Moving cautiously, I scooped up the letters and envelopes and got to my feet, frantically searching for an escape. When in doubt, punt, my dad always told me. Since punting wasn't possible, I did the next best thing. I tossed the envelopes high into the air. Then I ran.

"Shit! Why did you do that? Shit!"

I could hear his feet pounding against the floor as he raced after me. My heart slammed against my rib cage as I eyed the staircase ahead. At least I'd had the advantage of surprise. Another few yards and I'd be at the top.

Suddenly my head was jerked backward as he lunged at me and caught a handful of my hair. I lost my balance and nearly fell backward, but managed to right myself only to be dragged away from the steps like a cave woman captured by some heavy-browed brute. "That was stupid!" he cried. "I was going to let you go."

Was going to let me go? I grabbed hold of the corner of the wall. "There's no reason why you still can't."

"It's too late." He released my hair to wrap his arms around my waist for better leverage.

"It's never too late, Kenny," I gasped, struggling to keep my grip. "All you have to do is explain to the cops that Professor Reed lied to you and you just wanted to ask him to change his mind. You never meant to kill him. That's what happened, isn't it? You must have gone to see him right after I left, and found him in Puffer's office, talking on the phone."

"He brushed me off!" Kenny cried, his hold on me loosening. "I begged him to reconsider the clerkship, and he told me to grow up. He said I should stop being a coward and learn to face my father like a man. Then he turned his back on me, like I was a nobody."

"So you grabbed the phone from his hand," I prompted, "and then what?"

"I hit him," Kenny said in a cold voice. "He fell back against the chair, staring at me, and I knew he was thinking, 'You'll always be a coward.'"

"And that's when you stabbed him."

"I thought Professor Reed was different, but he was just like my father, an arrogant, lying bastard. You want to know the real reason why he rejected me for the clerkship? Because my father paid him to."

Wow. No wonder Kenny had snapped. Everything he'd worked for and counted on had been taken away because of one man's greed and another's need for control. But it didn't justify murder. A normal person might have been furious about the rejection, be he wouldn't have followed it up with a stabbing. Clearly, Kenny was not a normal person.

"So when you realized what you'd done, you ran out the back and took the elevator to the main floor?"

"That's right. Then I took the steps up to the computer lab, and a few moments later you called for help. I couldn't have planned it to work out that perfectly. When you shouted for help, I had to stop myself from laughing." There was no remorse or sorrow in his expression, only a look of immense satisfaction.

"But you didn't know Reed had already written the rejection letters."

"It was the only glitch. No one would have ever known I'd been rejected if you hadn't found that letter. But there's still time to fix that." He caught my arm and pulled me toward the computer lab, which I wasn't about to let happen without a struggle. Once inside the lab, Kenny could lock the door and make mincemeat of me.

"Police! Fire!" I yelled at the top of my lungs, wrestling to get free, hoping someone, anyone, was downstairs.

He clamped a hand over my mouth, so I clawed at it, but my short nails didn't even break the skin. I tried to kick his shins, but he only lifted me in the air, his arms squeezing my ribs so tightly I couldn't breathe. Finally, I went limp, making myself dead weight, slipping through his arms like a bag of wet sand.

Before he could react, I sprang to my feet and backed away from him. "Kenny, stop," I cried as he came toward me, the pencil a dagger in his hand. "You can still work out something with the prosecutor. Extenuating circumstances. Mitigating factors. A crime of passion. Don't make it worse by killing me, too."

He wiped sweat off his upper lip. "I was thinking along the lines of temporary insanity."

"For two murders? You can't use the same defense twice. It'll never wash with a jury."

No reaction. He wasn't thinking clearly. What would it take to get through to him?

"Kenny, listen to me. Do you know what your father will do when he finds out you've committed murder? He'll come to your defense. He'll be at your side every step of the way. If he gets you off with an insanity plea, you'll be indebted to him for the rest of your life. Or maybe you'll get life without parole, and then he'll come see you every week to remind you what a screwup you are."

I didn't know where those words were coming from, but they were working. Kenny used the back of his hand, with the pencil still in it, to wipe the sweat out of his eyes. "Then my father wins again."

"You can't let that happen. You'd better think of a new plan."

His eyebrows drew together as he considered my words, giving me the distraction I needed to dash for the staircase, nearly tripping in my haste to descend. But before I could reach the bottom he tackled me and we rolled down the last three steps, landing in front of the glass doors. I scrambled in the opposite direction and raced up the hall just as a ding sounded and the elevator door slid open. And there stood Puffer.

I gaped at him in surprise. He'd been upstairs the whole time—while I'd been defending my life.

Puffer grabbed my arm and dragged me inside just as Kenny lunged for me. Pushing me aside, Puffer shoved him hard, sending him staggering backward, then he shoved him again, until Kenny hit the wall and slid down, a stunned look on his face.

At once, the front doors burst open and cops poured in, with Reilly in the lead.

"Here's your man," Puffer thundered, as a mass of blue shirts moved forward.

I spotted Marco trying to get through, and, as much as I wanted to run to him, I had some unfinished business with Puffer to take care of first. "Professor, your light was out. I thought you'd left."

"As usual, you thought wrong," he snapped.

"You must have heard us struggling. Why didn't you step in sooner?"

He reached into his pocket and pulled out a minirecorder. "The man was confessing. Why would I interrupt that?"

"How about to save my life?"

"I did save your life," he said gruffly.

Which was amazing, now that I thought about it. Could there be a little softness under that crusty shell after all? Impetuously, I put my hand on his arm. "You're right. You did."

He glared at my hand until I removed it. "Well, someone had to do it. You were clearly incapable of doing it yourself."

I took the insult with my lips pressed together, then forced out the words that had to be said. "Thank you."

"You want to thank me? Stay the hell away from me." He turned to talk to Reilly.

"I'd be more than happy to oblige, Professor," I muttered. For a moment I just watched him—this harsh man who had caused me so many sleepless nights—and suddenly I realized that my fear of him had vanished. I wasn't afraid anymore. What an incredible feeling of freedom!

A hand on my back made me turn, and there stood Marco, looking good enough to eat. I threw myself into his arms and buried my head against his solid chest. "My phone call worked!"

"You bet it did. And I recorded the whole thing. Good job, Sunshine."

"Go, Abby," I muttered against his shirt, starting to tremble from my ordeal.

"Take it easy," he breathed into my ear, stroking my hair. "You're safe."

Yes. I *was* safe—from Kenny as well as from a fear of Puffer that had plagued me since I'd left law school. For some odd reason I started to giggle, and that turned into a guffaw, and then I was hanging on to him, laughing my fool head off as I tried to impart the hilarity of the situation. A dragon had rescued a Knight!

Marco held me away, searching my face in concern. "Are you laughing?"

I nodded, then burst into tears. Reilly came over to see what was going on, and Marco said, "I need to get her home. She's a little stressed."

"Understandable. I'll get her statement tomorrow."

That was the best thing anyone had said all day.

Because Marco had hitched a ride with Reilly, I let him drive my car home, which was especially helpful since my hands wouldn't stop trembling. Not only that, but I couldn't stop talking. It was like my brain was on fast-forward as I recounted my harrowing afternoon, describing how Reed's murder had unfolded, and how I had remembered too late that Kenny had been alone in Puffer's office with Reed's body.

I wrapped up my story just as we stopped at the China Cabinet to get some takeout. While Marco was inside the restaurant, I checked my cell phone and saw that Connor Mackay had tried to reach me. Connor! Oh, no. I hadn't canceled his appointment with Jillian. If I didn't do that quickly I'd ruin my plan. I checked my watch and saw that it was just a little after five o'clock—plenty of time to call it off.

"Hey, Connor, this is Abby," I said to his voice mail. "If you want the scoop on the murder, get over to the jail now. The killer has been caught. Oh, and Jillian said she can't see you tonight after all. Something came up. She'll call to reschedule. Bye."

That would keep him away for the evening. Then I called Nikki. "Hey, Nik, I need a favor. First of all, don't ask questions. Second, would you pretty please leave the apartment right now so I can have a few hours of private time with Marco? Third, you may hear some crazy stories about me being trapped at the law school with Reed's murderer, but don't believe them. I'll give you the real story tomorrow."

"Abby, oh my God! You were trapped with a murderer?" she cried.

"No questions, remember? I'm fine. Marco is getting some takeout and we'll be there in ten minutes. Thanks, Nik. Love you." I hung up just as the car door opened and Marco slid in, looking handsomer than any man had a right to. What was it about that dark, curly hair and five-o'clock shadow that made me want to eat him up?

He gave me a puzzled look. "Is everything okay?"

"It is now," I told him, putting away my trusty phone.

Back at the apartment, Nikki had left us a bottle of Yellow Tail with a note that said, *Enjoy!* Marco opened the wine while I spread the cartons of food out on the coffee table, then we sat cross-legged on pillows to eat.

As we chowed down on beef fried rice smothered in sweet-sour sauce, monk's delight, and cashew chicken, I said, "Okay, you've heard my story. Now it's your turn. Tell me what you found out from Reilly."

"There's not that much to tell. You and I had turned up the same information the cops had. In fact, they had already cleared Bea and Jocelyn and were in the process of eliminating Puffer when they got the lab results back on the phone. I told Reilly I thought you'd said that Kenny had been alone in Puffer's office. That's what we were discussing when your call came in. Then, of course, I heard Kenny confirm what I'd begun to suspect."

"Thanks to some quick thinking by yours truly. No applause, please."

Marco rolled his eyes. "Are you going to share that rice or do I have to give you a standing ovation first?"

I passed him the carton, then used chopsticks to pick up one last hunk of chicken. It immediately fell into my lap, while Marco deftly maneuvered a bite of rice with his. Why hadn't I ever been able to master those implements? Oh, well. Fingers worked just as well. "Who would have ever guessed that Puffer would come to my aid? I'm still trying to decide if it was just a knee-jerk military action or if he actually wanted to save me."

"This is Puffer you're talking about, Abby. Don't overthink it."

"Can you believe that Kenny's father bribed Professor Reed to keep his son from getting that clerkship? How low is that?" I sat up suddenly. "Damn! I forgot to tell Reilly that Kenny was stealing pets for Dermacol. You'll never guess why. To ingratiate himself with Reed. Do you believe that? Honestly, Marco, Kenny showed no remorse whatsoever about the pet theft or the murder. What kind of person can steal someone's pet or take someone's life and show no emotion?"

"It's your classic sociopath, Sunshine. I saw too many like Kenny when I was a cop. But you don't have to worry about the pets any longer. The photos I took plus the license number you supplied led the cops straight to Dermacol, where a suddenly cooperative Marvin Brown tried to pin the whole thing on Reed. I wouldn't be surprised to see the lab permanently shut down."

"That's terrific news!"

"The people from animal control went in this afternoon to rescue the animals, and pet owners are being contacted as we speak. And I believe he said they'd also found a little Chihuahua with an ID tag that said *Peewee* on it."

"Oh, Marco, that's wonderful! Mr. and Mrs. Sample will be so excited. See? One person *can* make a difference. Think how happy all those people will be when they get the good news."

"Ms. Knight," he said, as I settled beside him once again. "have I told you what an amazing woman you are?" He put down his chopsticks and raised his wine. "To you, Sunshine, for making a difference."

I touched my glass to his and took a sip, gazing at him with appreciation. His opinion meant a lot, as did Marco himself. No matter what happened, I knew he would always be there to watch my back, and that made me one very lucky woman. And how cool was it that a man with his combination of courage, integrity, and sensitivity could admire *me*? I lifted my glass again. "To you, Marco, for making a difference in my life."

We had barely taken a sip when the doorbell rang. I put down my glass and jumped up. "That must be Claymore."

"Jillian's Claymore?" Marco asked, following me up the hallway. "The truant groom?"

"He wasn't truant. Jillian has been lying about who left whom on the honeymoon. But don't worry. I've arranged a little surprise reunion for her."

"I have to see this."

I opened the door, and before Claymore could say a word, I grabbed his wrist and led him toward Jillian's apartment, with Marco following behind. "Good news, Claymore. Your wife is no longer missing in action. In fact, she's waiting for you on the other side of this door."

Cautioning him to keep quiet, I moved him off to one side. Then I rapped twice and called, "Jillian, your customer is here."

There was the click of heels on tile, then the door swung open. "Send him in," she said, stepping back, looking very sexy in a black silk pantsuit and bustier.

I propelled Claymore forward and quickly pulled the door shut behind him. "That'll teach her to mess with me. Now, Mr. Salvare, I believe there are two fortune cookies waiting for us back at my apartment. And after that? Who knows."

Marco poured more wine, then we settled on the pillows with our backs against the sofa. I gave him one of the cookies and took the other for myself, then we snapped them open and removed the little slips of paper. "This is amazing, Marco. Listen to what it says. *Even a dragon fears the knight.*" I turned to gaze at him. "Isn't that *cosmic*?"

He lifted a dark eyebrow. "Not half as cosmic as mine." He cleared his throat and read, "*Beware of short, busty, red-heads.*"

"It doesn't say that," I said, laughing as I snatched it out of his hand. "Here's what it says. *A friend will bring you luck.* Hmm. Do you suppose that friend is me?"

Marco gave me that provocative, half-lidded gaze that always turned me into a puddle of melted raspberry jam. "Let's find out," he said huskily, then tossed the slip over his shoulder and pulled me into his arms for a slow, steamy kiss that sent me soaring into the clouds.

Almost at once, Marco's phone rang, followed shortly by mine. "Now, *that*," he said, sending both phones skittering across the carpet, "is cosmic."

Read on for an excerpt from another
Flower Shop Mystery

Acts of Violets

by Kate Collins

Available from Signet

"You think that was funny? You think I don't know you did that on purpose? Well, I've got your number, shorty, so let me tell you something. Paybacks are murder."

Paybacks? Murder? Shorty! Hugging my purse against me, I gaped at the bad-tempered buffoon as he gathered his cucumbers, climbed onto his unicycle, and rode off to join his troupe. You wouldn't expect that kind of behavior from a clown named Snuggles.

Was it my fault he ran over my purse and fell off his perch? No, it was the bozo's behind me—pardon the clown pun—who was too busy stuffing his face with a bratwurst on a bun oozing pickle relish and mustard to notice the short redhead with an even shorter fuse standing in front of him. This was a small parade. He was a big guy. Did he have to be in the front row? And who eats brats at ten o'clock in the morning?

I turned my attention back to Snuggles, who was once again juggling cukes from his seat-in-the-sky as he pedaled up the street. My policy was to stand up to bullies—and that snarled threat was certainly bullying behavior—but before I could give him a piece of my mind (I was thinking along the lines of recommending a place to store those cucumbers), I was yanked back onto the sidewalk by my best friend/roommate, Nikki Hiduke, an X-ray tech at the county hospital, who had shared many childhood adventures with me and lived to tell about it.

"Abby, are you all right? You look dazed."

"Nikki, that clown threatened me! As if I elbowed myself off the sidewalk." I cast a glare over my shoulder at Mr. Oblivious, who had finished his bratwurst and was slurping mustard off his fingers. I was amazed he wasn't also talking on a mobile phone. Oh, wait. Yes, he was. He had an earpiece on.

"Snuggles the Clown threatened you?" Nikki stared after the troupe—three acrobats, two unicyclists, one stilt-walker, and the last (my favorite because of the huge purple violet atop a long green stem waving from her bonnet), a baby-doll clown pedaling a giant purple tricycle. "But he looks so harmless."

"Don't let that goofy smile deceive you." I scrubbed the black tread mark off the tan leather purse that I'd almost gone into hock for. "Beneath that grease paint is a nasty temper and a voice that would make a polar bear shiver."

"Abby, you have mustard on your shoulder."

Wonderful. I took a tissue from my tire-engraved purse and blotted the yellow stain on my white shirt. Why had I even bothered to come? It was a sunny Saturday morning, and although my flower shop, Bloomers, was open on Saturdays, this was my one weekend a month to sleep in. But no. Attending the annual Pickle Fest Parade was a family tradition, and to break that tradition was to incur the wrath of my mom, Maureen "Mad Mo" Knight.

Speaking of whom, where was she? I'd never known her to miss the start of the parade, when Peter Piper led his merry band of Pickled Peppers up Lincoln Avenue to the strains of a John Phillip Sousa march.

I scanned the crowd lining both sides of the street. Today was the start of New Chapel, Indiana's, fall Pickle Festival— a weeklong celebration of brine-soaked vegetables, attended by thousands of people from all over the state, some from as far away as Chicago, giving the local newspaper, *The New Chapel News*, fodder for headlines such as *Visitors Relish the Pickle Fest*. I had a hunch it wasn't so much the pickled produce as it was *getting* pickled that was the actual draw.

All four streets around the courthouse square had been blocked off to accommodate the huge crowds. Restaurant owners set up tables in front of their establishments to sell beer, hot dogs, bratwurst, dills, pickled beets, pickled tomatoes, pickled watermelon, and, yes, pickled peppers, to the hungry visitors. For the truly desperate, pickled herring and pickled pig's feet were also available. Shoe shops, gift boutiques, and clothing stores put out their wares, and even Bloomers had a display of mums, roses, asters, and greenery for sale.

Then there were the ever-popular arts-and-crafts booths that dotted the huge lawn around the big limestone courthouse in the middle of the square. Beneath the shady maples and elms, brightly colored canvas tents housed ceramicware, watercolors, oils, clay sculpture, silver jewelry, quilts, pottery, toys, metal sculpture, and even marble birdbaths.

My mother would have her work on display somewhere in that mix. In addition to being a kindergarten teacher, Mom now fancied herself an artist, having received a pottery wheel for Christmas last year. Before she grew bored with clay, she had produced a variety of weird sculptures such as the infamous "dancing male monkeys table," or the "human footstool." She had since moved on to mirrored tiles, with which she'd covered nearly every object in her house, making a washroom visit a truly frightening experience. I didn't know what craft she was into this week, as she often changed on a whim. My father would only say, "It's a tickler."

"Do you see my family?" I asked Nikki. Being a head taller (even more if you added in her cute, spiky blond hair), she had a height advantage. She also had a body advantage—slender, long-legged, and small-breasted, something I had aspired to from the age of thirteen. My brothers, both doctors, insisted that people stopped growing when they reached puberty, but they were only half right: I had never gone beyond my five-foot-two-inch frame, but I had gone *way* beyond my training bra.

"I don't see any of them," Nikki said, holding up her hand to shield her eyes.

Normally, they weren't hard to pick out, since Jonathan and Jordan had the same flame red hair and freckled skin that my dad and I had. My mother's hair was a soft brown, lucky woman, and my sisters-in-law—Portia and Kathy—had also escaped the curse of the red.

"There's Marco," Nikki shouted in my ear as the New Chapel High School marching band passed by. She pointed between green-coated band members to the opposite side of the street, but I had already spotted him. How could anyone miss a dark-haired, virile-bodied, extremely hot hunk like Marco Salvare, a former Army Ranger/ex-cop, who now owned the Down the Hatch Bar and Grill—as well as my heart?

"Who's that woman talking to him?" Nikki asked.

I eyed the attractive girl beside him. "I don't know. She's pretty, isn't she?"

"Pffft. No way. Ew. And would you look at those split ends?"

"Nikki, you can't see split ends from here, and besides, it's okay to agree with me. I don't feel threatened by the woman. I'm not the jealous type."

She burst out laughing.

Ignoring her, I narrowed my eyes at the pair, watching as Marco tilted his head toward the woman to catch something she said. She couldn't have been a day over twenty-five, and had an oval face with delicate features framed by long, thick black hair and a perfectly proportioned body. She was talking animatedly and pointing to something or someone up the street. The Pickled Peppers? The clown troupe? Someone in the marching band?

"Abigail, there you are!" my mother called. I turned to find her parting the crowd so the humongous feathered hat on her head could fit through. Normally she wasn't one to wear hats, let alone feathers, but she did have a way of surprising me. "We've been looking all over for you. Why aren't you in front of Bloomers?"

"Because we always meet here by the Clothes Loft. Where are Dad and the gang?"

"By your shop, which is where I thought you'd be."

"It's hard to see the parade from Bloomers, Mom. You know it doesn't go down Franklin. Besides, we always meet here. If you wanted to meet elsewhere, you should have told me."

"I would have told you if I thought there was a need to tell you. But since you're a shop owner now, I really didn't see the need."

I started to argue that my being a shop owner had nothing to do with it, but Nikki nudged me and coughed. That was the signal we used when one of us was expecting a family member to be rational.

"Shall we go get everyone and bring them back here?" Mom gazed at me from under the wide feathered brim of her hat even as her eyes scoured me for signs of illness or distress. Like a hawk, she instantly homed in on the yellow splotch on my shoulder. "How did you spill mustard on your shirt?"

"Ask him," I said, hitching a thumb toward Mr. Oblivious, who was now giving a running commentary to whoever was on the other end of his phone line. "He pushed me into the path of a clown."

"Well, thank heavens it was *only* a clown. It could have been that team of horses." She pointed toward the two grays hauling a circa-1860 fire wagon. Seated on a bench beside the driver was a giant inflatable cucumber dressed in an old-fashioned red fire hat and yellow slicker. Every entry in the parade had to incorporate something pickled, which could have gotten racy except that entrants also had to go before a review panel of six somber senior citizens.

"But *this* clown threatened me, Mom."

"A clown threatened you?" asked a familiar husky male voice from behind me.

My heart skipped a beat as I turned to see the owner of

the voice, Marco (minus the pretty woman), looking extremely macho in his tan Down the Hatch T-shirt, slim-fitting blue jeans, and dusty brown boots. He'd managed to cross the street between floats and was now holding a strawberry ice-cream cone, unaware that he was being ogled by every woman within a ten-yard radius.

Marco wasn't handsome in the movie-star sense of the word. He didn't have a straight nose, or baby blue eyes, or a wide, perfectly even smile. What he *did* have were deep, dark bedroom eyes, a masculine nose, a firm mouth that curved devilishly at the corners when he was amused, and an olive complexion that was rarely without a five o'clock shadow. He was tough and quick-witted, but amazingly sensitive to my moods and feelings. Maybe that was why he brought me the cone.

He held it out and I took it. Ordinarily I don't eat ice cream before lunch, but after being shoved and threatened and stained with mustard, I felt a strong need to soak my irritated nerves in butterfat. Once they were thoroughly saturated, I'd ask him about the woman.

"Morning, Nikki," he said with a little nod in her direction. "Mrs. Knight, new hat?"

"Yes. Thank you for noticing, Marco." Throwing me a *shame on you for not noticing* look, Mom gave him a hug. She gave everyone hugs. It was part of being a kindergarten teacher.

"Tell me about the clown," Marco said, watching me with that intense expression cops get when interrogating a witness. I knew that because my father had been a cop, and throughout my high school years my dates had been subjected to both the expression and the interrogation.

"He was just your standard bulbous-nosed, orange-haired, cucumber-juggling unicyclist with an attitude problem," I said between licks, "who mistakenly believed I threw my purse in front of him to knock him off his cycle. Who then went on to snarl something about paybacks being murder, as if he wanted to get even with me for tripping him. Go figure."

Marco rubbed his jaw, staring up the street after the departing fire wagon. "Not your typical clown behavior."

"His name is Snuggles," Nikki put in helpfully. "It's on the back of his costume."

"Snuggles," Marco repeated, as though storing it away for future reference.

My mother gazed at me sadly. "I'm sorry, honey. You've always liked clowns."

I swallowed a big glob of ice cream, nearly choking. "Mom, I've never liked clowns. I've had a fear of them since I was five years old, when a clown with bad teeth tried to toss me into a burning building. You must remember that."

"We were at the circus, and it was part of their act," she assured me. "If there had been any danger involved, your father would never have let your brothers volunteer you."

"They volunteered me?" I sputtered.

She handed me a tissue to wipe the cream off my mouth. "When Abby was little," Mom explained to Marco, and to anyone else who cared to listen, "she had imaginary friends who were clowns."

"They weren't my friends, Mom." I rolled my eyes at Marco.

"Then why did you play with little Jocko and Bimbo? Hmm?" To Marco she whispered, "That's what she named them. Jocko and Bimbo."

"I played with them because I'm a firm believer in the keep-your-friends-close-and-your-enemies-closer philosophy. It was purely self-protective."

"You were such a cute little girl," she said, tucking a lock of hair behind my ear. Mothers were forever tucking and straightening and—even worse—licking their palms to flatten hair that wouldn't lie down. Mom-spit, my brothers called it. My brothers the traitors, that was. I'd long ago made a vow to never inflict that kind of torture on my kids—if I ever had the urge to have any.

"Well," she said with a satisfied sigh, "shall we go? Marco, you're coming with us, aren't you?"

Of course he was coming with us. He'd promised to

watch the parade with my family. Then he and I were going to hang out together the rest of the day and enjoy the festivities.

"Thanks, but I have some business to attend to first." He put his mouth close to my ear and said huskily, "I'll catch up with you later."

I started to complain, but he was staring past me with a perturbed frown—the same frown he'd worn the time he'd cautioned me not to attempt the rescue of a young, captive Chinese woman, which I did anyway, then was nearly drowned in a hot tub. Or the time he warned me not to go back for the funeral rose I'd delivered to a dragon of a law professor, which ultimately led to my being the prime suspect in a murder case. It made me wonder what kind of business he was talking about now.

"Marco, you wouldn't be going after that clown, would you?"

"Nah."

"He didn't hurt me, you know. No harm done."

"I know that. I'll be back soon." He nodded a quick good-bye to Nikki and Mom, then slipped among the throng.

Oh, yeah. He was going after the clown.